IN A PROVINCE

" If thou seest the oppression of the poor, and
violent perverting of judgment and justice in
a province, marvel not at the matter."

Eccl. v. 8

IN A PROVINCE

A Novel by

Laurens van der Post

1980

THE HOGARTH PRESS

LONDON

Published by
The Hogarth Press Ltd
London
*
Clarke, Irwin & Co. Ltd.
Toronto

ISBN 0 7012 0240 8

First published 1934
Second impression 1953
Third impression 1965
Fourth impression 1971
Fifth impression 1980

Printed and bound in Great Britain by
REDWOOD BURN LIMITED
Trowbridge & Esher

BOOK I

"Le présent serait plein de tous les avenirs, si
le passé n'y projetait déjà une histoire. Mais
hélas, un unique passé propose un unique
avenir—le projette déjà devant nous, comme
un pont infini sur l'espace."

GIDE

CHAPTER I

AT the age of twenty-five Johan van Bredepoel fell seriously ill for the first time in his life. When he had recovered enough to be allowed out of doors, he found himself under doctor's orders to take a long holiday in some quiet part of the country. Some of his more intimate acquaintances, knowing that he was still far from well, talked things over among themselves and decided that he should be sent to Paulstad, a village in the remote Donkerberg district, and they began at once to make all the arrangements for his departure. One of them, Simmering, a violinist in the municipal orchestra of Port Benjamin, had argued the merits of Paulstad as a health resort so convincingly before the others that he was unanimously chosen to acquaint van Bredepoel with details of the plan.

Now Simmering, though he had known van Bredepoel for many years, had always respected him more than he had liked him, and therefore stood somewhat in awe of him. No sooner did he find himself being led to van Bredepoel by a hospital nurse, than he began to have doubts as to the best way of presenting the plan. His doubts were quickly strengthened by long habits of irresolution, and his eyes, never free from a shadow of distress, began to look as if he had just finished crying. Unconsciously his steps slowed down, and once he fell so far behind his guide that she had to stop and wait for him. Luckily he was too

9

busy with his doubts to notice the impatient look she
gave him.

Part of Simmering's trouble was that he was
absurdly sensitive. Out walking in lonely avenues,
he often slowed down his steps to avoid passing people
for fear that they might find something to laugh at
in his manner of carrying himself. Sometimes, in
moments of absent-mindedness, he did overtake and
pass other walkers, but as soon as he realised this his
steps became jerky and unequal; he either swung his
arms too much or too little and looked round wildly
for something to concentrate his gaze on. Often the
people happened to be laughing at a joke between
themselves as Simmering passed, and then he would
feel cloven with self-consciousness and for a long time
worry his perplexed head over probable sources of
ridicule in himself. Even at orchestral concerts, years
of training had not prevented him from dreading the
walk on to the platform, and he felt all the time that
everyone in the audience must be looking at him. At
times when he forgot himself in the climax of a great
symphony—for he had a genuine and intelligent,
though diffident, love of music—he would sooner or
later pull himself up, convinced that the whole
audience had noticed his abandon.

Simmering's respect for van Bredepoel made him
unusually anxious to secure his good opinion. When
he had left his companions, his task had looked easy
enough.

" Look here, van Bredepoel," he would say, " your
doctor has ordered you to spend some time, how long
depends on the speed of your recovery, in some quiet
and healthy part of the country. We, a number of

old and tried friends, have put our heads together
and decided to arrange for you to go to Paulstad.
You have not heard of the place, now have you ? "
And, of course, van Bredepoel would admit that he
had not. " But I, that is to say, we, know it well. We
can recommend both its air and situation to you.
It is remote and quiet, and has a background of
exceedingly beautiful mountains. The people there
are simple, old-fashioned, unspoilt, charming, and
fit into their surroundings as peacefully and naturally
as cows into an English meadow. Moreover, I know
an extremely cultured and intelligent German
family who live on a charming farm near by, and who
would be only too pleased to entertain you. We have
thought this over very carefully. We are convinced
that it will be in your best interests to go there. We
will hear of no refusal. Admit for once that your
friends "—and by friends he meant chiefly himself—
" can occasionally know best."

And yet . . . what if van Bredepoel knew Paulstad ? Or suppose he knew it well, and disliked it
heartily ?

" I will have to be careful, he is a fastidious
creature," he thought.

Just as Simmering came to this conclusion the
nurse, whom he had followed into the hospital
garden, stopped suddenly and turned. They were
standing on the edge of a lawn. Her uniform was
painfully white in the afternoon sunlight, and
instinctively Simmering's eyes sought the fresh green
of the trees beyond.

" You will find Mr. van Bredepoel over there," she
said sharply, and pointed to a deck-chair set up in

the shadow of a tree. But Simmering made no sign that he had heard. His doubts were sunk for the moment in the pleasure of looking at the quiet garden, and he was thinking how soothing it was on that brilliant afternoon to see green trees.

" It is almost as if that green puts one's eyes to bed," he thought.

" You will find Mr. van Bredepoel over there." The nurse's voice was sharper still.

" Oh! Thank you," Simmering answered mildly and started forward. She stopped him with an officious gesture.

" Mind," she said, her officiousness now fatally attracted to Simmering's diffidence, " mind you don't talk too much. It's strictly forbidden."

And she walked smartly away, the sunlight flaming on her uniform, the rustle of her skirts mingling with the stirring of leaves.

For a moment Simmering hesitated, then slowly crossed the lawn. So quietly did he approach the chair that he had a good look at van Bredepoel before he himself was seen. And what he saw agitated him a good deal, which made him more self-conscious than ever. Van Bredepoel was vastly changed. Simmering was not prepared, even though he had heard all the details of his friend's illness, to find him so much changed.

" Poor devil, he is all eyes and nose," he thought as he stepped forward.

Flesh had shrunk away from van Bredepoel's cheeks. His eyes were large and shone dully. His wide, full mouth had gone a dim purple colour, and seemed larger and fuller than before. A firm line of flesh which normally supported his underlip, and had always impressed Simmering as a sign of great self-control, had disappeared. He looked like someone whose whole nature had suddenly become clouded and who saw the world outside himself only as a blur. He sat there in the garden apparently indifferent to everything about him, and Simmering did not even suspect that he was conscious, as he had never in his life before been conscious, of the vivid spring afternoon.

Below them an avenue of slender poplars, shaking sunlight flake by flake from their trembling leaves, carried light into the heart of a sombre and dusty forest. Above them the sky was so blue that their eyes were almost hurt by such blueness, but beyond the forest, over the long curve of the cold Atlantic surf, that same sky sifted dim and yellow through a haze of dust and smoke. The hard lines of Port Benjamin were softly smoothed over. The harbour front was blurred; the haze, where it was thickest, pillared on the masts and smoking funnels of many ships. The roads between the harbour and the town were broad and shining and filled with inexplicably eager traffic, which fed the haze with thin, twisting clouds of dust. Here and there a factory chimney, a pretentious skyscraper or two and the top of a squalid apartment house rose above the haze, and there where the sky was bluest uncurled plumes of lazy smoke. The quiet air was shaken with the rattle of coal hurled into gloomy ships' bunkers, and clash of trucks, shunted and re-shunted over a glittering mesh of lines, the whistling of engines which left pure clouds of steam to fade on dirty air. A breeze, dry and warm and still guarding the memory of the heat and sand of the desert from which it came, stirred faintly over the town, flickered the movement of the dust and smoke and raised from the trees and grass around van Bredepoel and Simmering a low nostalgic murmur. Between Port Benjamin and the country surrounding it there was no gradual merging of one into the other. There where ended the last row of uniform houses, the shoddy products of democratic precipitation, began a low plain covered with lank untidy bush that concealed only faintly the drift-sand which covered its roots; a plain that still belonged more to the sea than to the earth and man. It gave evidence of an unexpected fertility only where it drew near a far-off range of mountains. There van Bredepoel saw yellow squares of cultivated land, houses flanked by long avenues of oaks, stable and graceful witnesses of a fruitful co-operation of Nature and man. Over the mountains the light was amazingly clear. Their steep volcanic sides were bare and grey, but occasionally streaked with layers of orange and red and black rock. The shadows in their ample laps were transparent and gave fullness to their form. Their peaks followed the horizon half-way round Port Benjamin. On an afternoon such as this they held the sky like wine in a cup; at night, like water in a pit. At one end the mountains pushed one massive peak slanting over the sea; the other one's eyes could never find, for, no matter how far one looked, the shadow of a peak, linked to a shadow just out of sight, still straddled the horizon. To van Bredepoel they looked as remote as if they knew no sound but that of the wind, no master but time; as

if in the calmness they gathered round their peaks
they pointed an inarticulate moral at the frantic town
below him. And he was reminded that Port Benjamin was only a small European pendant to a long
necklace of African land; that behind that barrier of
mountains lay the Africa from which he came and to
which he might one day have to return.

"You know, Simmerkins," he said to Simmering,
some minutes after he had greeted him, "I have
come to the conclusion this afternoon that only
adolescents, lovers and convalescents can really
appreciate a day like this. I, for one, was never so
moved by an ordinary spring afternoon when I was
well as I have been to-day. You see those mountains
over there? In all the years I have lived in Port
Benjamin I have never seen them show up so clearly.
Look, there is Booysen's Kop, the Snow Peak,
Fereira's Buttress; I could give you all their names.
Once, a long time ago, I climbed them all."

Simmering suddenly felt relieved. Many of his
doubts fell from him.

"Do you like mountains? I mean, do you like
climbing them?" he asked.

"No, I don't; but the doctor has ordered me to
convalesce in some part of the country well above sea
level. That's why I have been looking at those
mountains so closely this afternoon. I was wondering
if I might not do worse than go there."

"No, you mustn't do that." Simmering was
exultant. "I've got the place that will suit you down
to the ground, with none of your four-thousand-feet
koppies, but huge eight-thousand-footers. You
simply must. I mean to say, I wonder if you would

care to go to a place that I, that is to say we, know of. It's only a little place, but perhaps you know it already ? " And Simmering, faltering, began to put forth the attractions of Paulstad, not, it is true, with the conviction he had displayed before, but with less ambiguity than might have been expected. " And," he concluded, " if you want company, I'll give you a letter to a great friend of mine—at least, he was when I knew him a long time ago. He's an extremely intelligent German farmer, called Moller ; at least, he was when I knew him last, you never can tell how these small places change people. But I think you'll like him and his family, if they haven't changed, of course. It's just the place to send you back to your work a new man."

" It sounds good. But, Simmerkins," replied van Bredepoel, laughing at him, " I've never heard of Paulstad, and you've given me no idea where it is."

" It's on the borders of Bambuland," Simmering said, looking closely at van Bredepoel, as if reading indifference into his friend's remark. If he had any doubts, however, they were dispelled, for immediately he saw a look of keen interest appear on van Bredepoel's face.

" Near Bambuland ! Which part of Bambuland, Simmerkins ? "

" It's within a few miles of Masakama's Drift, the great gateway into Bambuland. It's one of the centres of European trade with the Bambuxosa. Sometime or other the whole of Bambuland comes to it. It's just the sort of place you would like, and I'm sure it will make you perfectly fit for your work again."

" Thank you, I will go there, Simmerkins."

And Simmering wondered both at the promptness and the firmness of van Bredepoel's decision.

Simmering was so pleased with his victory, a victory more over himself than over van Bredepoel —though, we suspect, he was not aware of any distinction—that he almost skipped out of the hospital gates.

"A good piece of work that. I'm glad I was careful," he told himself, and began whistling as he walked down the street. He did not notice that the fading light was giving the town a brief reprieve from squalor, casting on shabby and pretentious walls severely geometric designs, parallelograms of purest white light, cubes of gold, long pyramids of shadow, levered ever higher and higher by the slanting rays of the sun. In the avenue lingered a faint smell of receding winter which, now the sun was going, subtly discharged a cool putrescence into the air. Whistling, he walked to the bottom of the hill on which the hospital stood, and then suddenly noticed that people were looking at him from the other side of the street. He stopped whistling abruptly. Overwhelmed with shame, he made a dash for the nearest tram-car, nearly fell as he boarded it. " People must think me mad," he thought. Looking round furtively as he climbed to the deck of the tram, he saw that he was being followed by a man who seemed to be staring hard at some point on his posterior. " Heavens ! " He was at once in a panic. " I hope I haven't put my trousers on the wrong way round ! " Since he had done this once as a child, Simmering had never lost

the fear that he would do it again. He touched the
seat of his trousers lightly, deftly, as if he was
flicking some dust away, and as an additional
precaution looked slyly down his stomach. Re-
assured, he moved on to find a seat. It was some
time before he realised that he was on the wrong
tram, a tram which was carrying him out of Port
Benjamin, and out of this story. To this caprice-
ridden spirit, van Bredepoel owed a fateful journey.

Simmering's words : " It will make you perfectly
fit for your work again," had disquieted van
Bredepoel strangely. They drove him once more,
for the hundredth time since his illness, to take stock
of himself, in terms both of his past and of his
intentions for the future. That night he could not
sleep. He had never supposed that at twenty-five
his mind would be so uncertain. The last few years
of his life had been so regularly lived, cast in such a
definite groove, that he had unconsciously con-
sidered the question which now worried him as
disposed of. Yet the pivot of his thought at the
moment was : " Is it worth getting better to go
back to all that again ? "

Outwardly he was calm, and when the night
nurse came to see if there was anything he wanted,
his face, pressed back on a pillow looked so white and
composed that she had not the heart to disturb him.
But ten minutes later he was standing at his window,
looking out over the town towards the mountains,
where a grass fire was slowly mounting skywards.
The night was so clear that each flame stood out
sharply as the blade of a spear. In his present mood

the fire seemed like a beacon of distress. From the
town the only sound that reached him was the noise
of the surf on the beach ; silence in Port Benjamin
was always the sound of the sea. He thought of
another silence, somewhere beyond the mountains,
where through a long succession of nights it had
consisted of the songs of black people on a remote
hill, the stirring of restless cattle in a kraal. His
past was bound up with that : and if his present was
this, in Port Benjamin, it was because the first had
calmly—rather, with a certain quiet, ruthless logic—
wound into the second. But his future ?

In the first moments of lucidity that had come
to him in the course of his fever he had regarded
his illness merely as an unpleasant break in the
normal course of his life, which once he was better
could be taken up exactly where he had left off.
Now he was not at all sure. Illness gives one a
licence, a generosity and often a pity for oneself,
that in a precariously organised being can have the
most disconcerting results. It brings the individual
face to face with a purely individual problem. He
may have long lost sight of himself in the social
pattern, but in illness his eyes are turned inwards.
He is struggling with a condition that primarily can
annihilate or change only himself. And that private
inward world which has hitherto seen in the balance
of his actions merely an attempt to silence or to
crush it, finds in this struggle which he wages,
not for abstractions it cannot understand but for
himself, the hope that he is changed from an enemy
into an ally. It brings to his attention doubts,

desires, memories which his actions have long since
ignored, and clamours for a wider share in the
future life he is to lead. Van Bredepoel's case was
no different. That night he was more deeply
depressed than he had ever been, and across the
orbit of this depression fell shadows of the lives of
others, of one other in particular, who had once
diffidently set out from that very Bambuland of
which Simmering had spoken. To understand his
mood, however, now, after Simmering had left him,
within a few days of a journey whose consequences
he neither foresaw nor suspected, it is necessary to go
back many years.

CHAPTER II

MEMORY tears fantastic fragments out of the past. It is relevant not so much to life as a whole as to each of the many isolated movements of which life is made up. Looking back, van Bredepoel found that one of the first things he could remember was an amber necklace round the neck of someone bending over him. So clear was the recollection that he thought he would still be able to recognise the necklace to-day, but of she who had worn it one tranquil evening long ago his mind retained not the shadow of a memory. Then hard on this impression came others, though still not any of people ; he was surprised how little impression people had made on him at first. One large territory of his mind seemed occupied entirely by vague, impersonal things. There a faint nostalgia hung in the light of ample summer afternoons : the bleating of sheep at dawn and sunset, long trails of luminous dust drifting between him and the evening sun, yellow flowers in grass round a slime-covered pool, bats flapping in and out an avenue of pepper-trees, the bagpipe music of mosquitos, the far-off mutter of thunder and nights horizoned by lightning. In this world there were no footsteps and no faces. Even the first recollection of his room came to him by way of light streaming through the cracks of a faded green blind, the light of an afternoon throbbing like a high-powered motor-car at his window. How long had he lain there, how many years before the voice of his aunt woke him ? Was it really his aunt ? He knew for certain only that it was someone sitting beside him saying softly : " I see something that thou seest not ! " And he answered in a bright excited voice : " What colour is it ? " He could hardly contain himself for excitement. Was it the sail of one of the fleet of ships in the painted border of the wall-paper ? Was it the daddy-longlegs spider crawling down the wall, or was it the trembling reflection on the plaster of the light falling in the enamel wash-jug ? It was none of them, but all the time this someone at his side called encouragingly : " Cold ! Lukewarm ! Ice-cold ! Warm ! Very warm ! Thou art burning ! " And at last he found it. It was the first large blue letter of the text in Gothic print, which hung over his bed : " The Lord is my Shepherd, I shall not want."

There were recollections in which the voice was less soft, when it issued in sharp, commanding tones from a long, cold, white face with cool blue eyes. But even there the person remained vague : a mirage in the roaring summer light, a shadow fluttering in the wind of an oncoming summer storm. Summer storms ? He was kneeling on a chair, his forehead pressed against one of the windows of his aunt's parlour, looking out of wide-open eyes at a storm coming over the veld in wind and smoke, like a brigade of Tartar cavalry. Thunder filled the air, and dust beat against the tin roof of the house like a shower of sleet. The branches of the pepper-trees, which flanked both sides of the road in front of the house, bent low before

the wind and their pink and white berries were
blown in thousands to mix with dust and paper rags
and straw in the sky. The top of a blue gum-tree
scratched so persistently against the side of the roof
that it sounded as if a flock of black ravens were
trying to scramble up its surface. He felt then
vaguely that the storm was not the uncontrolled
thing it seemed, but a planned attack against the
house in which he was living ; those clouds, winged
with long plumes of dust, creatures of impulses and
terrible motives. Often he saw forked lightning
strike down into the same place three or four times,
just as if someone were controlling it and shrieking
at the earth : "Take that ! And that ! And
that !" His heart overflowed with terror, yet he
went on looking. When there came a lull in the
storm he heard the bleating of sheep being hurriedly
driven home and the sound of people moving about
behind him. He turned round and saw his aunt,
calm and self-possessed, helping the two black
servants wrap up in blankets all the cutlery, scissors
and knitting-needles, and hang linen sheets over
each of the many mirrors. She moved about quietly.
The black gown she wore was so long that it hid
her feet, trailed out behind her and disguised the
movement of her legs so well that she seemed to
glide rather than walk. The gown ended at her
neck in a high collar of very fine white lace, clasped
together with a brooch made out of one small gold
nugget. Whenever she came near a window the
light outside, a light both orange and grey from the
storm, shone dully on the brooch and made her face
look even whiter than before. But her eyes were

steady, severe perhaps, but cool and calm and
untroubled. For a moment Johan forgot the storm ;
he wanted to rush up to her and catch hold of her
skirts, but he dared not. She took no notice of him
until the servants had gone. Then she came towards
him quietly, raised his chin with a cool white hand,
felt him trembling, and looking down from far
above asked : " Art thou frightened, Johan ? "
He did not reply, but swallowed hard, and stared
at her.

" Fear," she said again, shaking her head gently,
" it is not a van Bredepoel's word."

She would have gone on speaking, but the storm
broke at that moment. Taking his hand, she led
him over to a small harmonium, smoothed her
skirt carefully underneath her, and sat down. The
noise of rain and wind and thunder was so loud and
so continuous that she made no effort to speak.
She merely made him stand at her side and began
playing as loudly as she could some old Protestant
hymns. Her eyes seldom left his face and he began
to feel calmer, though his fear did not disappear.
When the sound of the thunder was once more
remote and they could again hear the sheep bleating
outside, she closed the harmonium and said, like
somebody concluding a long address : " All the
same, God is very good to us."

On that day he definitely left the warm, luminous
impersonal world in which he had so long lived, and
linked up his thoughts and actions with those of
people other than himself. They were thenceforth
not beckoning figures on shining and remote
frontiers but strange, thrilling creatures in virgin

country. For the first time he became conscious
of a forward movement in his own life. Whereas his
life had hitherto appeared locked in a timeless and
tranquil lagoon, it now began to flow slowly forward
like a broad stream. Linked to the hours, a man
appeared at his aunt's side, a man with dark restless
eyes, who took disconcertingly long steps and read
in a grave, imposing voice out of a large, leather-
covered Bible. There was a long procession of
candle-lit nights in which he tried in vain not to
let this man's calm, sonorous voice lull him to sleep.
One moment he would be listening to this voice and
following the whirling candle-shadows round the
room, and the next he would be standing shivering
in front of the kitchen fire, looking with swollen
eyes at the cold, yellow light outside, watching his
uncle come in with wet, shivering lambs wrapped
in mealie bags and place them beside the oven to
dry.

He had vivid recollections of long Sunday mornings, when all the black servants filed into the
dining-room and squatted on the floor round a big
oak table, while his uncle read to them for an hour
out of the Bible and his aunt played psalms on her
harmonium. Afterwards the three of them always
went out riding, Johan in front of his uncle's saddle,
his aunt on a lively Basuto pony. They rarely spoke
to one another on these occasions. Johan's uncle
invariably led the way and his aunt followed in
silence. One of Oom Willem van Bredepoel's rides
was to follow an English gun-path to the top of a
very high hill, which overlooked an immense stretch
of country. On its summit was an old surveyor's

beacon, from which a ragged white flag still waved.
There they would often, all three of them, get off
their horses and sit for half an hour or so against
the side of the beacon. Johan, who had been there
on week-days as well, soon noticed that the atmosphere on Sundays differed from any other day.
The wind going through the brown bushes, the
cattle and goats feeding on the slopes of the hill,
all had for him a special Sunday sound.

" Do you hear that, Margrieta ? " he heard his
uncle say one morning.

" No. What is it ? "

" Listen ! "

All three listened carefully. At first Johan heard
only the bleating of the sheep. He looked down the
side of the hill and saw the wind go like a shadow
over the grass. Farther away, a flock of sheep were
rushing to a small red-earth dam to drink. The wall
of the dam was shaped like a crescent and covered
with blue-bush ; but in the centre stood three
willow trees, who seemed to have their roots thrust
into the quicksilver of a mirror.

" Do you hear that ? " his uncle asked again.

Very far away they heard the pealing of a church
bell.

" I've seldom heard it as clearly as that. Fifteen
miles as the crow flies. I must tell the verger about
that next time we go to church ; it will please
him," said Oom Willem, and glancing down below
them added : " We'd better get back or we shall
be late for dinner. There is old Koos' flock going
down to drink. It must be nearly one."

On another Sunday, a day so clear and hot that

the shining atmosphere reflected into the sky the banks of a river which was actually invisible from where they were sitting, Johan saw on the horizon a number of blue mounds and smoking chimneys, wavering in the air. He asked his uncle what they were.

"Those are the mines, the diamond mines, the mines the English wanted and took," he replied.

"But do they work on Sundays too?" Johan asked.

"Yes, on Sundays, and on every other night and day too. They never stop working."

"I was reading in the *Church Messenger* the other day," his aunt intervened, "that the moon must be simply stuffed like a turkey with diamonds. The moon volcanoes. . . ."

"Don't you believe it!" Johan's uncle exclaimed, a strange smile on his lips.

"But, Willem, the man who said that was a famous scientist," his wife said reprovingly.

"Don't you believe it!"

"Why not?"

"If there were diamonds on the moon the English would long since have annexed it."

They both laughed, but Johan went on looking at those chimneys. He had never associated the country in which they lived with things like that, and in later days, after one of the occasional visits they had to make to the mining village, he would lie in his bed at night listening to the sheep bleating in the kraal, to the jackals and striped hyenas barking in the veld, and wonder what the mines were doing in the middle of it all.

On Sunday afternoons there came to " Vergelegen"[1] visitors in black clothes from the neighbouring
farms, who were taken round the garden, and sooner
or later shown a large gold-framed picture, of which
we shall hear more. Johan had to follow them
dutifully round the garden and climb into fruit-
trees to pick all the choice peaches, pears and
pomegranates they wanted. One afternoon he said
good-bye to some neighbours very sulkily, and after
they had gone his aunt gave him a long scolding.
" The van Bredepoels," she ended severely, " have
always been gentlemen, and must always be gentlemen." For her a gentleman was little more than
someone who took off his hat politely to her sex,
and did not pass through a door until all the women
present had done so. But what her conception
lacked in breadth, it more than made up for in
faith. She never ceased to stress its importance to
her nephew, and he did not easily forget it.

Soon there came a day when he realised that his
relation to his aunt and uncle was not the same as
that of other children to the people who took care
of them. His curiosity and a vague disquiet was
roused. He began to ask questions. They were
answered evasively at first, but his persistence in the
end got at the truth. His father and mother were
dead. The black woman who looked after him
told him that they had both been killed by the
" Kakies." His aunt and uncle qualified this later.
His father, they told him, was killed at the head of
his commando at Dalmanutha ; his mother died
of hunger in an English concentration camp.

[1] An English equivalent would be "A Long Way Away."

Margrieta van Bredepoel claimed that she had
saved him from a similar fate only by getting her
brother, who was Dutch consul-general at the time,
to use every possible influence to have him sent to
her at the Cape, where she had found a refuge.
He did not understand easily what that word death
meant. Almost immediately after learning of the
death of his father and mother, he began to dream
at regular intervals that he was meeting them on
long railway journeys. He used to try and talk to
them, but something always prevented him from
getting near them. But all the people in the train
would be discussing them and saying : " They've
been hiding from the ' Kakies ' in the mountains.
They can't come back until the ' Kakies ' are
gone." Once he dreamt that his father and mother
were sent to him by parcel post, but he lost the
official slip, and the postmaster in the town near
" Vergelegen " refused to give him the parcel.
" It's because he too is a ' Kakie,' " he said in his
dream.

Thus early in his life van Bredepoel was brought
to think about death. He never afterwards lost the
habit. It became almost an obsession with him. In
later years he would be continually worried by the
thought that no man can live calmly unless he has
worked out the problem of death to his own satisfaction. " Death," he would say, " is always with
us. It's one of the biggest commonplaces of life.
Everyone expects death, and yet when it does come,
everyone is horrified. It's because they have not
faced the problem squarely, that they are horrified,
and being horrified, overwhelmed. No system of

life can ever be satisfactory unless it has an answer for the problem death poses, unless it can oppose a feeling of spiritual security to our sense of death."

And now he had another frontier to cross. It seemed to him that his childhood was beginning to recede as some lagoon-locked island in the Pacific falls away behind an outward-bound ship. Between him and that childhood lay a new frontier, marked not by reefs and placid lagoons but by a shadow. In this new world there was much talk of war. For him and his aunt and uncle there was only one war, there could be only one war : that in which his father and mother had died. It was blamed for many things. From the way people talked, he could easily have believed that it had cut them all off from a golden age, and had destroyed many more good things than had since been put in their place. His uncle was very bitter about the War.

One morning, Oom Willem took him up on the front of his saddle, and rode with him to the farthest sheep outpost. The outpost consisted of a couple of stone kraals, a ruined farmhouse, a small red-earth dam, and a steel windmill which pumped a thin spasmodic stream of water with a desolate noise. At the back of the house were the remains of a large fruit orchard. Its borders were traced by straggling and withered lanes of quince- and pomegranate-trees. The walls of the house were still blackened by fire, and Johan wondered if it had been struck by lightning.

" No," said his uncle bitterly, " the ' Kakies ' did it. They passed through here one fine morning, and in the evening the house was burnt down. They chopped down all the fruit trees, they speared all the sheep and laid waste senselessly to everything they could put their hands on. Isn't that so, Koos ? "

His uncle turned to the grey-haired black man who was in charge of the outpost. Koos, too, had been in the War. His right leg had been shot away and he limped round painfully on an ill-fitting wooden stump. His eyes were always red as if he had been crying and secreted at their corners a dry white matter which made Johan uncomfortable to look at them.

" Aye, Master," he replied slowly, in a grave evangelical voice, and shook his head. " As true as there is our Big Master in Heaven, it was the ' Kakies ' who did it."

As he spoke, the wind fluttered his loose and ragged clothes about him, until he looked more like a signal of distress than a man. When they rode away, he always leant on his stick, two mongrel dogs at his side, and stared after them for a long time. Often Johan looked round and saw him standing there quite still. Behind him were the blackened walls of the house and the devastated garden, and far away on the veld, sparkling like a crystal over the heads of the pepper-trees, the roof of the new " Vergelegen." Very appropriately old Koos stood between the old farm and the new, and Johan was convinced that the War must have been a terrible thing.

His aunt's reminiscences always confirmed what his uncle or old Koos told him about the War. There was one thing in particular that she had never forgotten and talked about with great emotion. Before the War she had had a small Bechstein grand

piano in the house at the cattle outpost. This house
had been the original homestead of the farm, and
had only been abandoned because his uncle, rather
than reconstruct a place which he had spent many
years of his life vainly perfecting, preferred to build
something altogether new. Talking of this piano to
Johan, she would describe sadly all the details of its
construction, the difficulty and expense she had had
in getting it sent out from Germany and transported
over an almost railless country to " Vergelegen."

" Yes," she would say, " the ' Kakies ' were
savage. They made war on women and children,
destroyed things which did not do them or anyone
else any harm. They passed through the farm one
fine morning, dragged my beautiful piano—the
President himself told me, when last he visited us
just before the War, that it was better than the one
he had in the Residency—yes, dragged and rolled
it out into the yard and chopped it up before my
own eyes for firewood."

If anything went wrong with the wool market, if
the magistrate insisted, very wisely, that old Mynheer
Willem van Bredepoel should dip all his sheep for
scab even when only three or four were infected, the
War was blamed for it. Johan would be told sooner
or later that before the War there was little scab,
that a kettleful of boiling dip had sufficed to extermi-
nate it. As he grew older, he realised more and more
that his uncle and aunt had never succeeded in
adapting themselves to post-War life. The War
seemed to have cut roughly through their psychological development, at the same time sealing it
arbitrarily. It lay like a wall across their lives.

They milled against it like thirsty horses, who knew
that there was water beyond, but could think of
no way of getting to it except by milling round and
round the place where they smelt it best. The
rhythm of their lives, in the fullest sense of the word,
had been broken, and they were incapable of taking
it up again. At the same time Johan noticed in
himself and in other boys that the parent generation
had conveyed to all of them its own special sense of
discord—a discord which had its roots not in the
lives of the children but in a life long since gone.
And because this discord persisted long after the
circumstances which had created it, it was the
source of much confusion, and gave the lives of
people like Johan an emotional content which they
could not properly possess.

As far as his uncle and aunt were concerned, Johan
was in later years surprised that the War had
affected them so profoundly. Like his own father
and mother, they were not of the country. They had
only emigrated to it from Holland as young people.
He knew that their emigration was the result of a
considerable decline in the fortune and position of
their family. He noticed later that a family in
a declining position communicates to its various
members its own sense of dislocation so strongly that
it makes it very difficult, sometimes impossible, for
them to rehabilitate themselves purely as individuals.
He wondered whether the War, by cutting across
his uncle's attempt to establish himself in a country
from which he had hoped so much, had not merely
brought a dormant sense of failure to the surface.
Before the War, his uncle had been a successful and

progressive farmer. Now it seemed that the effort
of reconstruction had exhausted him. Willem van
Bredepoel's interest in " Vergelegen " became more
and more perfunctory. The farm was not progressing
but standing still, which in the end is the same thing
as decay. The time that he should have spent on it
was more and more taken up by politics. After his
election to parliament, he left the farm for some
years almost entirely to his native servants. There
were long months during which Johan lived with
him and his wife in the capital, staying at more
expensive hotels than they could afford. When they
did return to the farm in the intervals between the
parliamentary sessions, Johan's uncle spent most of
his time not at home but in going round his constituency. His politics, like those of the party to
which he belonged, were only a protection, a
practical approximation of his private mood. All
the political and social problems of the country were
directly or indirectly caused by the War. The only
way to solve them was to make the country completely independent again, to wipe out the results of
the War. The opposition he met in his own province
was not strong enough to make him analyse seriously
his political attitude. Most of the people he liked
and esteemed felt as he did. His party and his
politics became a great provincial success. People
like him focused the outlook of an entire rural
post-War generation, not on the future but on the
War. The post-War generation believed firmly that
it had been somehow hideously maimed by the War,
even in some provinces where there had been no
war at all.

In the meantime, Johan's education was either
neglected entirely or of a very haphazard kind. Oom
Willem's increasing political energy and restlessness,
augmented by uncertain party ambitions and set-
backs, left him in the end without either the will or
the time to bother much about his brother's son.
Margrieta van Bredepoel was far too busy being
her husband's wife, far too busy giving his political
career a firm social foundation, to correct his
attitude to Johan. She had also in her character a
certain coolness which, coupled with a sense of
paramount duty to her husband, made detachment
comparatively easy for her.

Johan felt this instinctively. He admired his aunt
immensely, but he often wished he could love her
more. If only she had not been always so cool, so
collected, so very much master of both her own
feelings and those of others, he might have loved her
more. But even in those days he loved most strongly
when an element of pity entered freely into his love.
And Tante Margrieta never seemed to him obviously
a person to be pitied. He could never, for instance,
remember seeing her cry or hearing her complain
about her own life. Whenever she came back to
" Vergelegen " after one of her husband's long
political journeys, she would greet Johan, who
usually waited for them trembling with excitement
and pleasure at the gate of the grounds, as if she
had seen him only the night before, and would there
and then take up the clear threads of their relationship exactly where she had left them off some
months before. So Johan came to assume, as the
poet Blake assumed of people in general, that she

controlled her feelings so well only because they were weak enough to be controlled.

Years later, he often reproached himself for not having appreciated sufficiently that her devotion, though it had never seemed very warm, had always been constant. He felt for her then a belated tenderness and realised that if it had not been for her cool, silver-grey presence at Willem van Bredepoel's side, they might all have fared very much worse. He remembered instances of her spirit, her loyalty to her husband. There was one scene in particular which stuck in his mind. Willem van Bredepoel was addressing a political meeting in a red-brick school-house on a farm near " Verge-legen." His wife had a seat near him on the small platform at the back of the room. She sat there listening intently, her hands, which clasped some flowers presented to her at the beginning of the meeting, resting in her lap. Johan stood at the back of the room with some boys of his own age.

" They have taken away our country, but neither our pride nor our soul," Willem van Bredepoel was saying, deadly in earnest, his eyes shining with feeling and his voice raised in the best pulpit tradition. " Had we ten other countries beautiful as this, and were they too taken away from us, we would still have our national pride, our soul as a nation. For it is through adversity and sorrow that a nation becomes great. The unlimited possession of land has never yet made a people great. Think of the Jews, a great people, the Chosen Race. Think. . . ."

" I don't think," a sarcastic voice interrupted him from the front row.

Willem van Bredepoel's hand, ready to thump the
table at his side, wavered irresolutely in the air. His
mind never detached itself easily from the burden of
his feeling, and he was not at that time experienced
enough to have developed a formula for dealing
nimbly with hostile interruption. He could only
think of ignoring it, and try to go on. But Johan was
watching his aunt. She was looking intently at her
husband and had suddenly sat up very erect.

" Think of the Jews! " he began again, but once
more that voice below him interrupted: " I don't
think."

This time the supporters of the speaker began to
get angry. There was a mild uproar and shouts of
" Shut up, ' hands-upper '! " " Chuck the ' Kakie '
out! "

Again Willem van Bredepoel tried to go on, and
again a cool, unperturbed " I don't think! " interrupted him.

An outburst of counter-interruption followed, and
then suddenly ceased. Johan saw with amazement
that his aunt was on her feet, holding her hand up for
silence.

" You don't think, we know, Mynheer van der
Walt," she said in her best drawing-room manner,
looking steadily all the time at the man who had
interrupted her husband. " You don't think. The
trouble with all my husband's opponents is that they
don't think. Perhaps you'll be good enough to wait
until your mind has acquired the art of thinking
before you interrupt the meeting again."

A minute or two later Meneer van der Walt walked
quickly out of the building, murmuring something

to the effect that though he was ready to tackle any man on any subject, he was not given to quarrelling with women.

When after some years Johan's aunt and uncle found that politics were costing more than they could afford, while their income from the farm was rapidly declining, they felt their duty to Johan amply discharged by providing him with food and clothes and leaving his education in the hands of a consumptive old Dutch professor, who had come to them seeking no wages but a healthy farm to live on. It was also found convenient and cheaper than a manager to leave Johan and his tutor in charge of the farm when they went off on Meneer van Bredepoel's numerous political crusades.

The old professor, Meneer Pieter Broecksma, LL.D., had an interesting, lively, sceptical mind. Like many people with a lively disposition, he was contemptuous of orthodoxy of any kind and more concerned with leaping over traditional and conventional restrictions than with justifying or attempting to explain them. Hardly a day passed in which he did not draw attention to what he called " the inevitable stupidity of human beings." In the course of history lessons he would often stop dramatically, turn to Johan, shrug his shoulders, distort his features with an overstressed expression of disgust, and say: " Human nature again . . . my dear Johan, what else can you expect ? " Once, when he was explaining to Johan the mathematical hypothesis of the infinite, he concluded, " But a far better definition of infinity would be the human capacity for stupidity ! "

If any piece of gossip or any petty maliciousness

on the part of neighbours was reported to Meneer
Broecksma, he immediately generalised it into a
prevailing characteristic of the human race.

" Take the question of law, Johan," he often said,
for law was his own subject. " The only way we
managed to get a reasonably just administration of
law in the Western World was by dehumanising it
as far as possible. Experience taught us that the
human element in law was the chief enemy of
justice. Everyone recognised that there were certain
advantages in guarding the human element in the
administration of law, but everyone was convinced
that these were heavily outweighed by the dis-
advantages. If ever you are guilty of a crime,
Johan, choose to be tried by a jury—the last remaining concession to the human element, for a jury may
discharge you. But if you are innocent choose a
judge—someone as near a machine as we can get a
human being, for a jury might convict."

Until the arrival of Meneer Broecksma at "Vergelegen," it had never occurred to Johan to question
the rigid attitude of his aunt and uncle to religion.
It was as much a part of their daily life as eating and
drinking, and he would as soon have thought it
useful to question the one habit as the other. It is
true he did find family prayers twice a day irksome,
and was on that account tempted to be mildly
critical, but criticism of that kind seemed to him to
reflect more on himself than on religion. Meneer
Broecksma had no such reservation in his mind. He
made it quite plain to Johan, and as plain as he
dared to Johan's aunt and uncle, that he found
religion both stupid and boring.

One Sunday morning soon after Meneer Broecksma's arrival, he and Johan went out together to saddle up the horses for the family's ride. When they were alone he began to talk about the sermon they had heard just a few minutes before from old Meneer van Bredepoel.

" In matters of religion, as in all things that concern human nature," the professor lectured, " you can never be critical enough. Religion and faith are things about which man is least able to reason, and yet on which he holds the staunchest and most obstinate opinions. Consider the way your uncle talked, study the history of his life, and tell me if his comforting belief in everything being for the best has prevented the worst from happening to him."

Meneer Broecksma, moreover, had not been trained to undertake any education of a general kind. He was accustomed to lecture only on his own particular subject, so that he resembled a schoolmaster as much as an endocrinologist a general practitioner. Johan's instruction was supposed to follow that prescribed in government schools, but though he provided himself religiously at the beginning of each year with the standard text-books, Meneer Broecksma invariably used them only as jumping-off places for the most unprescribed flights of speculation. It only needed a sentence, a phrase, commonplace remarks which Johan himself took quietly for granted, to set Meneer Broecksma's thoughts soaring far beyond the green and red covers of the text-books. So that when Johan grew older, he found himself in possession of much interesting but quite unorganised and

unmarketable knowledge, together with a very deep
and wide sense of insecurity.

His tutor's sceptical, acid disposition, and, moreover, the wide difference in their ages, threw Johan
back on himself. He was gradually driven to seek
companionship in books rather than in people. No
control was exercised over his reading, so that
presently, although interested in many points of
view, he found he had none that he could strictly
call his own ; between his knowledge and his
experience there was a very wide gap. Then,
suddenly, his association with Meneer Broecksma
came to an end.

At the age of sixteen he had begun to keep a
diary. In this diary there were no people and no
records of his experiences on the farm. The entries
were uniquely devoted to, what he thought, a
collection of strangely generalised statements. One
of these entries was concerned with his aunt's
conception of a gentleman. But unlike Tante
Margrieta, Johan did not associate the word with
anything grand or worldly. He gave it a highly
individual and specialised meaning, making of
" Gentleman " a philosophic rather than a social
concept. In his diary, he had attempted to define
it like this:

" In a gentleman reason and feeling are kept in
strict, if strenuous equilibrium.

" Though he sees no purpose in life as a whole,
a gentleman contrives to live his own life as if it had
a very definite and obvious purpose. He finds,
indeed, that the only purpose life has is the purpose
he creates for it. His own life must be as highly

organised as he can make it. He must not allow any
sentimentality for himself or others to obscure his
just purpose, and it would be better, therefore, if he
treated his own life as some sort of business invest-
ment out of which he tries to secure the highest
interest for his purpose. He should, therefore, abhor
waste, excess, and a formless and undisciplined
existence. Though he is firm, he is not insensitive
or unsympathetic. He bears his own difficulties
without complaint, and if he cannot be enthusiastic,
he is at least conscientious."

One morning when he came into the schoolroom
he saw Meneer Broecksma standing at the table,
turning over the pages of his diary and chuckling
merrily to himself. When the old man saw Johan
enter, he stopped laughing abruptly and came
forward to meet him, the book in his hand.

" I owe you an apology, Johan," he said, " I
found this on my table this morning and thought it
was an exercise you had done for me. Look! The book
is not very different from your other exercise books."

" It's marked private, Meneer," Johan replied,
still blushing, for he had not yet forgotten the old
man's laugh.

" Dear me, so it is! But I assure you I didn't
notice it before, or I wouldn't have looked at it."

Johan took the book and turned away without
saying any more. His tutor's apology had completely
disarmed the anger he had first felt, and he would
probably have forgotten all about it if the old man
had not begun to chuckle again. He turned round.
His anger, confused by a painful self-consciousness,
had come back.

"Out of which book," asked the professor, still smiling, a look of worldly superiority on his face, "did you copy that piece about . . . er . . . gentlemen?" The word "gentlemen" sent him off chuckling again.

"I didn't copy it from anywhere; it's my own," Johan replied rather defiantly.

"Dear, dear me! it's your own, is it?" The old man was getting more and more amused. "We've been nourishing an infant prodigy in our breast, Broecksma, without knowing it. Well! Well! Well! Aged sixteen, 'no purpose in life,' and already a 'gentleman.' What immature maturity." Then noticing Johan's expression he suddenly became serious.

"Don't get angry, Johan," he said, "I was only joking. But speaking seriously, I think it's a disgrace that at your age you should write things like that. It's unbelievably prudish and false. You haven't the experience to come to conclusions like that. For you that is dead, dangerously dead, wisdom. You've no right to be contemplating your navel at sixteen, your vision should be focused a little lower down. You should be writing sonnets to the moon or to somebody's eyebrow. Have you so little appetite for life in you? Tell me, for instance, haven't you noticed what a good figure that girl Johanna has? I bet you haven't! But just look at her, there's something for you to write about."

"But, Meneer Broecksma!" Johan exclaimed, overcome with surprise. "She's black!"

"Black! Of course she is black; I'm not blind," the old man replied more warmly than seemed necessary. "But that doesn't make any difference to the fact that she is very beautiful. It's necessary to have grown up in this awful country not to have seen that. Every time I look at her, I feel that we lose a hell of a lot by being civilised. Look at her yourself and be inspired!"

"A black girl!" was all that Johan could reply. But he was conscious, all the same, of some inadequacy in his outlook. He felt that he was more surprised than he had a right to be at the old man's last remark, and this incident sank very deeply into his mind. It helped to link him to a future the shape of which he could not possibly foresee.

Some days afterwards, Meneer Broecksma was suddenly dismissed. Johan knew that the same girl, Johanna, had much to do with it. The evening before he heard the news, he saw Johanna's father speaking anxiously to his uncle. Within a week Broecksma was gone. But not before his tutor had contrived to say good-bye to him in private. Johan was upset, but not too upset to take in clearly one thing the old man said. "Johan, they are sending me away because they thought I would sleep with that girl Johanna. My only regret is not that I have wanted to sleep with her, but that I have not done so. You must be very careful of this silly superstition white people in this country have about the black. In your own case, the superstition has already got such a hold that it has deadened your sense of what is beautiful. The other day when I mentioned Johanna, the only thing you could find to say was, ' She is black!' And then you stood looking at me like a congenital idiot. There is nothing, nothing outrageous about being fond of a black person. I feel almost ashamed to have to say so obvious a thing; this is the only country I know in which it is necessary to say it. I want you to remember, in case you should one day meet people who feel about black women as I have felt about Johanna, that every white man who *does* sleep with a black woman commits a social act of the greatest value. Every white person who sleeps with a black person, merely by suggesting to the rest of the world that it is possible to want to do so, is helping to break down this wicked superstition, is helping incidentally the individual to realise an emotional richness in himself hitherto ignored."

He broke off, and smiled rather ironically at the slightly bewildered Johan.

" Johan," he said, " do you know what I would say if *you* talked to me like this ? "

" No! "

" I would say, that if a fellow wants badly enough to do a thing, no matter how bad the thing is, he will always find some fine sentiment to cloak it with."

Johan was henceforward left to continue his studies alone, and to take care of the farm while his uncle and aunt were away. While he thus became in one way accustomed to assuming independent responsibilities, he was left without a definite purpose and without ambition for the future.

His education obviously unfitted him for any established occupation except farming, and he would probably have drifted into this if something had not happened to prevent it.

Just before his twentieth birthday, his uncle
returned to " Vergelegen " strangely depressed after
a successful election campaign. Johan tried several
times after his return to make him discuss some very
necessary improvements on the farm, but he was
always put off vaguely. One day when Johan
insisted that the old man should listen to him the
latter replied abruptly, " It's no use discussing that,
I'm selling ' Vergelegen.' "

" Selling, uncle! Good God! Why ? "

Willem van Bredepoel began talking rather
apologetically.

" Yes," he said, " I'm selling. I don't want to sell
but I can't help myself. I'm sorry, because I always
meant you to have the farm. I had hoped that our
party would be returned strong enough to form a
cabinet after the last election, but though we've
done well enough, we haven't got a majority, and
I shan't have either the portfolio or the pay on
which I've been counting. Politics is an expensive
game. It has cost me much more than you know.
Of course, things will be better after the next
election, but until then I need more ready money,
and I must sell. But don't worry, you know that
everything I've got will one day be yours. If
anybody had told me before the War that I would
come to this, I would have laughed at him. God!
That War. . . ."

His old, old bitterness was coming back, a bitterness
so strong that it usurped the place of many more
legitimate explanations.

Johan himself felt that he, they all, were now cast
adrift. Before an irrevocable change, " Verge-

legen " appeared more attractive than it had ever been. It seemed to him that his uncle was selling not merely a farm but twenty years of their lives.

" And I, uncle ? " he asked after a time. " What do you want me to do ? "

" I've thought about it," his uncle replied. " When I was in Port Benjamin for our last party conference, I spoke to Karel Steyn, one of the heads of Steyn, Berger and Stumpfkopf—you know, the people who export all our wool for us. He's willing to take you on in their business. Everybody I've spoken to assures me that it's the most progressive shipping and wool broker's agency in the whole of the country. With your practical knowledge of farm produce, you shouldn't find it difficult to get to the top quickly. You'll start with a salary of twelve pounds a month—I'll let you have another three pounds a month in the beginning, but Steyn assures me that an ambitious young fellow can double and treble his salary in no time. I hope you don't dislike the idea, for there's nothing else we can do."

If Johan had many doubts, his uncle had none. The evening before he left, the old man took up the family Bible after supper and read out pointedly for Johan that chapter from Paul's letter to Corinthians which contains the text: " When I was a child I spoke as a child, I understood as a child, I thought as a child, but when I became a man, I put away childish things."

When old Meneer van Bredepoel came to this passage, which, like the rest of the chapter, he knew off by heart, he looked up steadily at Johan. His voice suddenly went very low and very deep, while his wife sat at his side, very still, her hands folded on her lap and her look fixed on the Bible. Johan tried to look steadily back, but he failed. He thought he saw twenty years of his life arrange themselves neatly round that scene like reflections of the earth and the sky round the light in a crystal. When the reading was over, his uncle asked them all to sing that psalm which begins in the Dutch version: " How shall the young man keep his path pure if not through God."

" Always remember that," his uncle told him when they had finished, " and you can never go wrong."

" Amen," said his aunt, rising from her chair and flicking a tiny speck of bread from the black velvet of her gown with a neat, fastidious gesture.

CHAPTER III

THERE is in Port Benjamin a large district which consists almost entirely of cheap boarding-houses and private hotels.

There, towards evening, when the smoke begins to tumble down among the housetops and the sky turns a feathery grey, and the harsh roar of the traffic has been subdued into a more leisurely, almost domestic noise, people gather in small, sheltered gardens or round obscure entrances in dusty side streets. In the deepening darkness you may see among the trees the tips of lighted cigarettes trace patterns whose involved designs, since the smokers are almost invisible, are mysterious as they are ephemeral. You hear the murmur of voices and the slow reluctant laughter that comes to people at the end of a dull day's work, until the forlorn tinkle of a dinner bell disperses first one group, then another. For half an hour or more, this district of Port Benjamin will be so quiet that if it were not for the distant clatter of knives, and those soft points of curtained light round which the voices gather like moths fluttering round candles, you might think these spacious, shabby houses uninhabited. But later the same groups will reappear in the same places, doing the same sort of things, until their boredom drives them indoors to form bridge parties in over-furnished common-rooms or casts them with books in their hands on lonely beds. Lights go out

in the biggest rooms, and smaller lights appear in
places which have been hitherto part only of the
shadows. Behind half-curtained windows occasionally there may flash a naked arm or shoulder, which
caught between the darkness outside and the yellow
light within takes on a glowing Rubenesque fullness.
And if in the late hours of the night you still paced
the streets here, and heard only the footsteps of some
belated being measure on the asphalted pavements
his anxiety to be wrapped in the rest these white-
walled houses enclose, you might feel that the night
has retained the memory of those bearded and
halberded old Dutch watchmen who, when Port
Benjamin was young, countered darkness with a
sonorous " All's well! "

Just on the edge of this district lie wide streets
which, filled with a stream of traffic, encircle it like
a moat. Each morning you will hear the latches of
innumerable side-gates click, the hurrying of many
feet, and presently, on the narrow lawns in front of
these islanded houses there will be left only people
too young or too old to work, with perhaps a visitor
or two from the interior of Africa, their faces
blackened by the sun. One old man will be saying to
another something like this: " A lovely morning,
isn't it ? But I fear it's going to be very hot to-day.
Did you notice how near the mountain looked last
night ? Always a sign of rain and thunder, old
chap." And both will turn their heads and look at
the mountain which overshadows and overhangs Port
Benjamin, noticing how its steel-grey rocks seem to
tremble already underneath the sun, how the morning vapours and smoke rise quivering to its summit.

Through the heart of the district runs Governor's Walk, a street which owes its name to a famous Dutch governor who less than two hundred years ago invariably took his evening walk along it. A German chronicler of that period has recorded with delight the beauties of that route. He assures us " that of all the many promenades for which Port Benjamin is so justly renowned, there is none that excels in all those qualities which a benevolent nature can bestow Governor van der Brande's favourite walk. To roam in its shade on a fine day and look at its vaulted verdure is the most perfect refreshment." The chronicler describes with considerable detail how Governor's Walk led from the " truly magnificent gardens of the East India Company into a dense indigenous forest," and emerged at a point on the slopes of the mountain from which he often looked down on the " cold Atlantic " on his right, and the " warm and sunny Indian Ocean " on his left.

" Nowhere have I seen the sublime and the beautiful," he states, " the tame and the terrible so well arranged as there. Everything grows with the greatest luxuriance. The oaks are large and tall, though twisted somewhat by the wind which often races down the mountain. Walnuts, chestnuts and many varieties of indigenous trees flourish in the greatest abundance, and among these last is the oleaster or wild olive, the wood of which is the most beautiful I have ever seen, and when polished is almost transparent. I have seen there within the space of a short evening's promenade more varieties of wild flowers than ever in the fatherland, and the

flocks of sheep I encountered are so well nourished
that their owners have to construct special little
vehicles for supporting their tails, lest the blessed
creatures should find it impossible to walk. I often
felt there that had it pleased the Good Lord to have
made Man out of African instead of Asian clay, he
could not have done better than to have placed his
feet on Governor van der Brande's Walk."

Since those far-off days the changes along
Governor's Walk have been enormous. The indigenous forest of which the chronicler speaks has
disappeared, and there is left here and there only a
twisted and rotting oak-tree, throwing shadows over
a cramped tennis-court where no one appreciates
them, or dragging its branches stiffly over the tin roof
of some boarding-house or private hotel. Nor is it
possible to look down to-day and see either the
" cold Atlantic " or the " warm and sunny Indian
Ocean." Between you and the two oceans are the
shabby walls and smoke of hundreds of houses built
neither at leisure nor with taste, and if you should
tell any of the people who inhabit them that where
now their tennis-courts and sickly lawns are, once
grazed sheep with tails so fat that they had to be
strapped to a little wagon, they would laugh at you,
say something about the tough and lean meat they
live on, and ask you to tell them another.

Of all these houses, 43 Governor's Walk would
remind you least of the period the German chronicler
describes. It has, it is true, a small garden, the
centre path of which is flanked by eight oak-trees,
but five of the trees have their trunks filled in with
cement to prevent them from rotting further, and

the branches of the others have been substantially
cut, so as not to interfere with the light on an under-
sized tennis-court. The house itself was built on a
modern instalment plan, and bears over the main
door the name " Eagle's Nest." It was originally
built for a retired sea captain and on his death
purchased by a Mrs. Harris, who made such a
success of taking in paying guests that 43 Governor's
Walk is to-day merely a small heart to a big web
of annexes. It is advertised in the Port Benjamin
newspapers as being " a home away from home,
fitted with every modern convenience."

One fine summer morning some years ago,
Mrs. Harris was in her sitting-room talking to her
sister.

" My dear, Gertie is getting awfully slack. I'll
have to give her a very good telling off. She hasn't
begun to do the Walter Street rooms yet, and
yesterday she forgot to do Major Mustard's slops.
She was out again last night with a French sailor,
and, of course, late this morning. Isn't it funny that
no matter how good these coloured girls are, they
will give their souls to go off with the worst of men,
as long as they're white. You wouldn't believe me
if I told you the number of coloured girls I've had
to dismiss for becoming pregnant, and mostly
through white men too. And by the way, my dear,
do remind me to talk to Mr. Radot about his
gramophone to-day. Yes, I've had another complaint about it from Mrs. Elstree to-day. He was
playing it until late last night, and I believe he had
some woman in his room too. And Mrs. Morrissette
must be told not to let her nasty little boy run about

naked on the tennis-court again. She told me that
she does it for his health, but I can't have my guests
complaining about it. Mrs. Songster spoke to me
about it at breakfast this morning. And do remind
me to move Mr. Blanchard from Walter to Brussels
Street to-day. This is the third time he's moving.
I don't know how people can be so inconsiderate.
They seem to think because they pay you a miserable
eight pounds a month they have the right to ask for
everything they want. Now, won't you sit down and
help me to write out these menus. Or, perhaps, my
dear, you wouldn't mind going to see if the maids
have aired the room for that young Dutchman who
is coming this evening."

Van Bredepoel arrived at Mrs. Harris' that evening
after sunset. He knew very little about " Eagle's
Nest," except that it had been recommended to his
uncle by a member of the Provincial Council, which
always had its sittings in Port Benjamin. His uncle
had said, " If it's good and cheap enough for a
member of the Provincial Council "—as an elected
Member of Parliament his uncle was always rather
scornful of its subsidiary bodies—" it will be good
and cheap enough for you. And don't forget one
must crawl before one can walk."

He was not surprised, therefore, to find it different
from anything of the kind he had ever seen, and yet
he was not unfavourably impressed. Mrs. Harris
saw him first from the window of her sitting-room,
coming slowly up the path of the small garden. He
had a suit-case in each hand, and was obviously a
little embarrassed by the stares of some of the
inhabitants of 43 Governor's Walk, who had

gathered in the garden. The moment she saw him, Mrs. Harris jumped up from her chair, threw her knitting on a table, and placing herself in front of a mirror made some quite unnecessary readjustments to her dress.

" Here he comes! " she exclaimed.

" He ? Who is ' he ' ? " Her sister knew perfectly well who it was but her question was both meant and understood as a reproof. She had always found Mrs. Harris' enthusiasm over a new lodger unbecoming.

" Anyone would think you were a common boarding-house keeper the way you go on," she had once protested. " You should show a little better taste than to treat your umpteenth lodger as though he was your first."

" Don't be stupid, Lily! " Mrs. Harris now replied. " You know perfectly well who I mean. Or if you don't, I can't stop to tell you," and she hurried from the room.

Immediately her sister rushed to the window and saw van Bredepoel about to ring the front door bell. She had only to look at his clothes to come to a conclusion.

" Phew! " she whistled, as she drew back. " Country born and country bred, and Dutch all along the line."

" Ah, there you are. Mr. van Bredepoel," said Mrs. Harris, appearing at the front door. " Come right inside, and don't bother about those suit-cases. I'll have them sent up to your room. I hope you've had a good journey. You're just in time for dinner."

" Are you Mrs. Harris ? " His manner was shy, his English diffident, and he hesitated on the doorstep. He picked up his suit-cases, then put them down again.

" Yes. Won't you come in ? "

He looked so bewildered that Mrs. Harris' excitement gave way to a feeling of sympathy, and she spoke to him in Dutch.

" I'll take you up to your room straight away. You must be tired. You must have been a long time in the train."

" Two days and a night." His tone was more confident, and he stepped into the passage.

" I won't bite you," Mrs. Harris felt like saying, but aloud she remarked, " It is really too much. I always feel quite ill at the end of a journey like that. You see, I once lived in the country you come from. My father had a farm. . . ."

Talking, she led the way down a passage, spot-lessly clean and shining with polish, up stairs covered with linoleum, down another passage, and right at the end stopped in front of a door, looking for a key in the bunch she had in her hand. The light in the passage was dim, and near the stairs soft-footed black menservants were moving about, jugs of water in their hands.

" May I help you ? " The new lodger stepped forward.

Mrs. Harris murmured her thanks, handed over the keys, stepped back and had a good look at him. " He'll stay a long time, won't be noisy, and will pay his bill punctually the first day of the month," she thought.

The door creaked open slowly.

" A little bit stiff ? " Mrs. Harris asked, and

added without waiting for a reply: " I'll have it seen to to-morrow."

The room was small. It contained a bed, chest of drawers and an iron wash-stand. It had only one window, which overlooked the servants' quarters and kitchen yard ; but Mrs. Harris ushered van Brede-poel into it as though it were a millionaire's suite.

" You will be quite comfortable, I think," she said, " but if there is anything else you want please let me know. There is always hot water in the kitchen, so please don't hesitate to ask for it. If the servants don't behave report them immediately. But as you come from the country I'm sure you'll know how to deal with them. It's only these town people who spoil the blacks."

She went, leaving van Bredepoel at the window. Waiting for his luggage to come, he had a good look round. The room was clean, the linen without a stain, but . . . .

" We'll have to see what we shall see," he said to himself.

He went to the window and looked out. It was nearly dark, and the half light revealed only endless numbers of grey walls and tin roofs, over which smoke drifted slowly. For the first time in his life he was conscious of the life of a big town boiling like a Niagara around him, and he thought, not without excitement, that linked to the noise were the lives of two hundred thousand strange people. He glanced down into the courtyard below him. The shadows were deeper there, except where the kitchen lamp shining through a doorway cast a long parallelogram of light on the stones. He made out the forms of some black servants standing against a wall. Well away from the wall was another figure, taller and stronger than any of the others, whirling round and round in a dance of wild abandon. Sometimes it whirled out of sight into the shadows farther in the yard, then reappeared in the light of the kitchen, stamped out a brief rhythm there, and once more slipped into the shadows. Every movement of the dancer was counterpointed by music played on a mouth-organ, stamping of the feet of the men against the wall, and every now and then a shout of " Oh, Ash Cake! "—evidently the name of the dance—" You beautiful thing! "

The tune itself was monotonous but its rhythm vivid and catching, and though there were hardly more than three bars to it, by the time it had been repeated about thirty times repetition lent a strange sense of wonder to its very monotony.

Van Bredepoel found himself deeply moved. At first he did not understand why. Then he realised that often at night at " Vergelegen " he had heard the native servants make music just like that. At the same time he was puzzled. He could not reconcile this primitive, direct rhythm with what he had so far seen of Port Benjamin. " Vergelegen " was more than a thousand miles away; the nearest native territories in which one usually heard music of this kind were almost as far, and Port Benjamin was an up-to-date and highly industrialised port.

Suddenly the group below felt that they were being watched. The youth stopped dancing abruptly and looked up. The light from the kitchen illuminated his features. Van Bredepoel looked down into a pair of large, vivid black eyes, a firm well-formed face with the healthy black skin of a native who is accustomed to live in the open air. Seeing van Bredepoel, he gave him a country native's salute, held his right hand far above his head, said " Eh! Inkosan '! " and then bolted, laughing as he went through the kitchen door.

" You are not from here," van Bredepoel told himself. " Like me, you come from the country and not so very long ago either." And he felt a certain sympathy for him.

He did not, however, think more of the incident that night, for soon he had to go down for dinner. He was put at a table with two other men, one young and of an athletic appearance, the other old, with waxed sandy-coloured moustaches and blurred blue eyes. The conversation between the two of them kept him for a time from thinking about himself.

" The food lately has been rotten; I absolutely refuse to eat this muck," said the young man, pushing a plate of green, pickled fish away from him.

" You are right," replied the older man, " but what do you expect ? All these places are the same." Turning to van Bredepoel he asked: " If it is not indiscreet, sir, may we have your opinion on this glaucous concoction ? "

Van Bredepoel hesitated, and then said with diffidence: " I don't think it's too bad."

" You're a new-comer, sir, but when you have lived in this den as long as we have, you will no doubt think as we do," replied the old man.

" She's given the room she promised me to Blanchard; if she thinks I'll put up with that sort of thing she's mistaken." The young man spoke as though he wished to impress both of them with his firmness and importance. " I'm going to give her notice right now." He threw his napkin down on the table and got up to go.

" Aren't you finishing your food first, young man ? " the other asked. " Too many carbo-hydrates and not enough vitamins, you know ? "

" No, no, Major. I've had just about enough of this, I'm going. Good night." And he walked out of the room like a dragoon.

" There, there you are," said the Major to van Bredepoel. " I'm an old soldier, sir, an old cam-paigner. I've had my share of times, rough and fair. I can rough it with any one of 'em. But what I don't like are these places which are neither flesh nor fish. But it's futile to behave like my young friend who has just gone. All these places are alike. He'll just jump out of the frying-pan into the fire." The old man leaned forward and spoke in a whisper. " It's the boarding-house mind he's got. He's annoyed that Blanchard has got the room he wants, not because he wants the room so much himself, but because he thinks the old girl has given it to Blanchard because she feels him to be the more important of the two. Take my tip, sir: if you don't want to develop the boarding-house mind—that expression of mine is rather good, don't you think ? What ?—if you don't want to develop the boarding-house mind, always observe a strict and polite neutrality towards your fellow lodgers. That fellow is an international foot-baller and would probably bear the loss of a father with fortitude and courage, but he can't bear a miserable pin-prick from a woman he despises. Why? The boarding-house mind. A polite and strict neutrality, sir, and you'll be able to live here happily for eight years as I've done."

With that the Major got up and left the room. Van Bredepoel did not at the time think it likely that he would be staying there eight years, but he was to stay long enough to learn that Major Mustard did not by any means observe the strict and polite neutrality he preached.

When van Bredepoel walked out of the dining-room he passed Major Mustard, Mrs. Harris and her sister in the hall. Major Mustard and Mrs. Harris nodded affably to him, but the sister ignored him.

" Who's the new guy ? " snapped the Major, when van Bredepoel had gone. " Where does he come from ? "

" Somewhere up country," Mrs. Harris replied.

" Looks and acts it, too! " her sister sniffed.

" He seems quite a decent sort," the Major said. He did not like Mrs. Harris' sister.

" Think so ? " Her tone was ironical.

" Yes, I thought he was quite an English type."

" You are funny, Major! " Mrs. Harris exclaimed, pleased at the last remark. And as the Major had been with her a long time she was not afraid to tease him a little. " Whenever you see anything you like in the Dutch you say how English it is; when there is something you don't like you say ' how very Dutch.' Now my mother was Dutch. . . ."

" My dear! " interrupted the sister, just as if she had heard it for the first time. " Are you sure ? "

"My mother was Dutch," Mrs. Harris repeated, ignoring her. "And you wouldn't say so to look at me!"

Major Mustard was vastly amused. He was still chuckling to himself as he walked away: "Doesn't she just! Doesn't she just!" And he did not forget to make a story of it at bridge that evening.

CHAPTER IV

" VAN BREDEPOEL, my boy! " Mr. Karel Steyn, managing director of Steyn, Berger and Stumpfkopf, had said to him at their first interview, " don't be in such a hurry to start work. Take a few days to settle down. Have a good look round and see how the land lies first. Then come back in a week's time and we'll have your work ready for you. Is that understood ? Excellent, then! Good-bye! "

And the big man had hurried van Bredepoel through his private door, leaving him none the wiser as to what he was to do or under what conditions he was to work. He had gone back disconsolately to his room. He would have preferred to start work immediately, but Mr. Karel Steyn had hardly given him a chance for even a faint protest. Now he was trying to write a letter to his aunt and uncle, but this was no longer easy. He was accustomed to write them long, impersonal, almost business-like accounts of what happened on " Vergelegen." Rarely had he attempted to discuss with them his more intimate feelings. He knew instinctively that such a discussion would only embarrass, that they were interested chiefly in his actions, and that his aunt in particular looked primarily on people as beings not with feelings but with certain obvious duties to perform. And as his present mood was full of misgiving about the new life he was to lead, he was utterly at loss for something to say. Ever since his arrival in Port

Benjamin he had felt like a person who has suddenly
been taken out of a quiet, primrosed country lane
and put to work in the engine-room of a vast and
very complex factory.

He had hardly begun writing when the sound of
some natives talking underneath his window made
him stop. They were talking a Bantu language van
Bredepoel could understand, and he was particularly
interested by one voice with a remarkably pure
accent. He got up from the table where he was
writing and went to the window. Below him were
six natives apparently teasing the youth he had seen
dancing on the night of his arrival. The youth was
taking the teasing in very good part and replying
easily to the sallies of the others. It was his voice
which had roused van Bredepoel's interest, and
listening he was once more struck by the facility with
which the boy spoke. Unlike the others he never
seemed at a loss for a word. Unlike them, too, there
was no trace of the kitchen jargon of their white
masters in his speech.

" It is the great water-serpent who has left his
home in the long yellow river beyond the Mountains
of the Moon," the boy was saying, with the emphasis
that speakers find necessary when they have repeated
the same thing four or five times. " There will be
much rain now. Look how his tail has beaten up the
clouds."

He pointed at the sky. Van Bredepoel leaned out
of the window to look up like the others and saw,
immediately overhead, a very strange cloud formation. At the back of the town loomed the summit of
the mountain, purple and gold in the afternoon sun-

light. But in the sky over the harbour, rising far above the highest skyscraper, was a long black cloud, grooved with shadow like a tunnel. From its centre was slowly descending a twisting pillar of rain, and the roofs of the farthest houses were already dark with shadow.

" Your words are foolish. You speak in ignorance. It is only the wind that has done that, and it will not rain," one of the other natives replied. But before the youth could answer, the man who had just spoken saw van Bredepoel. For a moment or two they were silent, while the youth looked shyly from van Bredepoel to his companions, from his companions to van Bredepoel.

" Joseph is an ignorant nigger, he does not know much, master," one of the natives said to van Bredepoel in English.

" He is very superstitious," remarked another, pronouncing " superstitious " with great difficulty, and seemed so pleased with his effort that he could not stop laughing.

" I heard what he said," van Bredepoel replied, and went back to his table.

But that night it rained a great deal, and van Bredepoel read in the newspapers the next morning that there had been a cloud-burst. Superstition, he thought, is often only the wrong explanation for the right observation.

Two days later, on his way to catch a train, he heard someone running after him. He turned round and saw the boy, Joseph, coming towards him, racing along as if running were his favourite means of locomotion. When Joseph reached him, he held

out a pound note and some loose silver (more than
he was paid in a month) and said with difficulty in
English: "Master, I found much money on the
table of the master this morning. It is bad, master.
Bad men there." He waved his hand in the direction
of 43 Governor's Walk, but to van Bredepoel it
seemed to pass over the whole of Port Benjamin.

"So you do my room?" he asked, after thanking
him.

Joseph seemed pleased by the question.

"Yes, master! I do the master's room, and make
shine the master's shoes."

Van Bredepoel watched him running back, taking
long graceful strides and pausing only to dance with
mock menace round a native who nearly walked
into him on a corner.

That evening van Bredepoel sought out Joseph and
called him to his room.

"Joseph!" he said, "I have something for you."
He took some money out of his pocket.

Unlike the servant who had brought up van
Bredepoel's luggage on the night of his arrival and
had received a tip very much as a matter of course,
Joseph held out both his hands cupped together,
taking a few shillings as though they were a glittering
pile of gold, and then raised a trembling hand above
his head as a salute of gratitude, just as the natives
on "Vergelegen" had done when they were paid.

"Joseph," van Bredepoel said to him in his own
language, "you are not of Port Benjamin. How
long have you been here?"

"Inkosan', it is four days and a night since I left
the kraal of my father," he replied.

"Joseph," van Bredepoel told him, "it is four days and a night since I left the hut of the brother of my father."

"Auck! Inkosan'," he exclaimed, as if over-whelmed with the significance of the coincidence, and then, as van Bredepoel said no more, he went from the room.

Van Bredepoel's tip, the first he had ever received, and the friendly way he had been spoken to in the language of his people, sent him dancing out of the house into the yard, in such a lively manner that Mrs. Harris came rushing after him to call him to order.

Thereafter van Bredepoel lost no opportunity of questioning Joseph. He was surprised to find that the black youth was easier to get on with and interested him more than anyone he had thus far met in Port Benjamin. He saw many analogies in their two lives, and contact between them seemed to become established by itself. He soon learnt that his real name was not Joseph, but Kenon Badiak-gotla. "Kenon" he discovered was actually, in the black youth's language, an exclamation of extreme gratitude, the equivalent of something like "Oh, I do thank you!" uttered in relief from a very great anxiety. Joseph told van Bredepoel that he got this name because his mother had borne him only after she had given her husband six daughters; she was so pleased when she heard that at last she had given birth to a son that she looked up at the roof of her hut and, forgetting her pain, cried out: "Kenon!"

"But what made you come so far away to Port Benjamin?" van Bredepoel asked him.

" Inkosan'," he replied, " my father is old. He has many daughters, but I am his only son. His daughters have not brought him in much cattle. Three of them are still in his hut, waiting for their men to come and fetch them. Last year the rain went away. It became very dry. There was no water and the sun killed all the crops of my father. He had to buy many bags of mealies from the white master's store. To-day he owes much money to the master at the store, and the taxes want much money and there is no money."

" You did not use your maize for making beer ? "

Kenon laughed, as if it were expected of him. Immediately van Bredepoel felt annoyed with himself. The question seemed to have come from his lips instinctively, and he realised with discomfort that if a white man had told him a similar story he would at least have expressed a polite sympathy. But had he not been trained as a child to be critical of everything black people told him ? It struck him, too, that his question was related in some way to a remark he remembered making long ago to his old tutor: " But Meneer Broecksma! She's black! "

" Go on with your story," he said quickly.

" My father told me," Kenon said, " that he wanted me to go out for a little time and earn money, and the teacher [missionary] told him that he knew of someone in Port Benjamin who would give me work. And so, Inkosan', I made ready to come."

CHAPTER V

THE kraal of Mlangene Badiakgotla lies against the summit of a hill, which is situated in a very wide valley. So vast is the valley, and so many hills does it contain, that when the Bambuxosa, the nation to which the Badiakgotla belong, saw it for the first time more than two hundred years ago they called it: " The Valley of a Thousand Hills." The white men who followed in their footsteps found the name not without charm, and to-day it is still displayed on the pamphlets of many tourist agencies and publicity associations which annually persuade hundreds of pallid travellers to rush through the valley in fast motor-cars.

At night and early morning in a normal season the valley is covered in a thick mist which fills it like a cauldron with steam, and overflows into the roads and plateaux that skirt the edges of the valley. But at sunrise a breeze invariably comes from somewhere in the direction of the sea, gathers the mist from roads and plateaux and drives it like a flock of sheep down through the darkest kloofs of the valley. Gradually as the mist unfolds one notices here and there in a patch of sunlight on the crest of a hill the neat brown circles of many kraals, from which smoke rises slowly skywards, dark blue against the misty air. Other hills appear with herds of cattle going slowly down the slopes into the valley to drink and women coming upwards along a dark red footpath, jars of water on their heads, gently carrying over their unchanging lives from a quiet night into a tranquil day. And an atmosphere of timelessness replaces the mist in the valley. The walls of the valley are like the frame round a picture in which life is sealed and transfigured in one calm, unperplexed and unchanging moment.

But the morning on which Kenon was to leave his father's kraal there was no mist in the valley. The mist comes only when the valley is moist, and on this day it was dry. The sun came up warm, and brought out the mamba and puff-adder and cobra two or three hours before they normally stir. When the Badiakgotla family were ready for their morning's meal, the sun was already so hot that they moved their pots round into the shade at the back of the hut of Kenon's father. For a time no one said a word. The women wanted to speak but they were silent, for they knew that their father had something to say, and Kenon's thoughts were far away from the kraal.

"My son," Kenon's father said after many moments, "you are going far to-day. Soon my words will not be able to reach you. You do not know this place you are going to, and I do not know it, but you are young. They say that there are such wonderful things as we have never seen. They say also that there are many bad men and many evil things. You will have to be careful of these evil things, and these bad men. See that you serve your masters well, see that you are honest and that you do not speak words that are not so, and your masters will be good to you. Hear and remember what I say to you, my son, and when the big rain comes, you will come back to the kraal of your father."

As he spoke, his daughters every now and then called out a polite approval of his words, but his wife was very quiet, and hardly took her eyes off Kenon.

" I hear," Kenon said, " and I will not forget."

Kenon got up and went away into the hut. There he took off his white-and-black blanket, his copper and bead bangles, most of which he had made himself, keeping out of them only two for his ankles and two for his wrists. He rubbed his skin well over with lion fat. Then when it shone to his satisfaction, he put on a long dress shirt, which the trader at the store had once given him. The shirt came down in front to his knees—behind, half-way to his ankles. He fastened it at his throat with a large shining brass stud, but he had neither collar nor tie. The shirt was so long that it made the wearing of any garments below it unnecessary, but, all the same, he did not part with his leather loin-strap. Over the shirt he buttoned lightly an old waistcoat and put on a black working-coat which had once belonged to the missionary. On his head he placed a small light blue serge cap on which was the badge of the mission school; picked out two of his favourite hunting-sticks and took them, together with an old umbrella, in one hand. The rest of his belongings, his beads, bangles, school books and a spare shirt, he packed in a chest, made out of pieces of old petrol cases and soap boxes.

His sisters clapped their hands when they saw him. They helped him to place the chest on his head, a burden which he hardly felt, so great was his excitement. They then followed him half-way down the hill on a footpath which led to the stream in the valley, running round him and shouting out his praises as they went. Long after he had crossed the stream their cries, in which there alternated grief, envy and admiration, reached him. They watched him climb up the far side of the valley, and saw every now and then the copper bangles round his ankles flash in the sun, and their spirits grew warm with pride and cold with sorrow that so splendid a brother should leave them. But in Kenon all such feelings were overlaid by his excitement. He did not pause to think that for a long time he might not tread again the footpath which led to his home.

Now, near Kenon's father's hut the soil is rich and red and warm, like blood, and when it rains the grass there grows thick and tall, the cattle big and fat. There from the beds of a thousand valleys you can see red footpaths twist up the grass-covered hillsides into a cloudless sky. You can see at evening the thunder-clouds of a storm two days before it fills the streams at your feet. You will hear at night the sound of wind which comes from the desert on the other side of the continent, the jackal, the stream flowing over smooth pebbles, and from many a light-tipped hill the sound of laughter and singing. And standing outside your tent, as you smoke a last cigarette before creeping into your sheepskin bag, you might be moved to quote even George Borrow's " wind on the heath, brother " nonsense. On the following morning looking around you from the cushioned seats of your motor-car, you will regret leaving such a fine country and might say, like many others before you: " What a happy, carefree country, people so like children. Yes! We pay "—and by " We " you would largely mean yourself—" far too heavy a price for civilisation, far too heavy a price." For you will see the country only like that. Your tourist agency would not recommend it otherwise. But will you know that there are far too many people even for so seemingly rich a soil, that often it does not rain, that the taxes are heavy, and that on the other side of the hill there is a Kenon setting out from his father's hut, envying you the speed of your car ?

That night Kenon slept in the hut of one of his sisters who had married into a neighbouring tribe. At dawn he was on the road again. He reached the railway siding at noon, just as there arrived by car the storekeeper, who had eaten his breakfast in comfort that morning at home. Kenon admired the confident casual way the storekeeper walked into the tin-walled office of the siding. With a great effort he ultimately solicited and obtained the storekeeper's help for the purchase of his ticket.

In the evening Kenon changed into another train at a bigger railway station farther ahead. He thought that nowhere in the world could there be more people and more trains than in this place. His new train was crowded with black people, not one-tenth of whom seemed to be of his own nation, let alone of his own tribe. The world seemed to him to have suddenly become unbearably complicated. There were Tamboukies, wrapped in red blankets, on their way to mines in the north; small but fierce-looking Pondos, heavily decorated and tattooed, on their way back from sugar plantations in Natal; there were other black people, whose race he did not know, some in blankets, some dressed up as fantastically as he was, some in clothes with exaggerated lines of the latest fashion, cowboy hats on their heads, canes in their hands, and pointed patent-leather shoes on their feet. Kenon was pleased to notice that although some of these coaches crowded with black people were put at the back of the train, his own and one other were given, as he thought, the pride of place, immediately behind the engine. But the white people in the first- and second-class carriages knew that they had a buffer of two crowded coaches between them and any accidents which might occur. And why not ? They had paid more, and after all they were white.

Next to him on a stiff-backed wooden bench Kenon found a grey-haired native, who was reading, half aloud, out of a small green book. Kenon looked over his shoulder and recognised immediately that it was the book he had been given at the mission school for his first primer. There were in it the same black-and-white illustrations of domestic animals, and little girls and boys in white frocks. The old man saw that Kenon was looking at his book, and asked him, in a strange tongue he could hardly understand:

" Boy, can you read ? "

" Yes, old father," he replied respectfully.

" You have been to school, then ? "

" Oh yes, I have passed my second standard."

" Then can you tell me what this is ? My eyes are not good; I cannot see well."

Kenon saw that he pointed to some large capital letters, whose outlines it was impossible not to see. To his great relief he knew them.

" S-N-A-K-E, snake," he said.

" I thank you," the old man replied, and went on with his reading, but after a time he looked up and remarked: " Your father must be pleased with you. What are you going to be ? A schoolmaster ? "

" Oh, no! " Kenon answered with some pride, " I am going to be a town boy."

The same old man later showed Kenon where the lavatory was, after Kenon had been considering relieving himself out of the window. The water-flushed lavatory pleased him very much. It was to him but one of the many wonderful things on that very wonderful journey. Every time he got up to go to the lavatory he took with him his two sticks, his umbrella and wooden chest, which he got into the lavatory with difficulty and often pushed accidentally into people. The old man, when he saw him do this, smiled at him over his primer—rather enigmatically, you would have thought.

Later, when the train pulled up at a station, Kenon saw ahead the outline of a long range of blue mountains. He heard someone shout out " The sea! " but though he looked out he could see nothing except far away a thin cloud of mist that was mounting slowly into the evening sky. While he was at the window he saw some white men get out of a coach farther back. They walked leisurely up the platform towards the engine, stopping only once or twice to light their cigars. Some of them had, as people often do on journeys, eaten too much, and repeatedly gave a forced dry cough to get rid of a sticky feeling in their throats. As they passed Kenon's window they turned up their noses and one of them said: " God! How it stinks here."

After a time Kenon, too, got out of the carriage and walked shyly up the platform. Two copper-coloured half-caste girls in bright green dresses and large yellow hats, seeing him, nudged each other and shouted out so loudly that many people laughed: " Oh! Nigger Boy, but you do look swell! " Kenon did not understand, but if he had he would have seen in that only a deserved tribute. He did not walk far, however, for soon there were people shouting out strange things at him, a whistle went, and a swearing conductor came to drive him running back to his coach. That night he slept with his head on the old man's shoulders, his feet between people on the bench opposite, and in his sleep his hand would often go into the inside pocket of his coat for the missionary's letter. Towards dawn he woke. His ears instinctively were tuned for that silence round his home, broken only by the noise of the cattle stirring in the kraal, the barking of dogs, and the sound of the wind shepherding a ghostly mist up and down the Valley of a Thousand Hills; but he was bewildered to hear hundreds of people shouting and talking loudly as they bundled out of the train. Quickly he sat up, grasped his luggage case, his sticks and umbrella, and joined in the crush at the door. There a white man was examining and questioning each man as he came down. When he saw Kenon's clothes he exclaimed impatiently: " What the hell's this ? You are not a Tambouki ! "

Kenon understood him so badly that he did not reply.

" Where the devil are you going ? " shouted the man, annoyed at his silence.

" Where ? " asked Kenon, still puzzled.

" Are you trying to be funny ? Where, you fool, where ? " The man caught him by the arm, and pressed it very tightly.

" Porto Benjamin," Kenon answered, now thoroughly alarmed.

" Then get to hell where you came from," shouted the man, and shoved him back so vigorously that he landed sprawling on the floor.

But all the Tamboukis had gone, and he found he could have a bench to himself. He looked out of the window, and saw in the dim morning light a strange country covered with forest, and in the south a sharp clear-cut range of mountains. Between these mountains and him the engine was casting a lurid light into the sky through which drifted dense clouds of steam. For the first time he had misgivings, and thought of his home. Two days later he arrived in Port Benjamin, the missionary's letter, safe but soiled, in his pocket.

CHAPTER VI

ON Sunday afternoons, when the servants at Mrs. Harris' had a half-holiday, Kenon would take off his uniform and wear with pride and fantastic elegance the clothes in which he had left his father's kraal. The moment he appeared in Governor's Walk, which on Sunday afternoon is always crowded with pedestrians, people would nudge one another, stare after him, and say: " God! Just look at that nigger! Have you ever seen such a sight in your life ? Trust a kaffir to make a fool of himself! " But it never seemed to strike Kenon that his dress could fail to excite admiration in others. His bearing did not lose any of its freedom because of the stares he received in the streets. Gripping his two hunting-sticks and an old umbrella firmly in his hands he walked on vigorously, with long graceful strides, carrying at the heart of him a warm feeling of satisfaction. Sometimes an elderly European, hot and uncomfortable in a close-fitting navy-blue suit, would be quite honest with himself and look after Kenon rather wistfully, admitting into his consciousness a pang of envy. And he would wonder how life could possibly burn so vividly, so spontaneously, so unshadowed by doubt and illness, in a human being. Even the day would seem to be made for people like Kenon, the brilliant summer afternoon, which discomfited most Europeans, devised to complete their happiness.

At the corner of a side street near Mrs. Harris' Kenon would meet other servants dressed rather like him, and they would all disappear dancing down the street, putting up such a realistic mock-fight with their sticks that pasty little white children out with their nurses would begin to weep with terror. Then the street echoed with the clash of their sticks and the sound of their laughter. Sometimes, even, policemen came running round the corner bravely prepared to break up a desperate faction fight, and Kenon and his companions would scatter, laughing at the curses heaped on them.

But in his free time during the week, Kenon was invariably to be found on the threshold of the servants' quarters at Mrs. Harris', carrying on lively conversations with the other black men. From the window of his room, in the gathering darkness, van Bredepoel would watch them squatting in a circle and drawing patterns with twigs on the loose surface of the yard while they talked. Sometimes when he had to go back to work in the evenings he returned to his room to find that small gesticulating group still in the yard. And how they talked! They were never at a loss for a subject and never in a hurry to exhaust one. The simplest incident was elaborately dramatised and presented with number-less variations. Each black man had a generous share of the conversation, and tended there to forget the jargon he was forced to talk in the kitchen. Van Bredepoel did not know which astonished him most, the ease with which they talked or the depth and richness of their memories. Things that had happened many years before were described as if

they were only a night old. One of the black men,
for instance, would tell how once he went out to hunt
a jackal, and there would come into his story the
names of his dogs, their respective peculiarities,
their behaviour on the way, an account of the
jackal, its history and the characteristics which
distinguished it from other animals of its kind. Van
Bredepoel would draw up his chair near the window
and listen to them for hours. The background of
their lives appeared to him very much like that of
his own, and as he listened a feeling of contentment
possessed him. He was relieved to find in Port
Benjamin people who were not wildly rushing about
from work to amusements, amusements to work,
but were content to spend the quiet summer evenings
in untroubled and luxurious conversation, indifferent
to the traffic surging outside in the streets. He
wondered if Europeans thrown together by hazard,
as these black men were, would conduct their
personal relations as well as these men did. On not
one occasion he could remember did they ever
quarrel or allow anything to disturb the unforced
cordiality of their relationship. They teased one
another often enough, it is true, but without any
irritation or anger resulting from it.

One evening as van Bredepoel listened to them
he decided to call Kenon to his room at the first
favourable opportunity, and to question him about
his people and the life he had led in Bambuland.

" I'm just as much, if not more, interested in what
he has to say as they are," he thought, " and I'm
far more lonely."

Kenon's first visit was followed by others until

there were few of van Bredepoel's free evenings on
which he did not invite the boy to come and talk to
him. At first Kenon was very reserved and replied
evasively to van Bredepoel's questions, often telling
him politely things that were intended to please him
but were not necessarily true. Once this reserve
broke down, however, his confidence was complete.
Then van Bredepoel was surprised to find how
little influence the mission school had exercised
over Kenon's mind and imagination. He talked
best about the legends of the Bambuxosa, and his
experiences with animals, of which not a single
characteristic seemed to have escaped him. From
him van Bredepoel learnt of that strange spirit
Tokoloshe—a sort of Bantu Priapus, who lived in
the rivers.

Tokoloshe, Kenon told him, was small but broad-
shouldered and unbelievably strong. His skin was
covered with long thick black hair, and he had a
phallus so long that he carried it wound round his
neck. He would be in wait there in the rivers where
he had his home, and when beautiful young girls
came with their pitchers, would catch them and
drag them under the water and they would never
be seen again. Sometimes when young girls suspected his presence and did not go to the river
for water, he would stalk out on a dark night and
steal them out of their father's huts, so quietly and
swiftly that not even the dogs were roused to bark.

" But are you sure that he exists ? " van Bredepoel
asked, careful not to show too much the doubts he
really felt.

" I am sure, Inkosan'," Kenon replied. " He has

dragged many a young girl into his hut underneath the river."

"But why are you so sure? Have you ever seen him?"

"I have not seen him, Inkosan', but the sister of the mother of my father's father was taken away by him. She never came back, Inkosan'."

"But perhaps it was a crocodile that caught her, and then she would not have come back."

"It is possible, Inkosan', for Tokoloshe takes many forms and he is very cunning. Listen! Inkosan', there was once a young girl of the Bambuxosa, one Mdabeni. Of all the young girls of the Bambuxosa this Mdabeni was the most beautiful. Her breasts were so round and small that you could hold and cover them with your two hands. One day when the women went down to the river with their pots, Tokoloshe saw Mdabeni, and when he saw her he knew that he would have no rest until he carried her into his hut. For many days he lay behind the bushes watching the women go about their work. Then one morning he saw the women go out to the fields, and Mdabeni was not with them. He crept round to the hut of Mdabeni's mother. Several times he walked round the hut, but he found no hole in the walls, and the entrance was shut. He tried to call with the voice of Mdabeni's mother: 'Mdabeni, my child, take, take these curds and eat.' But Mdabeni called back: 'Listen, listen, the voice of my mother is as soft as the voice of a sugar-bird, as that of the turtle dove when it comes to the water to drink, and your voice is like the voice of the jackal.' Then Tokoloshe knew he

would have to make another plan to get Mdabeni,
and, Inkosan', he made such a clever plan! He
took the steel of an assegai, and made it red-hot in a
fire and swallowed it, and his voice became wonderfully soft, like that of a mother. When he came to
the hut again, he called out ' Mdabeni, my child,
take, take these curds and eat.' Mdabeni thought
it was her mother. She opened the door, and she
was not seen again. Tokoloshe exists, Inkosan', he
is very clever."

" I would like to see him," van Bredepoel said.

" Auck! Inkosan'! " Kenon exclaimed, giving him
an amazed look, and shaking his head.

" But why not ? " van Bredepoel asked.

Kenon did not reply. He just looked at van
Bredepoel in a rather bewildered fashion and
wondered if he had understood.

Many, too, were the stories he told van Bredepoel
of Masakama, the great chief and founder of the
Bambuxosa. Kenon took no pains to hide the pride
he took in the history of Masakama. His imagination
was deeply stirred and van Bredepoel, listening,
sometimes imagined himself back in a lost world of
epic poetry, back in that old, old Africa, which lay
there beyond the mountains, its stony face turned
to the sun. He would listen intently, and from the
edge of his bed follow every gesture Kenon made.
The boy's gestures were often just as expressive as
his words. He sat on the rug on the floor at the foot
of van Bredepoel's bed, his legs folded in front of
him, one long black finger following the pattern in
the rug, the fingers of his other hand resting on a
knee and ready for any gesture he might want to

make. Always the gestures were calm, an inner tension showing only in a sight tremor of the fingers, a sombre glow in the eyes.

It was Masakama, Inkosan', he would begin, three fingers of the right hand raised to point at van Bredepoel when he uttered " Inkosan'," who brought the Bambuxosa to Bambuland. Until the days of Masakama the kraals of the Bambuxosa stood on the banks of "the long Yellow River on the other side of the Mountains of the Moon." Kenon pointed with his right hand at the wall and automatically van Bredepoel's eyes followed the movement. In those days, Kenon went on, the Bambuxosa were poor and surrounded by many dangers. They had not much cattle and very little crops. Their kraals and fields made only a small clearing in "the Forest of the Night." The trees in the forest grew so high that when the wind blew " their tops stirred round the stars. At night the forest spoke many words, but not the words of the Bambuxosa." By day there fluttered over the tree-tops the scarlet and yellow and green plumes of many birds, " and some of these birds, Inkosan', spoke like men, but not like the Bambuxosa." Sometimes a rhinoceros or a herd of elephants would pass through the forest like a great wind, charge out of it and trample through the fields and kraals of the Bambuxosa. Once, Kenon said, the women working in the fields came running back to their kraal, crying out that they had seen some yellow men not higher than a goat watching them from behind the trees. " And that, Inkosan', was not good." Then Masakama was born. He was so big

and strong that his mother died in giving him birth.
When the women came to nurse him they were
surprised to find he had been born circumcised,
"and that, Inkosan', was very good." Before Masakama was many months old, he startled his nurse by
walking suddenly. From that moment he never
again came to her for milk. Every morning and
afternoon he walked to the edge of the forest, where
there came a big white elephant-cow to feed him.
Everyone feared for him, but they did not stop him.
When he was a young boy, Masakama went with
other boys of his age to herd the cattle, and when
they drove the cattle back in the evenings, he would
call to them in a strange tongue, and the whole
herd would change colour. "Sometimes their colour
became red, Inkosan', sometimes yellow, sometimes
black, and at other times blue, so that when the
Bambuxosa first saw Masakama's herd they shouted
out in surprise: Look, Masakama has brought
home a strange herd of cattle."

In time the chief of the Bambuxosa became
jealous of Masakama, and feared that he would one
day kill him. So one fine afternoon when Masakama
was sitting at the side of a hut " making such a
bangle as the Bambuxosa had never seen," the chief
took his assegai and crept round the back of the
hut. It was a quiet day; the women were away in
the fields, the men out hunting. The chief took aim
between the shoulders of Masakama and threw his
assegai with great force, " but at that moment,
Inkosan', there came a great whirlwind and carried
the assegai into the sky." The chief knew then that
nothing could harm Masakama and he was sorry for

what he had tried to do, so he took Masakama into
his hut, and from that time honoured him. When
Masakama was a young man, he would take his
shield and assegais and go into the forest. "Many a
young man had gone into the forest, Inkosan', and
never come back, but Masakama came back. He
spoke with the birds and the trees, and the elephant
was his friend."

Only the Badimo (gods) were angry. They thought
that Masakama would learn their secrets and their
magic, and in their anger they spoke from the
mountains in thunder and smoke. Yet Masakama
had no fear. He went into the forest again and
again. "Then the Badimo sent some yellow men
with noses like the eagles, armed them with thunder
and lightning, and told them to kill all the Bambuxosa." But Masakama knew they were coming
and set fire to the grass and bushes, and they could
do nothing. When the Badimo saw this their anger
was terrible. "They bound the water-serpent in
the Yellow River so that he could not carry water
to the skies. For many moons there was not a cloud
in the skies. The ground became so hot that the
men of the Bambuxosa could not walk on it, and
the big Yellow River shrank into a few pools.
Even the lion and the leopard, the elephant and
the rhinoceros, the gorilla and the eland, Inkosan',
came to the kraal of the Bambuxosa to ask for water!"

Then Masakama called all the tribe round his
hut and told them what the Badimo had done. "The
Badimo," he said, "are jealous of the Bambuxosa.
I will lead you to a country where the Badimo cannot
reach the Bambuxosa. In this country there will be

many rivers and much cattle and food for the spears
of the Bambuxosa." And he led the Bambuxosa for
many moons, past a river over which lay "a smoke
that whispered," until he came into the country of
the Big Black Bull, a chief over many people. Now
at that time the Big Black Bull was at war with the
Big Black Elephant. He would not let Masakama
settle in his country unless he helped to kill the
Big Black Elephant. The kraal of the Big Black
Elephant was built on the top of "the Mountain of
the Night, so high that even the vulture feared to go
there." But Masakama took the best of his young
men, scaled the mountain at night, and killed the Big
Black Elephant and all his people, and the Big Black
Bull gave him much land and much cattle. The
women of the Bambuxosa bore so many sons and
their herds of cattle became so big that the Big Black
Bull became afraid that Masakama would become
too powerful and take all his land and cattle from
him. So one night he sent his best impis to kill
Masakama and all the Bambuxosa. Only the
daughter of the Big Black Bull, who had seen
Masakama and "whose belly had sickened for him,"
stole out in the night and ran many days to warn
Masakama. And Masakama was ready. He killed
all the impis of the Big Black Bull, killed the Big
Black Bull and burnt his kraal. "So Masakama
became the chief of all the land, Inkosan', and took
the daughter of the Big Black Bull into his hut and
she bore him many sons. Never have the Bambuxosa had so much cattle, never have their young
men been more strong and never their young girls
more beautiful."

" But how do you know all this, Kenon ? " van
Bredepoel asked him.

" Inkosan'," he replied, " the father of the father
of the father of my father's father was one of Masakama's indunas. It was to his son that Masakama
gave the name of Badiakgotla. For this induna was
a good man and a brave warrior, but he could not
hold his tongue. Often when Masakama was
holding his Kgotla,[1] this induna would talk and
talk until Masakama grew weary. One day he
talked all the morning and as the sun came over
the hills was still talking, when there came a young
boy to tell him that his wife had been delivered of
a son, and he talked no more. But Masakama,
hearing it, said to him, ' You shall call your son
Badiakgotla, he who has delivered the court.

" Masakama, you see, Inkosan', was a great chief
and a wise man. Never shall the Bambuxosa see
his like again, but the old men say that one day
Masakama will come back to his people on the clouds
with many warriors and much cattle, and then the
Bambuxosa will. . . ." Kenon suddenly stopped in
confusion.

" And then ? " van Bredepoel asked, but Kenon
said nothing and only looked at him with an
expression of dismay in his eyes.

" And then ? "

Still he made no reply.

" Shall I finish it for you ? " van Bredepoel
asked, and receiving no reply he went on: " And
then the Bambuxosa will take their shields and
assegais and drive the white man into the sea."

[1] Court.

" Auck! Inkosan'! " Kenon exclaimed distressed. " It is the old men who say that, not I. It is only a story."

When he listened to Kenon talking van Bredepoel found it difficult to picture him contented in Port Benjamin. It seemed to him that somebody with a background like that must be very unhappy in Port Benjamin, and he asked: " Do you like this place, Kenon ? "

" Yes, Inkosan'," he replied, " it is a fine place."

" But why do you like it ? "

Kenon looked puzzled, then gave a glittering laugh, and repeated: " It is a fine place, Inkosan'."

Some time after this conversation with Kenon, Major Mustard said to van Bredepoel suddenly at dinner:

" I wonder if you know an obscure English poet, who is not much admired nowadays, and who you may not like for his imperialistic tendencies, but who is quite good enough for an old soldier like me ? "

" Really, Major Mustard," he replied, " unless you can tell me more, I won't know who you mean."

" There you are," the Major replied, " I thought as much. You evidently don't know him, but if you did, you'd know a poem of his:

" ' Oh! East is East, and West is West, and
              never the twain shall meet.' "

" You mean Kipling ? "

" One can easily substitute for that, with as much justification," said the Major, ignoring his remark, " ' Oh! White is White, and Black is Black, and never the twain shall meet.' And if they do meet, by God, there shall be trouble."

" I don't think I know what you're driving at,"
van Bredepoel answered.

" I think you'll know presently," the Major said
mysteriously, and went on eating.

Van Bredepoel knew after dinner, for as he came
out of the dining-room Mrs. Harris beckoned him
nervously to her room.

" I don't like talking to you, Mr. van Bredepoel,"
she said, trembling with nervousness, " and I'm
sure, of course, there's nothing in it, but several of
my guests have been talking to me and complaining, not that I attach the slightest importance to it,
but you know what these complaints are, one must
attend to them if only to be tactful. . . . Oh, where
was I ? Yes! Some people have been complaining
that they often see that new boy Joseph going into
your room."

" It is perfectly true, Mrs. Harris," he replied,
and then sought the most plausible explanation, not
because he had anything to conceal but because he
knew it was quite hopeless to try to make Mrs. Harris
and her lodgers realise that he was interested in
Kenon as a human being. They would not have
understood. " You see, I'm very interested in native
folk-lore, and as this boy is still fresh from his
country it occurred to me that he might have a great
deal of useful information to give me. It's so rare
that one gets the chance of talking to a raw native in
Port Benjamin, isn't it ? "

" Oh! I'm so glad it's that! " she replied. " I'll
tell them that immediately, and I do hope you don't
mind my talking to you like this, but of course no
one would dream of interfering with your private

studies. But you know, Mr. van Bredepoel, you students are sometimes a little unconventional! "

The following night, at dinner, Major Mustard looked at him over his plate of soup and said: " So you are interested in anthropology ? " And before van Bredepoel could reply, added: " It must be an interesting subject that—ahem!—anthropology."

CHAPTER VII

For some months there was a look of joyful anticipation on Kenon's face. He seemed to have no care except a pleasant sense of bewilderment at the unfamiliar life around him. He did his work enthusiastically and was scrupulously honest. Happiness flowed from him, and there was hardly a morning in which one could not hear him singing in a low voice to himself as he polished the floor of the passage outside van Bredepoel's room. Often he would forget himself and sing louder than he had intended. Then the whole house was filled with a deep contented murmur.

" Eh! " he used to sing, moving his hands vigorously over the floor in time with the rhythm of his improvised tune: " Eh! the face of my missus is as white as the cob of a young mealie, the hair of my missus is yellow and long like the hair of a mealie. She eats her food with a long pin, and in her hut there are many precious things. There are iron pots and much copper and glasses of many colours. The floors are of wood and I make them shine. See how they shine these floors in the hut of my missus."

" There he goes again," the coloured cook would say in the kitchen, hearing the deep murmur through the ceiling. " That nigger will certainly drive me crazy."

" Suzie! " Mrs. Harris would shriek, quite unconscious that her praises were being sung upstairs.

" Go and tell that boy Joseph to shut up; he is driving the whole house mad, and Mrs. Songster is up there in her room with a headache."

For the rest of the day Kenon would sing no more, but the following morning he broke out again. And van Bredepoel, as he heard and saw these things, gradually lost the fear he had at first felt for Kenon, and became hopeful that the simple but exacting code of his tribe would uphold the boy and give him stability among the complex and persistently unsettling influences around him.

For many months Kenon came to van Bredepoel regularly for help in sending money to his father. His salary was little more than one pound a month, out of which he sent home at least fifteen shillings. But one month Kenon did not come. For about a week van Bredepoel expected him in vain. This was so unusual that he suspected Kenon of avoiding him.

Then one night, as van Bredepoel was just going to bed, he heard the sound of a very old and squeaky gramophone starting up somewhere in the servants' quarters. He waited patiently for the music to come to an end, but when some records had asthmatically unwound " My Sweetheart when a Boy," " The Wedding of Sandy McNab," " The Anchor's Weighed " and Sousa's " Stars and Stripes," and a fresh outbreak of applause threatened to prolong the entertainment indefinitely, he decided to go down. He found the door of Kenon's room open, and there by candle-light were Kenon and three other servants squatting round a gramophone with a large green funnel, like four ecstatic priests round an image of their god. On the

walls of the room were pinned faded illustrations
from newspapers. The plaster had once been smooth
and white, but now large brown cracks seemed to
trace everywhere on its surface crude maps like maps
of the British Isles. The bed in the corner had a torn
mattress but no linen; the only window was shut and
the spaces between it and its ill-fitting frame were
filled in with newspapers. The floor, unswept, was
stained with damp and bruised cigarette-ends. The
air felt oppressive and smelt of sweating bodies,
decaying plaster and dirty linen. Back in his room,
van Bredepoel could still smell the servants' quarters
in his clothes. The next day he waylaid Kenon.

" Do you want me to help you write to your
father ? " he asked.

Kenon replied only with a shamefaced look.

" Where did you get that gramophone ? "

" Inkosan', I bought it," Kenon said at last, his
eyes on the ground.

" What did you pay for it ? "

" Fifteen pounds, Inkosan'."

" Where on earth did you get all that money
from ? "

Kenon explained that a white man had come to
their quarters on the last pay-day afternoon, had
played the gramophone to him and easily persuaded
him to buy it. This Kenon had done by paying one
pound down and promising the rest in fourteen
monthly instalments.

" But the damned thing isn't worth two pounds at
the most! " van Bredepoel told him.

" But, Inkosan', it speaks and makes a most
excellent noise."

" Never mind that. If that most excellent noise keeps me awake again, I shall have something to say to you about it. But see that you call me the next time the fellow comes round to collect his money."

One Friday evening a month later Kenon came to fetch him. Van Bredepoel had already made up his mind that the man was a scoundrel, and, with the enthusiasm that comes to people when they feel that they are putting right an obvious wrong, had decided to tell him so. He was taken aback when he found himself confronted not with the villain he had pictured to himself but with an old man with thin grey hair, a round, red face, large, blue angelic-looking eyes and a big, wet mouth.

" Sir! " van Bredepoel said, and afterwards smiled at the pompous self-righteous tone he had adopted. " Sir! I find that you have tricked my personal servant "—an invention to justify his interference—" into buying for fifteen pounds a gramophone that isn't worth two."

" Personal servant, you say! " The old man seemed quite undisturbed. " Personal servant! Very personal, I should say."

" What do you mean ? " asked van Bredepoel, startled out of the prepared trend of his speech by this interruption.

" This boy," said the old man, pointing to Kenon, " is paid every month by the lady who runs this boarding-house. But if he's your personal servant, you must pay him as well. But as he does the lady's work, what do you pay him for ? Very personal, I should say."

" You are both dishonest and impertinent," van

Bredepoel replied, "and you seem to know far too much about the affairs of this boarding-house. I shall see that Mrs. Harris prevents you from coming here again."

"Steady there, mister, not so fast! If I've been rude I apologise humbly. But there are many others like me trying to make a living. If I hadn't found this boy, somebody else would've done so. What I say is he's lucky to have found a reasonable chap like me. It might easily have been thirty pounds, and business is business."

"Well, whether it is business or dishonesty or anything else doesn't matter now," van Bredepoel told him. "I'll pay you another two pounds for the gramophone, or you can take it away and get no more money from my servant."

The old man looked at him steadily for a moment or two, and then said, "Make it a fiver, mister."

"Two pounds or nothing."

"Four pounds or I lose on it."

"I will make it three pounds but no more."

"All right!" the old man replied, shrugging his shoulders. "It's very little, and you've spoilt my market here."

"I'm so glad!" said van Bredepoel.

"Look here, Kenon," van Bredepoel told him afterwards, "if ever you want to buy anything like that again, see me about it first."

And for a time again, Kenon resumed sending instalments to his father. But though van Bredepoel did not notice it then, the episode of the gramophone marked the beginning of a profound change in Kenon. He now began to realise that all white men were not alike, that they varied among themselves at least as much as his own people did, only with this difference, which he felt but did not understand: whereas he could treat his own people more or less as circumstances demanded, everybody expected and, indeed, forced him to treat both the worst and the best of white men in an equally respectful and obedient way. He had also a genuine and deep desire to improve himself, which exposed him to all sorts of dangers of which he was not aware, and made him particularly vulnerable to the disdain of his more sophisticated companions by creating in him an acute consciousness of his shortcomings. It did not take him long to realise that, in the strange and complex life in which he found himself, the traditions of his people were no longer certain guides. All pride and self-respect are based ultimately on personal achievement. And on what could he pride himself in Port Benjamin? He could no longer take any pride in the fact that he was taller, faster, stronger and better at hunting than most young men of his age. Among his new acquaintances small, sickly, pimply creatures with quick, clever, lying tongues, who would have been despised by his own people, were often the most admired, because they imitated the manners and dress of the white man better than others.

Then one night he went with some other servants to a cinema. The out-of-date news bulletin he understood fairly well, for it consisted chiefly of magnificent pageants, reviews of troops in all parts of the world, and he instinctively warmed to these vast and well-ordered displays. But the feature film

puzzled him completely. He looked round respectfully at the people who knew when to shout: " Eh!
Tomma Mixi, Tomma Mixi!" It was, it is true,
exciting enough to watch how illusion was made on
a linen sheet more real than reality itself, but he did
not understand half the time why the men fought
like wildcats and drew their revolvers on one
another so easily.

When the climax of the film came, Kenon made a
thorough fool of himself. It was the moment when a
young mother was separated from her baby by the
wicked men of the film, and the baby held out its
arms to her appealingly, shedding large, glycerine
tears. The hall was silent when this great moment
came. Now Kenon, to whom babies and their tears
were, as a rule, rather a joke than a tragedy, could
only see this incident as something unrelated to the
rest of the film, and laughed out loudly. In vain the
men next to him nudged him and shouted: " Be
silent, you big baboon!" To compare a man to the
clever, enterprising baboon was, in Kenon's tribe,
if anything, a compliment. Even the chief of the
tribe was addressed as the Big Baboon, and Kenon
had been taught as a child to greet strangers
politely by saying to them: " Good day, Baboon."
So he only laughed more. But when his companions
spoke to him about it afterwards and sneered at his
ignorance, he felt that he had done something very
wrong. He was not by nature brooding and intro-
spective. All his vitality pushed outwards to a life
of movement and action. He seemed almost
incapable of thought without at the same time
expressing his thought in speech, or of feeling

without translating it into singing and dancing.
But now, imperceptibly, his old confidence was
shaken with misgiving, and he began to be distress-
ingly conscious of differences between himself and
others. It seemed to him that nobody in the world
could be as ignorant as he was, and he spoke no
more about what he had done at home. Van
Bredepoel still tried to make him talk, but it became
more and more difficult. Often he looked in vain for
Kenon among that small group of talkers in the
yard. Kenon was there less and less often. It would
grow dark in the yard without Kenon appearing and
like most of the people at Mrs. Harris', like most of
the people in Governor's Walk, van Bredepoel would
throw himself on his bed, to read books as they are
read only when we know books to be a substitute.

" What on earth does he do with himself ? "
van Bredepoel wondered. He was able to answer
the question for himself the following Sunday
afternoon.

Van Bredepoel had been out walking, and was
returning to his room when he saw Kenon ahead of
him, moving in the same direction. He was still
wearing the clothes in which he had left his home.
Van Bredepoel thought first of overtaking him and
talking to him; then he noticed that Kenon's steps
were halting and uncertain, as if he had in mind two
directions for his feet. Soon he saw the cause of
Kenon's indecision.

On the other side of the street, walking in the
same direction, was a half-caste woman with a face
almost the colour of sulphur. Her legs were
elephantisic in shape and size, and she had a large

protruding posterior which she wobbled so much and
so persistently that one might have thought something was continually tickling her bottom. Her
breasts were large and loosely hung and each movement she made caused vibrations in every part of
her body. Van Bredepoel thought also that she
had the bridgeless nose of the congenital syphilitic.

As she wobbled along she kept on looking sideways
at Kenon, laughing shrilly at him with ostentatious
but obviously sham disdain. He could see that Kenon
was getting more and more excited. Van Bredepoel
thought at first that he was going to run away, but
in the end Kenon crossed the street with a few rapid
strides, took the woman by the arm and jerked her
round to face him. It would have taken normally
a much bigger force to upset her but now she fell
heavily against Kenon.

"What are you laughing at ?" Kenon asked in an
angry voice.

"You! You flat-faced, naked Kaffir!" Her in-
solence was more assumed than felt, but to Kenon
it seemed so unexpectedly real and firm that he was
startled, and only asked.

"Whom you call Kaffir ?"

"You! Flat-face!"

"Why do you that ?"

"Well, aren't you a flat-faced, naked Kaffir ?"
She looked coyly at his legs.

"Maybe, but I don't like you calling me Kaffir."

"All right, big, strong man."

Her voice had suddenly softened. She made no
attempt to withdraw her arm from Kenon's clasp.

Van Bredepoel watched them turn down a side

lane, from which latched gates gave between tall
hedges on to neat lawns, and led beyond to open
fields over which lay already the heavy shadow of the
mountain. His eyes followed them until they
disappeared into the shadows and silence of that
quiet Sunday evening.

"So you don't like being called a Kaffir," he
thought. "Oh, Kenon! I fear your mother said
'thank you' too soon."

On the following Sunday afternoon Kenon
appeared in shabby grey flannels, a tattered blue
blazer and a dirty pair of worn tennis shoes. And
this time the half-caste girl did not laugh, but waited
anxiously for him to come.

CHAPTER VIII

A WELL-PRACTISED attitude to life does not disappear in a day, as little indeed as a new one arises overnight. Yet Kenon's feet were definitely set in a new direction; whither, he neither knew nor seriously attempted to find out. Around him were thousands of black people, some better and many worse, all going the same way, and all he did was to surrender himself gradually to his instinct for imitation. To have taken a different course would have demanded the qualities of a leader, and he was only intensely human and very young, desiring chiefly to avoid pain and to improve himself. Still, in spite of himself, in spite of the new environment of his life, his old habits of living persisted for a long time. Sometimes when he seemed to have discarded them entirely they reappeared with sudden, unexpected power. His life appeared to lose any remnant of continuity it might still have had, and he was profoundly perplexed. One habit he never gave up, however, was the sending of monthly instalments to his father, but this habit was more a tribute to van Bredepoel than to Kenon's goodness.

The look of pained and inarticulate perplexity which Kenon often wore now as he went about his work struck van Bredepoel more and more. Sometimes it seemed to appeal to him for help, as if Kenon thought his bewilderment could be straightened out as easily as the affair of the gramophone.

But van Bredepoel was too unsettled at the time to do anything more than try to treat Kenon, when they did meet, as if nothing was the matter.

One night, some months after the Sunday afternoon on which he had met the half-caste woman, Kenon was sitting on his bed, playing his gramophone. He had just been paid his wages. He had one of his moods of reversion on him, and was only waiting for a light to appear in the window above, to go and ask van Bredepoel to send money for him to his father. Van Bredepoel, who had been kept working late that afternoon, was at that moment sitting down to dinner with the captain of a ship that had just come in. While Kenon was waiting, three of his fellow servants came into the room and suggested that he should go out with them for the evening.

" I know a good place," said one of them, " where there are some fine Bushman girls," and he gave Kenon an ecstatic description of their charms.

" No," said Kenon, shaking his head emphatically.

" You are afraid ? " The other simulated great surprise.

" No! "

" Oh! Leave him alone," the second said. " He is a boy, he has not yet dried behind the ears."

" He has not been circumcised yet, there is no hair on his body," the third remarked gravely, as if stating a fact which is always and permanently true.

" He is longing for his mother," added the one who had spoken first.

" No," replied Kenon still firmly. The matter would have ended there, for he was sure that they were merely trying to shame him into going, only he could not prevent his pride from rebelling and felt forced to add: " I have had a Bushman girl better than any you could show me." And he bragged eloquently about the points of his half-caste whore. The others were impressed, but did not show it.

" That is nothing," their spokesman said, " the girls I know are better. They are fatter and their bellies are softer than those of hippopotamuses."

" They can't be," said Kenon with much scorn.

" Well, you come and see," the man replied.

" Oh no! they can't be better."

" Well, then just come and look at mine and afterwards you can show us yours, and we shall see then whose words are bigger than his eyes."

" If I don't go now," Kenon thought, " they will think I have lied and am frightened." So he said aloud: " All right. I will let you show me and I will look, but nothing else."

When van Bredepoel returned to his rooms an hour later, he wondered why the servants' quarters were so quiet on pay-day night. By that time Kenon and his friends were knocking at the door of a dark, three-storied building, which faced a large gravelled square surrounded by squalid houses. This square had been the site of a number of other houses no less squalid, which the police, who knew them to be the centre of an illicit drink traffic, had destroyed some time ago. They still regretted that all the hundreds of tumbledown houses in the neighbourhood had not been pulled down as well. Periodically the Commissioner of the Police would tell members of the Primrose League: " We shall never succeed in making decent, sober, and, last but not least, law-abiding citizens out of our native and coloured people while this eyesore, this blot on the escutcheon of our beautiful city, remains in our midst."

On one side of the door at which Kenon and his companions were knocking was a dirty glass window, the old green blind drawn carefully. The light from a street lamp found its way through many threadbare patches in the blind. Looking through one of them Kenon saw a dusty shoemaker's shop. There, during the day, offering as convincing an example of industry as the bee or the ant, worked the owner of the house they wished to enter. He seldom spoke, and inside his shop one rarely heard more than the sound of his needle, the tapping of his hammer, and a dry chronic cough. But at night the zeal that had gone into resoling the shoes of respectable citizens of Port Benjamin was diverted into a trade at least as old. He was known to the police as the very skilful runner of an illicit brothel.

Suddenly the door opened a few inches. It happened so quietly that Kenon, hearing people whisper close to him, looked up with a start. From behind the door, someone he could not see was talking very softly to their spokesman. For a moment he had a feeling that they had been followed, and turned round to face the square. He was sorrier than ever that he had allowed himself to be persuaded to come. But the square was empty and not a sound came from the tumbledown houses on every side. Far away in the docks he could hear the coaling of ships going on ceaselessly, and over the town hung the dark shadow of the mountain. He looked at his companions, and felt that the night had communicated uneasiness to them too, for they were very quiet, shuffling restlessly on their feet and looking anxiously at the door. After a time the whispering became louder and Kenon heard the man behind the door say: " I don't like it. You know it's Friday night. Everybody in the world knows you people get paid on Friday nights. It's a good night for the police, but not for us."

" We are early," the spokesman replied. " We'll be back in bed long before the police think of coming here."

There was a moment's hesitation. Then, reluctantly: " All right! Come round the back way and mind you don't make any noise or I won't open the door."

They tiptoed into the backyard. It was small and surrounded by high walls, the tops of which were cemented in with broken glass. In one corner of the yard the kitchen garbage of many months was rotting; in the centre its concrete floor was slippery with the overflow of a stopped drain. They went softly through an open door, climbed up a few creaking steps and then found a white man, whom the spokesman called, to Kenon's surprise, just " Tommie," waiting for them in a disordered kitchen. On the walls were some Christmas almanacs, gaudy portraits of the King and Queen of Greece in their coronation robes, and shelves filled with cheap crockery on which were the faces of other kings and queens. It was some time before Kenon was able to see Tommie clearly, so sudden had been the change of light.

Tommie's face was long and yellow, and when he

was asleep had a sensitive tortured look; altogether a face El Greco might have painted. But Tommie seldom slept, and years of practice had taught him to use certain features independently of the others and of his real feelings, so that he could smile while the rest of his face retained its tortured neutrality. He seldom went out into the fresh air, and like the furniture in his house he looked as if he had been rotting for a long time, and would rot for a long time to come. Kenon felt he had never seen a more repulsive human being, and again regretted having come.

Tommie's practised eyes soon noticed Kenon's uneasiness. "A greenhorn," he thought, and smiling slightly, sensitively, held out to him a narrow, long-fingered hand.

"Pay up!" he said.

"That's all right, Tommie," the spokesman intervened, "we see the girls first and then we pay."

"What will you pay?" asked Tommie in a matter-of-fact voice.

"Half a crown, as usual."

"That's not enough," said Tommie. "What do you take me for? You pay five bob."

"Half a crown or . . ." the black man turned as if to go.

"Wait a moment," said Tommie, "there is no hurry. We can leave that until later. Let's have some wine first."

He went over to a kitchen dresser, and returned with four green, unlabelled bottles.

"How much?" asked the black man, who evidently knew Tommie well. Tommie immediately began to bargain again, and it was some time before the price was decided on, the money paid, and they sat down to drink.

Kenon's recollection of the evening was afterwards very faint. He remembered that the drink burned his throat, that he coughed and his companions laughed, and that after a time he laughed with them. Then five or six women suddenly stood in the room. He had not seen them come in. He remembered only the face of the woman who came and sat next to him. Her lower lip, he noticed with disgust, was terribly swollen. It was covered with sticking-plaster, and at the corners of her mouth some pus was collecting. He jumped up and started to walk to the door, but she came after him, gripped his buttocks with her hands, shook them and said: " Poor little boy, he is frightened."

That angered him and he went back, and drank a great deal to show her how much he could stand. After a time he wondered why he had thought her underlip so swollen.

" Why, it is only a little pimple, the tiniest little pimple you have ever seen," he said to himself.

He was fascinated, too, by her necklace of bright blue beads. It had the prettiest sparkle. He could not keep his eyes off it. Somehow he did not mind how much the woman kissed him on the lips as long as he was allowed to play with her beads. They were beautiful enough to justify anything.

" And Masakama was making such a bangle as the Bambuxosa had never seen," he tried to say to her, but she kissed him and he tried no more, did not even notice that the sticking-plaster on her lip had gone, and that round her mouth was a yellow froth.

" It's hot in here, boys," he heard Tommie say, " Let's take off our coats." He saw Tommie take off his coat and like the others did the same.

" Come upstairs with me, little one," the woman said.

Slowly he came to his feet, and in that moment time stood still for him. The room was an immense plain of light, the people in it a flicker of shadow, stone and wood and brass the sparkling insubstantial reflections of a reflection. Deep in one's heart is a longing to clutch something more than a shadow, to pass over into a moment where neither memory nor desire can torture, where no fear or courage is asked for, where "Now" holds in the core of the shrinking flesh a pool of calm. For all flesh and blood is weak and lonely, and like sheep on a winter's night must come together for warmth; so one follows the beads, and their sparkle keeps illusion warm in the shadows beyond, while in Tommie's kitchen the clock on the mantelpiece ticks on.

But Kenon Badiakgotla, have you forgotten that the path of the Bambuxosa is dangerous and long, and leads from the Yellow River on the other side of the Mountains of the Moon ? Once the grey volcanoes heaved in their sleep and bannered the sky with smoke at dawn over the kraals of the Bambuxosa. Then the forest of many voices was hushed and bent its branches low behind Masakama's impis, as they stepped out with a heavy grace in the tracks of the lion and the elephant, the buffalo and the kudu. At evening the glow of the sun on their spears is red and they wade through blood. Neither water nor thirst, neither fire nor ice, stops them. Life is dark with danger, the mind sombre with shadow, but the flame of feeling is clean and clear like the blade of a spear. Love and hate do not mingle and he who is not a friend is an enemy. They carry your seed, over rivers that are no more, through ruined cities of stone in deserts of sand. They pass over plains that rise, winged with dust, to meet thunder in the skies, and they scale hills on whose crests sits the black cobra, its neck ringed with foam, swaying in a somnolent rhythm in the sun. Dawn comes up in fire on the wings of flamingoes to meet them, noon beats on tattered parasols of karee-thorn over them, and the moon trails coolness and the cries of the jackal and hyena in the wake of the sun. From the other side of the world they march and the corridors of history reverberate with their footfalls. But is it for this they come, these creatures of shining skins and glittering limbs? Is it for this they called out Kenon? Is it here the journey of the Bambuxosa ends?

CHAPTER IX

WHEN Kenon and his companions had gone upstairs
and Tommie had seen the last of them into an attic,
he hurried back to his kitchen and went through all
their coats with a light, deft, sensitive Greek touch.
His face as he went about this work gradually
became more composed, and his actions seemed to be
governed increasingly by a great and very sensitive
gentleness. Yet it was a gentleness more repellent
than any blatant coarseness, for it served merely as a
very nicely timed and smoothly working machine
for placing the exact commercial value on each
human situation. Carefully he collected all the wine
left in the glasses and bottles into one vessel; placed
what he had found in the coat pockets into a small
black cash-box. His actions were never more gentle
and sensitive than when he locked the box and
pushed it slowly underneath an old sofa. He was
not displeased until there came on the door outside
a loud peremptory knock and someone shouted:
" Open! Police! " Then he quickly turned out the
lamp, hid the coats in the kitchen dresser, put on
an old dressing-gown, and waited in a chair until the
knock had come a third and a fourth time. He got
up, opened the kitchen door, switched on the passage
light. Feigning a sleepy air, he walked to the door
thinking: " Thank God I made them go to the
attic."

Outside in the square a police van had drawn up.

Prostitutes had seen it and signalled to the scented pimps who trailed them everywhere that the " picking-up wagon," as they called it, was out, and then had disappeared quickly from the streets.

" How long is it since you raided Tommie ? " a police inspector asked the officer in charge of the van.

" I think about five months," he replied. " But I have had his place watched very carefully and he seemed to me to be very quiet nowadays."

" I think I will look in and call on Tommie," the inspector said.

" Well, Tommie," was his greeting, when the door was at last opened, " you sleep very soundly nowadays. Your cough must be better."

Pushing past Tommie, he asked: " Where have you put Mabel Riempies and Sarah Gampies " (two stock police names for prostitutes). " Come on, I've no time to waste. I know they're here." But Tommie had done his feigning and his work well. The police did not notice that an attic window gave on to the fire-escape, and they prepared to go after only a casual search.

" Look here, Tommie," said the inspector, when he was at the door again, " when are you returning to Greece ? "

" Soon," replied Tommie, " I need only a few pounds more, and I won't be sorry. In Greece the police are gentlemen."

" Why don't you wait just a little bit longer ? Wait just a wee bit longer and the Government will pay your fare back."

The inspector was such a wit, and his men thought it good policy to laugh.

" And Tommie," he added, " I would recommend you to take a smaller house. For a shoemaker and a bachelor you keep rather a palatial establishment, you know."

Before they reached the police van, the inspector heard soft footsteps behind him. He turned and recognised a well-known police informer.

" Baas! " she said, " I saw black men go in there a while ago, and they've not yet come out."

She pointed at Tommie's house.

" So Tommie thinks he can diddle me! " exclaimed the inspector, ignoring the fortuitous source of his enlightenment. " I'll learn him! "

A few minutes later the police van drove off at a great speed, but soon it returned quietly by another way and was parked in the shadows of a side street near Tommie's house.

From the window of the attic Kenon and his companions watched the police drive off, and laughed and jeered at them for their stupidity. They felt that they themselves had outwitted and triumphed over the white men, and they returned boasting to their women. Only their spokesman remained at the window. The wine had turned him sulky, the presence of lascivious women aggressive. He stood there boasting and crying out softly old battle-cries. Suddenly a noise outside drew his attention to three white men crossing the square. He became very quiet and watched them intently. They walked up to Tommie's house and away again to the other side of the square. Then they came back.

" It's four voyages since I was here last, but I think this is the place," he heard one of them say.

The black man saw them make for the door and heard them knock. He could control himself no longer. Some deep racial memory woke; the man in him fought the slave and in a rage greater than he had ever known he shouted out: " Here come some white men after our women! " and ran for his sticks. Hearing his shout his companions seized their sticks too, and bounded down the stairs. Kenon wanted to follow but his woman struggled with him.

" Don't be a fool; you'll just get into trouble," she said. Kenon had to wrestle with her for some time before he got free, and then stumbled blindly down the fire-escape.

The white men were on the point of knocking again when they found themselves surrounded by three dancing black men.

" You think you can come here and take my woman! " shouted the spokesman. " Well, take that! And that! And that! And that! " With each " that " he hit them over the head with all his might.

" This is better than killing jackals," thought the other two, and did the same.

" Go for them, you fellows," shouted the inspector, drawn from the side street by the noise. One of the black men saw the police come running across the square, and instantly sobered up.

" Take care! The police! " he shouted to his companions and ran away hard. The other two bolted after him and before the inspector and his men had reached the house were out of sight. Just at that moment Kenon, dazed and stupefied by the wine, came stumbling round the corner of Tommie's house into the arms of a policeman.

" Here! I've got you, you beggar! " yelled the man, pleased and a bit scared at the same time. And as Kenon put up an arm to ward off the blows immediately aimed at his head: " Oh, you're cheeky, are you ? You won't come quietly, will you ? Well, take that, you son of a bitch! "

He stopped for a moment, as one of the sailors staggered up, wiping blood from his face, and declared hoarsely:

" That's the bastard who did me in! Lemme have a sock at him!"

CHAPTER X

ON Monday mornings the first criminal court of
Port Benjamin is always overcrowded. From the
witness-box, one sees in this dimly lit room, on whose
dark oak panelling the brilliant sunlight outside is
reflected only in a cheerless shine, a great number
of black people pressed tightly against a wooden
railing and looking up with dark anxious eyes at
the magistrate's bench. They are either witnesses,
or relations of people who are about to be tried.
Often in the course of a trial some among them lose
control of their feelings, and a low cry of despair,
anger or bewilderment fills the court. Then a
white policeman marches down menacingly on them,
glares severely, parades up and down for a few
minutes, and goes back to his stand near the witness-
box, where he whispers to the Clerk of the Court
that these niggers really stink far too much. So big
is the crowd of black and coloured people who
desire admittance to the court on Mondays that it
usually overflows into the quadrangle outside. There
they sit on the stone floor, waiting with a patient
despondence, or lean against the pillars, talking
anxiously to someone who knows the court better
than they do, while all the time policemen and court
officials and lawyers wade impatiently through their
ranks. Occasionally a policeman appears in the
doorway and shouts out a name. Then one of these
waiting figures comes instantly to life, draws his

tattered coat carefully round him, snatches his hat off his head, and rushes as energetically as he can to the door.

People who are on trial, however, are kept apart from the rest. They are placed in a carefully barred yard, from which a passage underneath the floors of the building conducts them directly into the witness-box. A warder with a pistol in his belt carefully guards them there and unlocks their handcuffs only as they are about to go down the passage to the court. To Kenon's dismay, on the Monday after his visit to Tommie's, he was the first of the prisoners to be sent for. He had no idea what was going to happen to him, but he was feeling overwhelmed by the disaster that had already overtaken him and profoundly sorry for himself. He wanted to talk to the other prisoners and ask their advice, but the moment he opened his mouth the warder silenced him. He wished he could remember what had taken place on the Friday night. Between the time he had gone into the attic and the moment when they dragged him into a brilliantly lit suburban police-station, there was a wide gap in his memory. When his name was called out, he was so pre-occupied that he did not hear it. One of the prisoners nudged him, but he thought it was only an attempt to talk to him, so he did not respond.

" Here, dreamer! " called out the warder, a big fat man with a good-humoured face, coming up to him. " You're wanted."

Kenon held out a pair of trembling hands to the warder, and when his handcuffs were unlocked quickly followed a policeman down the passage.

In a few seconds he came out in the witness-box. As he looked around him his bewilderment increased. The number of people about, the policemen in shining uniforms, and the lawyers sitting at their tables, gave such an air of importance and gravity to the occasion that he was frightened and could hardly shut his mouth properly. He longed for someone to talk to, to confess all his difficulty about forgetting what had happened, to ask what he had really done; but one look round the court, full of strange and severe faces, and he realised that that was impossible. When the interpreter came and stood next to him and asked him to take the oath, Kenon repeated the words with dry lips in a low, trembling voice, and his despair was complete. He had seen the interpreter, a fat, sleek native in a shiny black suit, with pince-nez glasses in his hand, talking so familiarly to the other officials in the court that Kenon thought he must be very learned and very good, and could have no sympathy for someone like himself. The magistrate, moreover, had such a look of synthetic gravity and severity that Kenon read a terrible punishment for himself in his first words. Yet all he said, in a low, spiritless voice, was: " Does the prisoner know with what he is charged ? " Then murmured to himself as he looked through the long list of cases before him: " The usual blue-Monday crush."

" The magistrate wants to know," said the interpreter with a business-like air, squaring his shoulders and putting his thumbs in his waistcoat pockets, " if you realise that you have nearly killed three white men ? "

The interpreter had already judged Kenon.

Kenon did not know, for he could not remember what had happened, but he did not think that men like the magistrate and the interpreter would lie. He thought it better, in any case, to agree with them, and said submissively:

" Please tell the master that I know."

" Does he plead guilty or not guilty ? " the magistrate asked.

" Do you want to deny that you beat the three white men ? " asked the interpreter.

" No! But I cannot remember," Kenon answered.

" The prisoner pleads guilty, your Worship," said the interpreter, looking at the clock. He had a long day before him.

The magistrate felt relieved. So there was at least one case that promised to be over quickly. Still, formalities had to be observed. Is it not a principle of Port Benjamin law that a man is not guilty until he has been proved guilty ?

The inspector and two of his men were called to identify Kenon and described the assault. In the course of his evidence the inspector stated that the police had tried all the week-end to trace Kenon's companions, but that the prisoner had " obstinately refused " to give them any help.

" Don't you think, inspector," the magistrate interrupted, " that it would have been wiser to postpone the case until you had made an attempt to find the other men implicated in this charge ? "

" In normal circumstances, your Worship," he replied, " it would certainly have been so. But the assaulted men's ship must sail to-day for the Philippines, and we thought it best to get this part of the charge over immediately, in case there were things arising out of the trial which make it necessary to examine them again. The police, moreover, have done their utmost to trace the boy's companions, but without success. In the circumstances, your Worship, I submit there is no reason why this part of the case shouldn't be treated separately, for the prisoner has pleaded guilty."

Affidavits by the sailors, who were said to be in the ship's hospital, were submitted to the court. The district surgeon was called to describe their wounds, and he testified in a dry technical manner that these " could only have been caused by a long rounded piece of wood about four feet long."

" Do you think," the prosecutor asked him, " that the wounds you have described are consistent with wounds that might have been caused by a native hunting-stick, like these ? "

And the prosecutor passed Kenon's two sticks over to the doctor.

" Perfectly," replied the doctor without taking up the sticks.

" The doctor says," the interpreter told Kenon, " that he thinks it is your sticks that made the wounds and he says you're lucky the men aren't dead."

The magistrate questioned Kenon very closely about his companions, but he could not, apparently would not, say who they had been, a fact which the magistrate duly recorded.

" Ask him once more," the magistrate told the interpreter, " who his companions were. This is the last time and he may be sorry later if he does not reply more frankly."

" The magistrate gives you one more chance. Who were your companions ? He says you will be sorry if you don't speak the truth."

" I do not remember," said Kenon.

" Ask him if he doesn't think it is strange that he can't remember who his companions were. I can't think that anyone in his full senses would go off on an expedition like this with strangers," the magistrate insisted again.

" The magistrate doesn't believe you, and asks if you were blind that you could not see who was with you," it was translated to Kenon.

" I am sorry," he replied, " but I cannot think now; I had wine to drink and I. . . ."

" The prisoner says he was too drunk to see, your Worship," said the interpreter, and Kenon had to swallow the rest of his sentence.

" Has he anything to say in extenuation of his crime ? " the magistrate asked.

" Do you know of any reason why the magistrate should not punish you for the rogue you are ? " The interpreter was getting bored with the case.

" I have done wrong," said Kenon, " but I am young, and I was misled by older men I trusted. I have always been a good boy and went to this place against my wishes. I do not remember what happened, but I had wine to drink and my head is not accustomed to. . . ."

" Hurry up ! " snapped the interpreter, " we've heard all that before. You're just wasting his Worship's time."

And Kenon, interrupted just when words were coming to him more easily, could only add: " I am unhappy over my great misdeed, and I know that the master will do what is good for me."

" He is sorry for what he has done, your Worship. He says it's his first crime, he says he was misled by bad company and had too much drink."

" Unfortunately he doesn't give us a chance to judge how bad the company was," murmured the magistrate, smiling cynically and going over his notes. For a few minutes nothing was heard but the scratching of his pen. Then he summed up:

" Kenon Badiakgotla, I have taken into consideration the facts that you are young, that this is your first offence, and that you were led into this by men who have been mean enough to leave you alone to bear the responsibility of a crime in which they were at least as much implicated as you yourself. I have not forgotten, either, that you had too much to drink, that you were not entirely responsible for your actions, and that your crime was not preconceived. But taking into consideration all these things, and remembering, too, that you have helped the course of justice by openly acknowledging your crime, I cannot ignore that your murderous assault on three white men was unprovoked. Nor can I ignore the fact that you have shown a strange and suspicious reticence as regards the identity of your companions. I cannot believe that you would go off on an expedition of this kind with men who are strangers to you. Had you been more open on this point I might have dealt more leniently with you. But unprovoked assaults by men of your race on white people are becoming far too common in this district, and in the circumstances—taking into consideration your youth, and that you are a first offender, I can do no less than sentence you to six months' imprisonment, with hard labour, and without the option of a fine. Let this be a lesson to you to keep out of bad company in future."

"The magistrate says that it's a pity that you lied about your companions," said the interpreter complacently, "but that in his kindness he has not forgotten that you are young and a first offender. He says it is lucky that you've not been before him in the past and that as your companions are getting off bird-free until he can lay his hands on them, he will sentence you only to six months' hard labour."

"He speaks good," replied Kenon, raising his hand above his head and saluting the magistrate, "and I thank him."

As he was rushed down the steps which led from the witness-box into the prison yard another black man was hurried into his place, and no one thought it strange. But an old woman, standing in the crowd at the back of the court waiting for the trial of one of her sons to come on, began to sob so loudly that a policeman had to call out: "Silence in the court!"

CHAPTER XI

" AN unprovoked and murderous assault on three white men ? Ridiculous! I don't believe it! " Van Bredepoel was sitting on top of a tram, the Monday evening newspaper open in front of him. He had only just come across a short account of Kenon's trial, and was quite incredulous. He could not reconcile what he knew of Kenon with " an unprovoked and murderous assault." But as he read carefully through the evidence he began to admit that there appeared to be little chance of a mistake having been made. Adding what he knew of Kenon to the facts given by the newspaper, he was moved more deeply than he would ever have expected to be moved, moved both by the boy's readiness to admit his guilt and by his obvious helplessness.

" I am a white man," he thought, " and I have been brought up under the law of white men, but I would not know how to set about defending myself in a similar case except to send for a lawyer. But he, poor devil, how was he to know what to do ? "

At the same time van Bredepoel suspected that there was much more to the case than had come out in court. " The law," he said to himself, " is, after all, concerned only with the law. It sees the human being only at the point where he comes into conflict with the law. Kenon passes before its vision only as a drunken native who suddenly comes spurting into a square with two unknown men, assaults three sailors, is arrested, sobers up in gaol, pleads guilty in court and disappears for six months into prison. But I would like to know what went before. I shall try to find out."

Had the evidence contained any allusion to Tommie's brothel he might have understood more quickly; but the Greek had so obstinately denied all knowledge of Kenon that the police had come to the conclusion that his evidence would if anything weaken their case.

Looking out of his window that evening, van Bredepoel saw in a doorway of the servants' quarters three black men bending attentively over a newspaper. They frequently made remarks to one another, but their voices were too low for van Bredepoel to hear. He looked at them closely for some time, and then something occurred to him. Quickly he went down into the yard.

" April," he said to the eldest of the three servants. " Where did you and Joseph go on Friday night ? "

" Pardon, master! " April replied, without looking van Bredepoel in the face.

" April, you are a Makatese, but you speak the language of the Bambuxosa," said van Bredepoel, speaking to him in Kenon's language, and deciding to change his tactics. " Listen, this is what I have seen. On Friday night I saw you and Joseph and a man I do not know walk out from here. At midnight I saw you and the man I do not know come back, but Joseph was not with you. What happened to Joseph ? "

" Master, there were three of us who went with Joseph——"

" It was dark and I could not see well and perhaps there were three of you who went out with Joseph, but I saw only two come back," van Bredepoel qualified his subterfuge.

" That is true, master," he replied, " we got separated when the night was still young, and I came back alone with this man here," April pointed to one of the servants.

" But what happened to Joseph ? " All three servants were now looking at van Bredepoel, April most attentively of all. They knew of his interest in Kenon, and did not know how to answer.

" Joseph is young, master. He is of the Bambuxosa, and I am of the Makatese. Between the men of the Bambuxosa and the Makatese. . . ." April began a long evasive reply, but van Bredepoel stopped him.

" If someone went, April, and told the police that on Friday night you went out with Joseph, but that when you came back Joseph was not with you, what would the police do ? "

" Many police have been here, master, and we have spoken to them, and they have gone away, and we are still here," April said.

" But if someone told the police what I know, wouldn't they come back ? "

" But the master will not tell the police ? " April turned sharply to look at his companions.

" I am not a policeman, but I want the truth, April," van Bredepoel told him. Yet it took him more than an hour to get April's story, and when he had heard it he was still puzzled.

" You say you have spoken the truth, April, and

I believe you; but why do the police say there were only three men, when you say there were four ? "

" Master," interrupted one of the other servants, speaking for the first time, " we drank many bottles of wine, but of us all, none drank more than April. Now I remember that when I turned to run, I saw only three of us, and Joseph was not one of them."

" You also had too much wine to drink," broke in April, " and my head is better than yours. I was angry but not blind. There were four of us."

" It can be that April does not remember," said the third servant, " and I am not sure that I speak the truth, but I think we left the house before Joseph and maybe he was not there when the fight took place."

When van Bredepoel at last knew all, he was dismayed by his inability to do anything for Kenon. He tried to persuade the other servants to go to the police with their story, but they steadfastly refused. He had to content himself with getting Mrs. Harris to promise to take Kenon back into her service when he came out of gaol, and by sending his instalment to his father for him. To his surprise, Mrs. Harris consented readily.

" He has always been a good worker," she said, " and after what you have told me, of course I will take him back."

CHAPTER XII

TIME flows subtly, paradoxically. From day to day it seems to drag with an extreme reluctance, seems almost, if we submit ourselves entirely to its movement, not to move at all. And yet if the mind is withdrawn consciously and fixed on Time's cumulative effect, the impression received is one of unbearable swiftness, of a terrible uniformity of speed. One feels that one is passing from the day into the night, clutching only the reality of a twilight transition. Nothing, it would seem, could be swifter; yet if this inexorable movement is married to an absolute uniformity of existence, one is bowed down with terror before the speed with which even Time accelerates, until the years seem to be darkening around the world like a tropical evening. The shortest life, one knows then, is the most uniform life, and one prays to be preserved from uniformity.

To van Bredepoel, caught up in the routine of the affairs of Messrs. Steyn, Berger and Stumpfkopf, the months between Kenon's imprisonment and his reappearance passed only too quickly. In his employers' ornate offices in the Buite-Cingel Street, the wool season merged imperceptibly into the bunkering season, the bunkering season into the mealie season. And outside, the haze of heat which had hung against the mountain all summer disappeared; clouds of mist collected round its summit and nightly flowed down over the town. Low-flying showers of rain began to gather over the harbour and ships faded into heavy sea-fogs, the long Atlantic swell breaking over their bows. In the avenues the oaks shed their leaves, which the wind carried down into the streets, lifting and dropping, dropping and lifting them among the wheels of the traffic. Dawn became only a faint illumination of mist-clouds, evening a gentle transition from half light into utter darkness. Rain dripped steadily from barren trees, robbed even of their shadows, and at night drummed on the world like an Antarctic wind. Soon the mountains beyond Port Benjamin were covered over with snow. Masses of hungry sea-gulls flew low before the rain over the town. Governor's Walk at twilight became deserted; those little groups of people who in the summer had filled its gardens with laughter disappeared. Lamps were lit in bedrooms two or three hours earlier, and there held against the rain dull yellow rectangles of light. Pianos that had long been closed began to be delivered night after night of the same tunes and with the help of innumerable gramophones, hurriedly bought on hire-purchase, filled evening, already the most nostalgic hour, with music-hall nostalgia. Fires were lit in halls and common-rooms, and at Mrs. Harris', when van Bredepoel came home at night, the copper vases and bronze trays shone with a warm domestic glow. Never had the day and night seemed so close, and yet as they ranged themselves imperceptibly into this grey procession of the hours, no one thought of change.

And then one evening as van Bredepoel, who had just come in, was about to go upstairs to his room,

Mrs. Harris called out: " Mr. van Bredepoel! Is that you ? "

" Yes, Mrs. Harris, it is," he called back, and halted on the stairs.

" Ah, I know your step by now," she said laughing, and came towards him from somewhere out of the darkness. " Could you spare me a minute ? "

Van Bredepoel followed her through the dimly lit hall into her bedroom. Their feet made no sound on the heavily carpeted floor, and the steady beat of rain on the roof mingled unhindered with the crackling of the wood fire, until Major Mustard's gramophone overhead suddenly released:

" Dere's an ol' man call'd de Mississippi,
    Dat's de ol' man I'd like to be;
    What does he care if de world's got trouble ?
    What does he care if de man ain't free ? "

" Mr. van Bredepoel," said Mrs. Harris, closing the door carefully behind her. " It's that boy Joseph I want to speak to you about."

" Joseph, Mrs. Harris ? I don't understand ? " replied van Bredepoel.

" Yes, Joseph. I don't like the look of him nowadays."

" But why ? Have you seen him ? "

" Good Lord, Mr. van Bredepoel! Didn't you know ? He's been back a fortnight."

" I am sorry you didn't tell me, Mrs. Harris. I would've liked to know," he answered, and thought: " So Kenon has been avoiding me."

" Oh! I thought you would be sure to know. You were always questioning him and taking such an interest in his doings. But if I'd realised, I would've told you."

" What's the matter with him, Mrs. Harris ? "

" That's just what I want to find out, Mr. van Bredepoel. You know what a cheerful good-natured creature he used to be. Well, now he goes about this place like a thunder-cloud. I can't complain about his work exactly, but there's something I don't like about him. He has been having the most awful rows with the maids in the kitchen. I'm just a bit afraid."

" Why afraid, Mrs. Harris ? "

" Oh, I don't know exactly why myself, but he's so touchy. So many of them get like that when they've been in town some time. For a year or two they are perfect servants, and then something goes wrong and they're devils. I often think it's a pity they come here at all."

" A great pity; I don't know why anyone comes here at all."

" Why, Mr. van Bredepoel! " she exclaimed, thoroughly alarmed. " I hope you are not uncomfortable here ? If I. . . ."

" No, it isn't that, I'm very comfortable here," he replied. " It's this town. Anyway, Mrs. Harris, I don't suppose it's much good discussing Joseph until I've seen him."

" No, I suppose not. But do tell me what you think when you've seen him."

Van Bredepoel took his leave and went upstairs.

In the passage outside his room a servant was moving about, placing jugs of hot water at each door. It was so dark that van Bredepoel could not see clearly who it was, but he thought the man's bearing familiar.

Close by, a negro baritone was still singing on Major Mustard's gramophone:

"You an' me, we sweat an' strain,
Body all achin' an' wracked with pain:
Tow dat barge; lift dat bale;
Get a little drunk an' you land in gaol.
Ah gets weary an' sick of tryin';
Ah'm tired of livin' an' scared of dying. . . ."

"Is that you, Kenon?" asked van Bredepoel, as the servant stooped to put a jug outside the door next to his own.

The man paused, the jug half-way to the floor, and replied without moving:

"Yes, Inkosan'. It is I."

"Come in here for a minute," said van Bredepoel, opening the door of his room and putting on the light.

Kenon came slowly into the room. He looked to van Bredepoel very tired and subdued, an object of pity rather than of fear. His face seemed less dark than before, and there was a strained look round his eyes. His clothes were wet through, and he stood there shivering in the doorway.

"Come in, and close the door behind you," van Bredepoel said gently.

Kenon did as he was told and then looked at his feet. There seemed to be no vitality left in him, his old vividness was dulled. This Kenon was a strange person. Van Bredepoel felt with dismay that the way he had followed towards understanding him no longer existed, and a reproach at the back of his mind made way instantly for a deep feeling of pity.

" I am so sorry, Kenon," he said, " about what happened. Why didn't you ask the police for me or Mrs. Harris ? We could have helped you."

" Inkosan', I did not know, and there was no time."

" But why didn't you tell the magistrate you were innocent ? "

" Inkosan', I did not know. I was not I. There was a cloud in my mind, and I was sure the magistrate would know the truth for me."

" But he didn't know, or he wouldn't have sentenced you."

" There were many men who spoke against me, Inkosan'. I did not think they would lie, for they were men I had done no harm."

" It is a great, great pity. It was a misunderstanding from beginning to end, and you must think no more about it. No one will think any the worse of you for it. Mrs. Harris knows you are innocent."

" I will think no more of it, Inkosan'," Kenon said, but there was no conviction in his voice.

" Is there anything I can do for you ? " van Bredepoel asked him, but his voice was lost in the sound of the dinner-bell ringing vigorously below his window. Kenon turned to go, but van Bredepoel signed to him with his hand to stop.

" You have to go and I won't keep you, but isn't there anything I can do for you ? Think it over. I'll see you to-morrow if I can."

" There is nothing the Inkosan' can do for me, and
I thank him." Kenon raised his hand above his
head and left the room.

" A pity, a great, great pity," thought van Bredepoel, when he was alone. " I must see if there isn't
anything I can do. I must talk to him again soon.
Perhaps he will pull round."

But the winter is a difficult season for Messrs.
Steyn, Berger and Stumpfkopf. It is the time when
most of the employees take annual leave, and as the
routine of the business can never be slackened, those
who are at work have to do more than their normal
share. For three days van Bredepoel returned to
Mrs. Harris' so late, and had to be away so early in
the morning, that he had no chance of seeing Kenon.
Then when he did have time to look for Kenon, an
agitated Mrs. Harris met him in the hall with the
words:

" That boy, Joseph, has gone, Mr. van Bredepoel.
He didn't tell you he was going ? "   Mrs. Harris
spoke in an injured tone and without noticing van
Bredepoel's look of surprise, as if he were responsible for Kenon's departure.

" No, I did not know. Why has he gone ? "

" Well! Nobody knows, then! " she said petulantly.
" I had a little row with him this morning and he
hasn't been seen since, though his baggage is still
here. It's strange; I've often rowed with him. It
couldn't have been that. It *must* have been something
else. I told you there was something the matter with
him."

Her manner annoyed van Bredepoel.

" Of course there was something the matter with

him," he replied. " Six months in gaol for something one hasn't done must be, to say the least, very upsetting."

" Oh no, Mr. van Bredepoel! Not for a nigger! Punishment upsets them as much as water a duck. It's not the same thing for them as it is for a white man. They've no shame, these blacks."

" Perhaps he'll come back. I suppose it depends on what you said to him this morning." Van Bredepoel was talking more to himself than to her. " What did you say exactly ? "

" Oh, he's just been impossible lately. If it hadn't been for you I would've sent him away days ago. And he was such a good boy, too. He used to have no objection to washing the dishes and helping in the kitchen. But this morning when I told him to help with the washing-up he refused point-blank, said cheekily that he was a bedroom-boy, not a kitchen-boy. Fancy all that to me, who had taken him back and given him another chance when no other woman would've had such a gaolbird about the place. I told him straight I wouldn't stand any nonsense from a nigger. ' You either help in the kitchen, Master Joseph,' I said, ' or you get out of my house.' If I ever get hold of him again, I'll tell him what I think of him—leaving me short-handed like this in the middle of the month. There's no holding these niggers nowadays. I'm sure these agitators have got hold of him! I've a good mind to set the police after him."

" But, Mrs. Harris, you told him to go ! " exclaimed van Bredepoel.

" Ach ! That was just my way of telling him off.

He ought to've known better than to think I would let him go without a month's notice," she retorted crossly.

Van Bredepoel soon discovered there was more to Kenon's disappearance than Mrs. Harris had told him. The next morning when one of the servants brought him his tea, he questioned him about Kenon. He learnt that for some time there had been a bitter feud between the black menservants and the half-caste servant girls whom Mrs. Harris employed in the kitchen and dining-room. The half-caste girls, highly conscious and proud of their European blood, had given themselves a privileged position in the household, and each one's behaviour was subtly calculated to remind the black men constantly of their racial inferiority. The girls used any dispute as an excuse to call out jeeringly: "Naked Kaffirs!" Knowing the strict taboos the black men had in their own country controlling the relations between men and women, and the undisputed priority of man over woman, van Bredepoel was not surprised that the men resented it strongly.

The day before he disappeared Kenon had gone down into the kitchen after breakfast to help with the work as usual. Afterwards he sat down at the table with the women servants to have his own meal. One of them had arrived late, and seeing all the places taken came up to Kenon and stood glaring at him truculently. He behaved as if he had not seen her and went on eating. Suddenly she tapped him on the shoulder and said: "Give me that chair, nigger."

"Humph!" he replied and went on eating his porridge.

"You don't expect any manners from a Kaffir, do you?" remarked another girl opposite him.

"Humph!" Kenon grunted again.

"Get out of my way, damn' nigger!" the first woman shouted, and tried to push him off his chair.

"I am nigger," he replied, settling firmly into his chair. "You are not nigger. Oh, no! You are not white. Oh, no! You are Bushman girl."

"Good Lord!" she screamed. "Here's this naked Kaffir calling me a Bushman girl! Me! The daughter of a Highland Scotch soldier! I tell you get out of the chair, nigger!"

"Humph!" said Kenon and clung to his chair.

"Oh! God hears me; I will kill you; just wait and see what I do to you," and she looked wildly round as if she meant to snatch a knife from the table, but instead she leant forward and spat twice on his head. The quarrel might have taken a serious turn if the noise had not brought Mrs. Harris running into the kitchen.

"She didn't tell me that," thought van Bredepoel, satisfied that he was nearer the immediate explanation of Kenon's disappearance. "And I don't expect she'd tell that to a policeman; though I don't suppose if she did it would make much difference."

But at the same time he realised that six months ago it would have taken considerably more than that to upset Kenon.

CHAPTER XIII

IT was Sunday afternoon in Port Benjamin. The sun was beginning to break through the heavy rain-clouds that had hung over the town so long, and for the first time in many months people had ventured out into the country in such numbers that the streets were nearly deserted. Governor's Walk was particularly quiet and a solitary taxi coming up it sounded so loud that a young man sitting in a patch of sunlight on the lawn in front of Mrs. Harris' raised his head to watch it. Abruptly it pulled up at the gate, and thinking a new boarder must be arriving, the young man continued to stare. He saw the white driver of the taxi lean out of the window and fling open the door. Out of the back stepped a young native, dressed in a new double-breasted suit of a rich purple material. The coat was cut very short and well tucked in at the waist so that the trousers, which were exceptionally wide, filled out like a skirt behind. On his feet were a pair of white and brown suede shoes, narrowly pointed and very high-heeled. A bright red, yellow, and black tie hung loosely over his coat in front, and as he started to walk the wind fluttered it round his neck. He wore also a wide-brimmed cowboy hat and swung a Japanese cane in his hand. Carrying himself like a shy chorus boy marching for the first time alone across a stage, he walked up the garden path to the front door and rang the visitors' bell.

" Is Mrs. Harris at home ? " he asked the servant who opened the door and who was struck dumb by the combination of the strange and familiar in the visitor's bearing. " Tell her that Mr. Badiakgotla, Junior, has called for his luggage."

Mrs. Harris, roused from her after-dinner sleep, made for the front door like a battleship going into action.

" Rang the front-door bell, did he ? " she muttered as she came. " Wants his luggage, does he ? I'll luggage him! "

" What do you want, and what do you mean by ringing my front-door bell ? " She was so astonished by Kenon's appearance that she failed to put as much dignified anger as she could have wished into her voice. And faced suddenly by the hard and sleepy-faced old woman, Kenon's memory of her authority and his habit of unquestioning obedience proved too much for him. He took off his hat respectfully and said: " Good afternoon, madam."

" Don't you ' good afternoon ' me, you naughty, naughty boy! Where have you been all this time ? And what do you mean by ringing my front-door bell at this time of the day ? "

" I have come for my luggage, madam," he said meekly.

" You want your luggage, do you ? Of all the cool-faced impudence I ever heard! You're lucky I haven't put the police on to you. What do you mean, going off like that, without giving notice ? "

And Kenon, forgetting that she had told him to go, could only say shyly: " Auck, madam: you know how a man is, sometimes he just goes wild."

"Here," she said, getting really angry, "get out of my sight, and don't let me see you again. If you want your luggage go round to the back and ask the maids to give it to you."

"But madam, please, I want a reference." Kenon spoke anxiously, for he saw her already withdrawing into the passage.

"Bah! a reference? You won't get one from me."

"Haven't I been a good boy, madam?"

"Haven't you been a good boy!" She forced herself to laugh. "A gaolbird, I should say."

"Can't I see Mr. van Bredepoel, madam?" he pleaded as a last resort, moving forward as she stepped back and grasping the edge of the door firmly.

"Mr. van Bredepoel is very angry with you. He doesn't want to see you ever again." And Mrs. Harris slammed the door in his face.

Yet when she related this incident to van Bredepoel afterwards, she told him neither that Kenon had asked for him nor how she had replied. Now Mrs. Harris believed in being firm with servants, and as she usually had something which they needed and wanted badly, she succeeded in being firm with them very well.

Ten minutes later the man in the garden saw the taxi drive off, loaded up with two wooden cases, an old gramophone, a box of records, some hunting-sticks and an umbrella. He gaped at it and then burst out laughing. "I've seen many dressed-up niggers, but that one takes the bun," he said to no one in particular.

But for Kenon it was no laughing matter. He

returned that afternoon very silent to the room of the half-caste girl with whom van Bredepoel had once seen him. He had meant to ask van Bredepoel for advice, and van Bredepoel had told Mrs. Harris he did not want to see him. He did not think van Bredepoel's attitude unjust, but it upset him profoundly. He felt that something had just happened once more which he could neither have foreseen nor avoided, and he felt resigned, without hope or despair, yet so bitter. He tried to think about his bitterness, and there was no end to it. It existed, though over it in his mind lay a cloud.

" I am not I," he said to himself, shaking his head.

Early the next morning he took a train back to his home, but the journey was no longer exciting. He seemed to be going farther and farther away from something he wanted, he did not know what. He felt almost as if during the journey he were seeing himself in a film, which started at the end and finished up with the beginning. The walk from the siding to his father's hut seemed very long, his shoes pinched, and the sweat round his neck made his collar cling to his skin until it seemed to choke him; he carried his wooden chest and gramophone, one under each arm, which was not at all comfortable, but he had to take care not to spoil his hat.

Though his parents and sisters were very pleased to see him, obviously still thought him wonderful and killed two goats to celebrate his arrival, he was no longer happy at home. For some weeks their admiration of his dress and manners flattered and pacified him. He took to hunting, dancing and singing, with a good deal of enjoyment, and even liked helping to

brand the young cattle, but soon his restlessness
returned. He would do nothing for hours on end,
except sit in the sun against the wall of the hut,
playing on his gramophone the same records over
and over again. Often he would take one of his
father's horses and ride down to the railway siding
to see the trains go through, and to show off before
the passengers in his best clothes. When he returned
from excursions like these he was more moody and
depressed than ever. He responded to the well-meant
attentions of his family with a graceful, but twisted
smile, which seemed to say: " It is all very kind of
you, but it doesn't really do any good, you know."
He no longer seemed fond of walking and would
not go anywhere unless he could ride.

One day he rode to the foot of a hill about six
miles from his home, and after looking at it for some
time from his seat underneath a broom bush,
realised that it was not so very high after all, and
proceeded to climb it. He reached the top short of
breath and sat down on an old surveyor's beacon.
The atmosphere was very clear and he was surprised
to find how far he could see. His vision rested for a
long time on some mountains, whose peaks rose over
the horizon. " Those must be the mountains I saw
from the train when I left home," he thought. " How
small they look; I could almost cover them with the
palm of my hand."

Below him on the crest of every hill in the valley
were the neat brown circles of huts, and round them
irregular patches of cultivated land. Here and there
someone wrapped in a white and black blanket was
walking at a steady unhurried pace on a red foot-

path. None of these people seemed to have an obvious destination and the country over which they were walking was so big, and so much of it was exposed to the eye, that Kenon felt as the look-out on a steamer must feel when he sights in mid-Atlantic some small dinghies. The feeling that, no matter how far they walked in that wide fertile land, they could never reach any final destination, came to Kenon and depressed him unutterably. Sometimes a group of calves broke away from herds grazing below him. Their hooves stamped dust from the grass, but the wind appeared to lack the force to carry it skyward, and the dust fell back among the hooves which had raised it.

" If I got on my horse now," thought Kenon, " I wonder how long it would take me to get to those mountains." But he made no effort to go, and found himself thinking instead of Port Benjamin on a Friday night. On Friday nights, like thousands of other servants, he had always had the evening off and had walked about for hours in streets bright with electric light, looking in at shop windows which seemed filled with everything that one could want to make one happy. He remembered the cheerful crowds, weaving and interweaving in the complicated mesh of their intentions, and there came back to him the excitement he had felt walking amongst so many strange people, seeing them at their best, not knowing the sordidness they came from and would go back to before midnight, but projecting both forwards and backwards in his mind a picture of them in the same attractive clothes, the same care-free mood. And he began to feel that if only he could walk there again, surely there would come to him from the depths of the crowd a voice, and someone would take him by the arm and say: " Come, you are he I have been looking for and never found till now. Come, and we shall be happy together."

Some days later Kenon's parents woke up to find that both he and a horse were gone. They discovered later that he had sold the horse to the trader at the railway siding, but they did not find their son. Kenon's sisters still think of the gramophone he had with him. To them it was one of the many wonderful things about that very wonderful Port Benjamin, but they never speak of it to one another, for since they heard it last, they have not seen or heard of Kenon.

As for van Bredepoel, he was scarcely more fortunate than they. That afternoon when Mrs. Harris told him that Kenon had come and gone a second time, he had a foreboding that the two of them would not meet again. And how the foreboding distressed him! Once when one of the black servants repeated to him a rumour that Kenon was doing a long-term sentence in a gaol somewhere inland, he was visibly agitated. Far down in his mind were sown the seeds of a disturbing sense of guilt, a feeling that Kenon's situation during those last days at Mrs. Harris' had demanded from him something more than an expression of sympathy. He blamed himself for not seeing sooner how desperate the boy's plight had really been. After all, he had been in a better position to observe Kenon than anyone else, and the hints he had received from Mrs. Harris should have been sufficient warning. He saw now the significance of all sorts of small things which had made no particular impression on him at the time.

One image of Kenon, above all, he could not forget. Van Bredepoel had brought some work back with him to his room one Sunday afternoon. Not a sound reached him from the servants' quarters, which he believed to be deserted. But when he got up to open his window wider he was surprised to see Kenon sitting on the threshold of a servants' room. Kenon must have heard the window open, but his attitude did not change. He went on sitting there, his head in his hands, looking out of large black eyes straight before him; not a sign, not a gesture, that he was aware of anyone watching him. Van Bredepoel concluded that he was waiting for someone, and went back to his work. But some hours later, when it was getting dark, Kenon was still sitting there. It grew quite dark without van Bredepoel seeing him move. The picture in his mind of this still, black figure lost in the shadows of a backyard in Port Benjamin haunted van Bredepoel; it became the symbol of his failure to help the boy when he alone could have helped. He did not try to justify himself as once, to his tutor, he had justified a complete lack of interest in a native girl with the mere exclamation: " But, Meneer Broecksma, she is black! " Since those days he had moved far.

And this would appear strange only in Port Benjamin. For how often it happens, in the lives of people, that a purely human interest immediately creates a corresponding concentration in the field of ideas. Here you see a man very fond of a woman and there a woman very fond of a man, create out of their

love for one another attitudes of mind totally in-
compatible with the former trend of their lives.
This feeling for another becomes, indeed, a rallying-
point for interests and ideas which have hitherto been
scorned, and soon what had first possessed little more
than position and no size, snowballs into an ava-
lanche which threatens to overwhelm the old self.
Van Bredepoel's relation with Kenon had never
gone so deep. But it had been deep enough to
destroy the traditional barrier between white and
black. For whereas through the mind of white Port
Benjamin runs a bleak and deserted corridor which
separates European from black and coloured people,
a secret lock seemed to have been sprung in the walls
of van Bredepoel's mind and a figure, savage from
the knees down, resplendently civilised above, had
entered furtively, acquiring as it came a white man's
gesture or two, but the mentality, the feelings . . . of
what ? And once a way is opened, who knows what
may follow ?

BOOK II

" Pour la première fois depuis dix mille ans,
l'homme est à lui-même, totalement et sans
aucun reste de connaissance, un problème.
Car il ne sait plus ce qu'il est et il sait en
même temps qu'il ne le sait pas."

Scheler

CHAPTER I

WINTER passed swiftly from Port Benjamin, and in its wake came at night colossal winds that shook the town like a ship caught in a gale. On the black and sodden bark of the trees appeared small explosions of green. Soon the avenues were covered in shade. The sky hardened and stretched taut over the town, until life seemed imprisoned in a sphere of steel. An atmosphere, vivid but insubstantial like that of a dream, gathered over the houses. Wood and stone and steel lost their look of solidity and appeared only violent vibrations of colour on planes of smoke and vapours of heat. All day long ships uncurled long motionless plumes of smoke over the sea and the long Atlantic swell dissolved not in breakers of water but a surf of light. With the nights came a profound darkness and clearness of stars, but no coolness. At Mrs. Harris' the sun began to blister the paint on the window-sills and twist even the wood itself. Often van Bredepoel thought he could hear the day vibrate, like a low-pitched tuning-fork in his ears, and a deep restlessness communicated itself to him and the people of Port Benjamin. On Sundays the streets filled with traffic moving rapidly out of the town. Looking at the white, set faces of the drivers, the cargoes of joyless and perspiring passengers, van Bredepoel was reminded of fugitives fleeing from a sudden insurrection.

One Sunday afternoon, he was in his room trying

to read. Outside in the servants' quarters a gramophone was releasing loud monotonous circles of
music into the shimmering air. Van Bredepoel
suddenly thought of Kenon and remembered that
Mrs. Harris had attributed his disappearance to the
influence of agitators.

"Why did she do that?" he wondered. "I think
I'll go and have a look at these agitators. I shall
never settle down to anything in this atmosphere."

Outside, the afternoon bombarded both his eyes
and ears. A young couple were approaching him from
the other end of the street; the man, dressed in a
navy-blue suit and pushing a pram, walked with a
tired and depressed air, as if the high hopes he had
placed in the companionship of the woman at his
side had been utterly frustrated. The woman was
dressed in black, had on a large black hat with a
cluster of cherries at the side, a sulky expression lay
in the corners of her thin white mouth, and she, too,
looked as if the man had disappointed her. Neither
of them made any attempt to drive away the flies
crawling round the eyes of the chalk-faced baby in
the pram. When he saw van Bredepoel, the man
suddenly realised that it was a long time since he
had said anything to his wife, but all he could now
think of saying to her, in a quiet spiritless voice, was:
"Darling, isn't it hot? My underpants are wet
through with sweating." And he tried to laugh as if
he had made a great joke, and as if they were the
happiest couple in the happiest possible world. But
once they had passed van Bredepoel he was silent
again.

Van Bredepoel walked on slowly until he came

to a square called Shepherd's Place, where native
agitators were usually supposed to congregate. At
first he thought the square deserted and he was not
surprised, it was fully exposed to the sun, and heat
vapours were mounting from its gravelled surface.
But a sudden burst of clapping drew his attention to a
T-shaped row of shuttered fruit-stalls on the far side
of the square, and in the corner of the row, in the
only shade the place afforded, he saw the backs of a
great number of people. These, he noticed when he
came nearer, were mostly black men dressed with
varying degrees of completeness and success in
European clothes. There were also a few European
youths with coarse faces and open-necked shirts,
standing in groups of two and three in the crowd.
Whenever a black speaker, who stood on a table
right in the corner of the stalls, said anything definite,
which was seldom, the Europeans jeered him loudly.
Near the table were numbers of black men wearing
red badges in their button-holes, and a purple-faced
white man, who was very busy making a shorthand
note of everything that was said. It was obvious that
the black speaker was only a minor figure at the
meeting, for he was continually being interrupted by
good-humoured shouts of " Where is the Doctor ?
We want the Doctor! " It was some time before van
Bredepoel followed closely what was being said, for
when he looked at the glittering landscape beyond,
he felt that the only force that mattered, the only
personality almost, was this cruel and twisted afternoon.

Presently, however, he heard the speaker say:
" Ladies and gentlemen "—there were no women

present—" before I call on the Doctor to address you, I want you to sing a little song. When we go to the meetings of the European he makes you sing ' God save the King,' and you have to take off your hats and stand to attention until he has finished. But that melody is not ours. We sing our own song and I hope you will all give it the same tokens of respect. Hats off, ladies and gentlemen, to the African National Anthem! " All except the Europeans took off their hats, and began to sing in deep baritones a song which began like a hymn, worked up towards the middle with quickened rhythm and ascending notes into something like a battle song, and faded away again like a hymn. The words were in a native dialect van Bredepoel could not quite understand, but part of it he translated as: " Long have you waited, long have you slept, O Africa! But now you shall awake! "

" God, how these niggers give themselves airs," a white man near him said. " Look at that fellow getting on the table, he is quite the big meneer."

A very carefully dressed native had just climbed on to the table and was looking round him importantly, like a pompous professor about to begin his first lecture to a new group of students. He was bareheaded, but his chin was so tightly supported by a high, stiff collar that he could not turn his head without turning his body as well. Round the collar was tied a black silk kerchief in the fashion of the 'nineties. His chest was puffed out, his stomach drawn in, and his posterior projected so much that the lines of his figure resembled those of a stuffed and corseted pouter pigeon. Drawing himself to his full height, he held up his hand for silence. The crowd greeted him with loud shouts of " Auck! The Doctorr! "

" Ladies and gentlemen, if there be such present." he began, putting his hands underneath the tails of his coat, and moving himself from his toes to his heels, his heels to his toes. " I have to-day an important announcement to make. I would not be far wrong if I called it an epoch-making announcement, and I assure you that it has never been heard before. But before I begin my oration, I want you to sing once more the African National Anthem. Your last performance was egregiously disappointing. Now, hats off everyone, and the European brothers present will, if they are at all conversant with the laws of international etiquette and free from base and ignoble prejudices, do the same."

Van Bredepoel noticed that the Doctor pronounced English better than he himself did, and he heard a white man near him say: " Phew, what a mouthful! Do you know what ' egrejusly ' is, Bill ? "

When the song was sung, the Doctor began again:

" Ladies and gentlemen, if there be such present, this announcement I have to make to you to-day is the result of many long and arduous studies on my part. I may modestly say that in order to arrive at the conclusion which makes it possible, I have often burnt the midnight oil; yes, on very numerous occasions even the candles at both ends, and I can give you my personal assurance that it is no white elephant being dragged across your trail, but the truth, the fruit of exact and conscientious labours. Gentlemen! Gentlemen! Gentlemen! And, of course, ladies too, if there be such present. This announcement is that we, the black men of this country, are the natural Christians of this country, and the white men the heathen, the Philistine, the Moabite, the Vandal. Gentlemen, if God sent me to-day a wireless telegram to tell me that the white man was a Christian "—he spoke as though it were the most natural thing in the world for God to do— " I'd send that wireless telegram back to God and say, ' Now, God, just put that nonsense in your pipe and smoke it.' I'd say to him, furthermore: ' God, have you forgotten that when the white man came to this country he came to us with the Bible in his hand ? Yes! He had the Bible and we had the land; to-day he's got the land, and we the Bible. Don't you think, God, that that's a pity ? ' I'll ask him, and never will the wireless be so busy as that day on which I begin telling God a few home truths. ' God, do you know why the atmosphere of hell is like a railway station ? ' And if he doesn't know, I'll say to him: ' Because there are so many Smuts in it.' I'll ask him: ' God, do you know why the road to hell is like a dirty table-cloth ? ' If he doesn't know, I'll say: ' Because there are so many Steyns on it.' Now I ask you, gentlemen, isn't it just right that we should be Christians ? Aren't we in trouble and going through parlous days ? Aren't we oppressed ? All right. But there is another reason why we are of the true Christian race."

The Doctor paused like a conjurer who is about to produce a rabbit from someone's empty hat.

" Christ himself," he said, while the officials round him cheered the announcement, " was black! This

may surprise you, gentlemen, but my scholastic
endeavours have convinced me that on this point
there can't be any doubt, no doubt at all. I have it
on the highest authority, the authority of the great
Tertullian himself, and in case our white brethren
present don't know who Tertullian was, I had
better state that he was one of the founders of the
Christian Church, and near enough the time of
Christ to know what he was talking about. This
Tertullian, this big noise of Christianity, once
declared (I won't give you the Latin equivalent
because it will only puzzle our white brethren) that
the Virgin Mary, the mother of Christ, ' was black
but pretty.' Note the use of the word ' but,' gentlemen. To my mind, it ominously strengthens my
announcement. It shows that the great Tertullian
would've preferred the Virgin Mary not to have
been black, but that like a true Christian and an
honest man he felt in honour bound to state it. I
submit to you, gentlemen, there can be no doubt on
this point. Doubt would be an idle superfluity, a
luxury in which the licentious European can indulge,
but of which we hard-working, suppressed Christians
must divest ourselves. When I hear the so-called,
quasi, pseudo-ministers of God in this country
talking about converting the black man, I laugh at
the back of my neck, because they are the sinners
who need conversion. If God asked me to-day what
his ministers are doing in this country, I will say:
' God! Both the Anglicans and the Dutch predikants
are trying to get the bun for prayer and hypocrisy,
and do you know what the bun is, God ? The black
man and his capacity for honest labour and the little

land and sheep left to him, the crumbs that the rich
man wants to take from the poor man's table. Isn't
it a shame, God ? ' Now, gentlemen, the legs of
this country are out of joint and we must pull
together to set them right. We have God on our
side, for his son was black, and all we need is to
organise and tell the white man that we will take
from him what he has taken from us. Let him bring
his machine-guns and tear bombs, his bayonets and
policemen, we are not frightened, we have God on
our side. Our needs are Christ, Combination and
Co-operation. We have Christ. All we need is
combination and co-operation, and for all three,
gentlemen, all you have to do is to join right now
the African Workers' Union and to put as many
pennies as you can in the hat which is coming round."

As van Bredepoel listened to the Doctor, he
wondered if any of the natives could understand one
word of this long-winded speech. Yet their faces
looked attentive enough; they all seemed to feel
that someone was at last getting to the roots of
the grievance and had brought them there. Only
the white men were gaping like dead cod-fish at the
speaker, and had forgotten to jeer.

" It doesn't matter," van Bredepoel told himself,
" if a man like that states the wrong grievance,
the real grievance remains; and as long as it remains,
people conscious of it will gather and, if necessary,
die, even round the wrong soap box." And he felt
dismayed to think that it was to men like these that
Kenon had come searching for help.

After a time he decided to ask one of the men with
red badges for the words of the song they had sung.

The man was just beginning to tell van Bredepoel, when another official stepped in between and pushed them roughly aside, hitting a pencil out of van Bredepoel's hand as he did so.

" What the hell do you want, white man ? " he shouted.

Van Bredepoel, startled and controlling himself with difficulty, picked up his pencil, and tried to ignore the fellow.

" What is that you said ? ' Vuka,' was it ? " he asked the other.

" I don't trust no white man," the truculent one said again, but this time with a faint note of apology in his voice. Still van Bredepoel took no notice of him.

" I do not mean you personally, sah," he began again, a trace of dismay in his bearing. " I'm referring to white men in general." And then, as van Bredepoel still paid no attention to him, added : " I meant no offence, sah. Excuse me, sah. Au revoir."

He walked bashfully away.

But van Bredepoel could not get the first native to give him the rest of the words of the song. The incident, slight as it was, made a deep impression on him. He thought it a bad sign. Start out with a colour prejudice and the native and coloured people will sooner or later counter it with a white prejudice. He wondered which was worse.

As he walked home the great tide of life was ebbing back to Port Benjamin. The streets were streaming with traffic and most of the people in the cars carried on their faces the sunburn of far-off beaches. On the pavements were servants dressed in their best, hurrying home to serve cold Sunday

suppers, young men and women in white sporting
dresses with tennis rackets and golf-bags, and many
elderly people in black on their way to church.
It was still hot, but the air over Port Benjamin
seemed to be stirring in revolt against the heat which
had oppressed the town all day. A sudden and
powerful wind was streaming over the mountain
top, pouring dense, twisting formations of cloud into
the town below. So dense and moist were the turbu-
lent winds over the mountain, and so still and light
the air immediately over Port Benjamin, that the
clouds dropped precipitately down the cliffs, re-
bounded and scattered from the rocks below like
the spray of some vast, unimagined Niagara. And
on this turning, twisting air was thrown the sound
of many church bells, loud, metallic, shaking and
pealing, pealing and shaking like things in the throes
of a violent hysteria. So the bells of some mediæval
city might have rung, calling its inhabitants to
prayer in face of a disaster which no human effort
could avert.

And he felt deeply disturbed. What had come
over him ? Why could he not take the life around
him, the scene he had just witnessed in Shepherd's
Place, as the other Europeans there had taken it;
as no problem, that is to say, but as something one
could dismiss with a laugh, at most a jeer. Had his
vision been so slanted, so specialised by the coming
of Kenon into his life and by his own sense of loneliness, that he could not lift his eyes from human
frustrations ? Perhaps in this he was not alone.
Perhaps many other people's vision had come to be
concentrated and specialised in the same way. He

thought immediately of Shepherd's Place and the
crowd gathered anxiously about a pompous wind-
bag, not because it believed him to be really wise
or helpful but because it felt he was circling in his
vague bombastic way round the mysterious source of
its frustrations. People may have no very definite
faith in doctors yet be drawn to seek their help in
illness, if only because doctors, however fallible, do
try to get at the roots of disease. He remembered
his uncle telling him when he was little how the old
Boer farmers used to sit all day, calmly and happily,
on their stoeps, drinking coffee and smoking their
pipes, never a word of bitterness about themselves,
content both in their past and their future. And he
could not imagine one of that pretentious crowd
which filled the eating-houses and cinemas of Port
Benjamin to suffocation sitting still alone for even
half an hour. Their thoughts, the moment they
were alone with themselves, would follow a slant
just like his own, turning inevitably to the secret
sources of their common misery, and thoughts of this
kind were just what all wanted to avoid. They
clamoured daily for more time, more leisure. Yet
the moment they got what they wanted they enslaved
themselves to a new precipitation. The rush, the
stampede for soporifics began. They fled from
themselves, from the reality of their lives, to games,
to cinemas and books which lifted them into a world
where human beings were miraculously free from
the natural consequences of their actions. The
gaiety, the cheerfulness of everyone, except perhaps
children, seemed to him but a disguised and painted
joylessness.

Here, he believed, was the emotional substance
out of which churches and revolutions are made, and
mentally he began to divide it into two. On one
side he placed the set of feelings which drove men to
gather round soap boxes; on the other, the feelings
which sent them to pray in churches. One seemed
born out of the sense of frustration imposed by
society on the individual; the other out of a dim
belief that the individual, that both the individual
and society, indeed the whole of life, would be
subjected continually to interference, even annihilation, by capricious forces of Nature, were it not that
his fellow men prayed to a god. Was this the clue
to the calmness of those old men his uncle had
described ? Did they owe their calm to the fact
that they believed in both their society and their
prayer ? For in Port Benjamin people had lost
faith in both. So that the value of the service society
and religion rendered them had declined; the price
they paid for it remained the same. " Here," van
Bredepoel thought, " the form of our lives is order,
but their content is chaos."

He thought suddenly of a painting that used to
hang in the passage at " Vergelegen." This picture
had originally been brought from Holland by van
Bredepoel's father and had passed, on his death, to
Uncle Willem. It had always had a great fascination
for Johan. As a child he could not help being
attracted to it because it received, as the only
original picture in the house, more attention than
any other. The canvas was enclosed in a very old
and massive gold frame, which seemed to draw out
and support the subtlest and faintest tones in the

painting. His aunt would never allow any of
the servants to go near it, and often spent as
much as two hours polishing and cleaning the
frame and the glass, carefully, sensitively, almost
reverently.

Whenever strangers came to " Vergelegen," sooner
or later Margrieta van Bredepoel would say: " But,
my dears, I must show you our de Groot, a real, a
genuine de Groot." And conducting them down the
long passage inlaid with tiles that had come all the
way from Holland, would draw herself up in front
of the picture, tall, proud and erect like the governess
of a royal family, and say: " Now, don't go too
near, my dears. Come and stand next to me. You
will get the best view from here. Now, isn't that
splendid ? I don't honestly think, although I say
it myself, that there can be another picture just like
it in the world. Such beautiful detail. Such sure
and accurate drawing! You see just the suggestion
of a vein underneath the skin. Isn't that so, so
amusing ? And look at the nail of the middle
finger of the little girl's hand. Do you see how it
shines ? Isn't that too, too sweet ? "

How well he remembered that picture. It showed a
section of a street in Leyden on the banks of the
Schildersgracht, whose waters, just visible, were
shining and still with a tragic intensity. The branches
of two very old trees leant over the Gracht, interweaving and touching high up in the picture until
the house which formed the centre-piece was seen
as if through an embroidered net. There, high up
in the picture, was a gable unwinding a somnolent
rhythm against a partially clouded sky. Lower down,

the brick walls of the houses burned among the
smoking tree shadows; at the side of the house, in
the centre, a wide-open door gave on a dark passage
leading into a pebbled court-yard, dimly visible at
the back. At the door a charming but very ordinary
scene was being enacted: a mother, dressed in the
clothes of the early eighteenth century, handing to
her small daughter a porcelain flask. Both faces
were bright with contentment, the mother looked
the best mother of the best daughter in the best of
all possible worlds, and even the bricks behind
them took on a warm domestic glow.

There in that picture, van Bredepoel thought, was
everything the life around him lacked: faith,
security, calm, contentment. He was convinced that
the picture did not owe these qualities to the painter,
who had been, as Johan's aunt was so fond of pointing
out, a wild disorderly fellow. He thought it a clear
case of a painter giving expression, involuntarily
perhaps, to the salient characteristics of the life of
his time—a life of which the calm and security were
so strong that they annihilated, or placed in a
tradition of order, his own sense of disorder.

He remembered the occasion when Margrieta van
Bredepoel was showing Meneer Broecksma round
the house for the first time. Johan, following them
diffidently, saw the old man swing round so quickly
that he nearly slipped on the tiles and make for the
picture before Tante Margrieta had really meant to
draw his attention to it.

"God! Mevrouw!" the old man said. "Maar
dat is toch een meesterstuk! Extremely good! A
genuine de Groot! Who on earth would have

expected to find so much light in so dark a
continent?"

Unaware that he was not only paying a back-
handed compliment but poaching on Margrieta van
Bredepoel's pet preserve, the old man continued, in
the same manner:

"Charming! Charming! It pleases me a great
deal. Yes, there can be no doubt it pleases me a
great deal, and pleases me all the more because it
is unexpected. Yes, and I like it all the more because
it reminds me that our national genius has not gone
only into trade and the creation of more trade and
still more trade, but also into the elaborate organisation of our homes, their complicated but comforting
life, their cheerful domesticity."

That was the old man all over, looking at what
was simply a picture from the most complicated
angles.

"There's no doubt it pleases me. Ach! Mevrouw,
it has everything that was real and outstanding in
our life in Holland. Look how the faces of the people
there suggest its intrinsic lack of perplexity, its
steadiness and certainty. Think of that successful
struggle we put up against Philip of Spain—it began
there: I see the one great cause of our strength in
that, in the fact that we were not perplexed about
and did not doubt for a moment the truth and justice
of our cause. Had we been dissatisfied and some
Bolshevik of that day had jeered at us saying that
we were fighting after all only about one interpreta-
of the Bible as opposed to another, and not about
the veracity of the Bible itself, that we were all just
quibbling about the right to quibble about religion

and not the reality of religion itself, had we worried
our heads, for instance, about the incompatibility
of our doctrine of predestination and free will, we
would have dispersed like smoke in the wind before
Alva's forces. But we were then, we were still when
that picture was painted, a people for whom all the
mysteries of life were clearly and definitely worked
out like a scientific theory or a field of tulips. There
was no mystery, no problem, no perplexity which our
doctrines did not solve for us. What conviction,
what untold contentment and prosperity our faith
gave us! For think how far we had moved when
that was painted from the sensibility of Rembrandt,
who could never shake his imagination free from
those dark ages out of which we had so slowly come,
whose mind was always sombre with shadows,
broken only by a beam of light falling on a cross in
Palestine. Then suddenly the shadows are gone and
we are here in this world of light and tranquillity.
And look at the staunch row of houses! Look how
simply and harmoniously they are conceived! You
don't see houses like them now. Contrast them even
with any genuine piece of Gothic architecture you
know. There you'll see evidence of a mind tortured,
swaying flame-like between hope and despair,
between mystery and enlightenment, until hope,
despair and a tortured anxiety for relief dominate
thought as the spire a Gothic cathedral. But here
the houses, this picture, give you peace, the quin-
tessence of peace—order. Look at those clouds.
There's a north-west gale brewing somewhere, but
even if it comes, that Gracht will hold calmness to
the sky; and that house with its wide-open door:

it holds peace, quiet, and contentment against this dark and mysterious universe. Ach! Where is that world now ? "

The old man's lyrical outburst, like many of his speeches spontaneous and unpremeditated, had slightly humiliated Johan's aunt, who only thanked him with: " Very interesting, I'm sure, Mynheer Broecksma." But after they had gone, Johan once more had a look at it, and yes, the door of that house was wide open, plainly and invitingly open, and he envied the people who had lived when that picture was painted, because they must have had thousands of doors like that, through only one of which they had to pass in order to find everything the old man had described.

Nowadays this mood underlay all his thoughts and feelings. He lived in the same punctilious, conscientious way, but neither his work nor his leisure satisfied him. He awaited the end of the day's work with anxiety, yet once back in his room found it difficult to stay there. More and more often he would wander aimlessly through the streets of Port Benjamin, watch people stream out of cinemas, theatres and restaurants, see them swirl into little units whose members fell at once into an easy companionship. How mysterious all that was! His own friendships, made with people like Simmering, were neither numerous nor satisfying. He found his friends as a rule too much an embodiment of all the diffidence, doubts and disgusts he carried in himself ever to go farther than just liking them. He felt that if for a moment he relaxed his vigilance over himself, he could only too easily become another

Simmering, and rather than be like a self-conscious, dissatisfied and second-rate musician, he would remain a first-rate shipping clerk. But at the same time he knew his life was missing something which it could not afford to miss, was rapidly running dry in the sink of Messrs. Steyn, Berger and Stumpfkopf. Yet what could he do about it ?

This question was always with him when he wandered about alone at night. Often, as he walked along the Esplanade at Port Benjamin, he would feel that he could not return to his room until he had found a solution. On the sea-front were green iron benches, on which slept men in ragged clothes, their knees drawn up underneath their chins, covered with old newspapers for warmth. He would sit on one of these benches and listen to the swish of the sea on stone, the same sea which, if Herodotus is to be believed, once tossed the cockle-shell ships of the Phœnicians, and brought up the fleets of Albuquerque and d'Almeida. Behind him Port Benjamin was a branch of fire burning at the end of a long continent of mysterious land; while somewhere, eight thousand miles above, in China and Japan, six hundred million people were going about their lives in bright sunlight. And he would feel as if a black tide of nothingness, of annihilation, were creeping over him. He would consider that nearly half of his life was already spent. " And what have I to show for it," he thought, " except the facts that I am a nuisance to no one but myself, have a certain amount of patience and conscientiousness, twenty pounds a month, no convictions and a hell of a lot of doubts ? But perhaps I am worried only because

my mind is on a slant, and I see outside me only
what is already in me."

Yet he went back to his room, night after night,
his question still unanswered. And in the end, by
accepting his restlessness he came to question it no
longer, forgot even to hanker for peace, or to dream
that peace was possible.

CHAPTER II

FIVE years had gone by since he came to Port Benjamin, five years which are so little in time and so much in the life of the individual. Many changes had come about. On the outskirts of the town the large old oak forests were being cut down hurriedly, and in their place rose row upon row of little red-roofed houses, all built on the same precipitate plan. Their newness did not prevent them from conveying an impression of unutterable dreariness and squalor. The harbour front had expanded; statistics, cited with pride, showed that ocean-going traffic through Port Benjamin had been nearly doubled. Daily, trains came in from the north, bearing loads of bewildered and unsophisticated black people to augment the local labour supplies. Every set-back in farming released hundreds of destitute, unskilled, uneducated white families into the town. The port of Port Benjamin near the main working and business areas overflowed with an indescribable mixture of peoples, thrown together only by a common mis-fortune, held together by a common defencelessness. At night the public squares were filled with shabby, hungry, bewildered, heavy-hearted crowds, listening hopelessly to glib exponents of the latest social panacea. Clashes between workers, mostly black workers, and police became more and more frequent. Yet the Municipal Council of Port Benjamin claimed that the town had never been so prosperous, and quoted figures to show the success of its loans abroad and the increase in its rateable value.

Every main street in Port Benjamin now had its cinema, built on childish conceptions of a Moorish palace, with velvet and cushioned seats, thick carpets and plush curtains, electric organs and uniformed ushers. Many cinemas instituted baby-crèches, where mothers who had regularly taken their children for walks in the park now placed them in the care of a uniformed nurse, while they went and looked at the pictures inside. Enormous balcony cafés looked down on the main streets, and catered for unending crowds; all day long there were people sipping iced drinks and listening to fat and bald musicians dressed up as " Barcelona Bull-fighters," " Roumanian Gipsies," " Spanish Min-strels," and " Tyrolese Mountaineers."

Messrs. Steyn, Berger and Stumpfkopf prospered. Old Karel Steyn was now rarely seen at the office, being too busy working on public committees and addressing Rotary Club meetings on " Service before Self."

Over the week-ends, Port Benjamin overflowed into the country and the roads were black with traffic. Every shaded place had its picnic party complete with thermos flasks and gramophones. The churches became practically empty, but the number of Spiritualists, Total Immersionists and Hallelujah Highsteppers steadily grew. Only one thing did not seem to prosper, so the Municipal Council said, and that was the Orchestra, in which Simmering played. The revenue from its concerts was steadily declining, and the Council frequently

warned the director of the Orchestra that unless it
too was run on business lines it would be scrapped.

At Mrs. Harris' the changes were less violent, but
not less real. In the place of Kenon and his companions there was now double the number of
servants. The web of annexes extended beyond
Governor's Walk and the price of board and lodging
had been raised.

Major Mustard one night entertained an old
regimental contemporary of his, and the next
morning was found dead in his chair. Mrs. Harris'
sister still came yearly to visit her, but the little girl
she had once brought with her was now almost a
woman. Van Bredepoel, who had seen her annually
for five years, was shocked one day to notice that
she was no longer a child. The transformation was
most natural, and yet he was surprised and a little
depressed.

One evening van Bredepoel came back to Mrs.
Harris' to find a telegram waiting for him. " Uncle
died yesterday funeral to-day, Aunt," it read.
Since it was too late to think of attending the
funeral, he wrote that he was going to ask for leave
immediately and would join her. A letter came by
the next post begging him to do nothing of the kind.
She was very grateful for his intention but would not
dream of interfering with his work. There was
nothing he could usefully do. His uncle was buried
and the estate was in a good lawyer's hands. When
everything was settled she would no doubt pay him
a visit.

Some months later she did come to Port Benjamin
and spent a week with van Bredepoel. She would

have liked to stay longer, she said, but there was an
aged brother in Holland who might die at any
moment, and she had to see him again.

Only once had she shown any traces of bitterness
about her past, but these had been so faint, and had
revealed themselves in circumstances so provocative,
that it seemed dangerous to build too much con-
jecture on them.

Johan was saying good-bye on the ship that was to
take his aunt to Holland. For the second time in her
life she was going on a long voyage, and she was
telling Johan of her first voyage more than forty
years before. She had been a young married woman
then and had made the voyage to Port Benjamin in
the company of her husband and Johan's father and
mother.

" There were no proper docks," she told Johan,
" and all the passengers were taken from the ship
and rowed in a small boat right to the edge of the
surf. There huge negroes waded in to meet us and
carried us in enormous baskets to the shore. All
went well until your mother's turn came. She was
so terrified of a huge, grinning black creature who
came to fetch her that she cried out to your father:
' Oh! Please don't give me over to the devil!'
And. . . ." Suddenly she had stopped and taken
Johan's arm. Whether it was a sudden realisation
of the fact that she alone was left of the little band
of four, who once when she was young had arrived
full of hope and excitement in Port Benjamin, or
sorrow at leaving Johan that upset her, he could
not tell. But her eyes, those cool blue eyes that had
left on Johan's mind a memory of enduring calm

and steadiness, had suddenly moistened. Before she could speak the ship's gong had boomed out close to them, the siren had given one long, hysterical shriek of warning. She had tried hard then to regain her self-control, and said in a low voice to Johan: " Hanske, we all made a terrible mistake coming to this country. It hasn't done us any good. I don't think it does anyone good to uproot themselves like that. One's mind can readjust itself, but one's blood not so easily; one's mind can forget, but one's blood never forgets. I must try to get you to come and join me soon."

Johan did not see Margrieta van Bredepoel again. Within a few years she too was dead. But her going left him with an added feeling of loneliness—a loneliness that seemed to belong more to his blood than to his mind.

Sitting on a tram on the way home one afternoon, thinking of these and similar things, a movement near van Bredepoel made him look up. His seat was almost at the back of the top deck of the tram. There were no other seats vacant except one or two behind him on the four benches which the law of Port Benjamin allocated to native and coloured people. A young woman had come on to the tram and was hesitating, as if she meant to sit down on one of the empty seats behind him. She stood there for a moment, evidently in doubt, until the sight of the black man who would be her companion finally decided her to stretch out her hand for a strap. Commonplace as the incident was, van Bredepoel found himself instinctively watching her. The other passengers, mostly middle-aged men, were also looking round, now at the girl, now at one another. At first he thought this was merely a prelude to the usual scene in which four or five men jump up and offer a woman their places. But something unusual was afoot. The men continued to stare in the same direction. A minute or two, and the atmosphere on the tram had become electric. Suddenly two of the white men who had been sitting together jumped up and walked down the length of the car silently with set faces, until they reached the bench beside which the woman was standing. Then one of them said to the black man on the bench, a young Indian with a lean face and soft brown eyes: " Say, will you come out of that ? "

" What for ? " asked the Indian, a bewildered look on his face.

" You know damn well what for ! " Van Bredepoel was bewildered in his turn by the anger in the man's voice.

" This lady wants a seat," said his companion, who was the more timid of the two and therefore a more conciliatory type.

" Well, there's plenty of room ! " the Indian replied, a racial instinct putting him on his guard and giving him an impertinent air to hide his sense of dismay. Van Bredepoel felt sorry for him. He looked so trapped between pride and fear.

" You know damn well that she can't sit there now ! " shouted the man who had spoken first. " Come on out of it, and no nonsense."

" If you're so anxious for the lady to be seated why not give her your own seat ? " said the boy truculently.

" By God! You'll come out of it, chat or no chat,"
shrieked the man, catching hold of the Indian's coat
and trying to jerk him out of his seat.

" These seats are reserved for non-Europeans,"
said the boy and clung more firmly to his seat.

" Please, please don't make all this fuss! " pleaded
the woman, tears in her eyes.

" No, madam! " replied the man, beneath his
breath, tugging at the Indian, who was now hunched
up in his seat and clinging to the rails at his side.
No, madam, no. It's high time these blacks were
taught their places."

He gave a great heave at the Indian's coat. The
collar of the jacket gave way and the white man
staggered heavily back against the benches on the
other side. Van Bredepoel saw a glitter of pleased
smiles on the faces of the other black men there.
The white man either saw or felt it, too, and his anger
was fed by the knowledge that he was being made
to look ridiculous. He rushed back and again caught
hold of the Indian, going white and breathless in his
efforts to dislodge the boy. But the young man clung
to his seat so effectively that his assailant succeeded
only in tearing his clothes more.

Just then a young white man got up from his
seat in the front and approached the struggling pair
with a determined though none the less nervous
air. He was exceedingly tall, so tall that in order to
avoid bumping his head against the roof he had
to stoop considerably, and this strengthened the
impression of an essentially nervous, almost furtive,
organisation underlying his cool, deliberate manner.
What struck van Bredepoel most were his eyes.

They were not only unusually large and slightly protruding like a horse's but exceedingly vivid and lit by a sort of mystical ardour. They were the eyes, van Bredepoel was sure, of a nature which was never in repose, and yet had faith. With it all, there was something girlish in his appearance. His clothes were rough and studiedly of the people, but the skin of his face and hands, and his hair, had the transparent delicacy of a consumptive girl's. Like his features, his hands appeared to know no rest.

He reached the struggling men just as the European, despairing of dislodging the Indian, straightened himself and gasped: " Well, if you won't listen, you can damn' well take that! "

He hit the Indian in the face. Immediately the Indian released his grip on the seat, and as the man prepared to strike again, fell against him and caught his arms. But the white man put his knee in the Indian's stomach, pushed himself free and raised his fists again. Before the blow fell, however, the tall youth caught his arm and said in a clear high-pitched voice: " Stop that! You swine! "

Amazement possessed the white man's face. For a few seconds he looked dumbfounded, and then, without saying a word, caught the tall fellow by the shoulder and pushed him violently aside. Whatever the feelings of the white men on the tram may have been, their actions had hitherto been strictly neutral, but now every one, after the first shock of astonishment, seemed impelled by a desire to intervene, not between the white man and the Indian but between the two white men.

" Damn you, man! " someone shouted. " That's not cricket, taking sides against a white man!"

" Here, nigger-kisser! " shrieked the Indian's assailant, seizing the boy and throwing him against his champion. " Take your brother! "

It seemed to van Bredepoel that everybody was trying to get at the struggling men. He feared for the Indian and his champion. But suddenly the tram stopped with a violent jerk. The conductor, followed by a policeman, rushed on to the deck.

" Steady there! Steady! " said the policeman, laying his hand on the man nearest him. " Get back to your seats, all of you." Then, dryly, to the three struggling men, who were still trying to get at one another: " Now, what is the matter with you three? What's all this fuss about? "

They all began to speak at once, but pulling out a note-book he cut them short: " One at a time, please."

Turning to the Indian's assailant he asked: " Name, occupation and address, please? "

" Look here," said the conductor, " I can't stop here all day. We've held up the traffic long enough."

" You don't think I'm here to give you a ticket for exceeding the speed limit, now, do you? So just hurry up and tell me what's your trouble."

" Keep your shirt on. I only want you to see to these chaps here and let me get on with my job."

" But I have several things to say," began the tall youth, but before he could get any farther the policeman interrupted, eyeing him disapprovingly, " Oh, you have, have you? Now what might your trouble be? "

" I want to testify that this man has committed
an unprovoked and malicious assault on this Indian
youth here."

" That's a damned lie! " exclaimed the Indian's
assailant. " I was just teaching him manners.
Wasn't I, Bill ? "

" So he was, that he was, I swear! " agreed his
companion timidly.

" Just a minute, not so fast, you two," the policeman intervened, and turning back to the youth he
remarked: " The Indian can speak for himself.
Have you any complaints to make for yourself ? "

" Yes ! " came the reply in an angry voice. " I
object most strongly to having my journeys on a
public conveyance disturbed by meddlesome brutes.
I object. . . ."

" That's enough for a start," said the policeman,
smiling ironically, " You'd better all three come
along with me to the station."

" I appeal to all of you." The youth, ignoring the
policeman, turned round to the other white men on the
tram, and spoke with passion. " I appeal to all of
you to come with me and testify to what you have
seen."

His appeal was met with jeers; only van Bredepoel,
hating the youth for his appeal, for forcing him to
enter into a public dispute, forcing him out of the
indifference of his life, got up and walked over to
join the group. He felt extremely disconcerted and
self-conscious as he stood up, and a foolish busy-body
when the policeman stopped him at the top of the
stairs and said: " Your name and address will do."

A little later van Bredepoel saw the Indian, the

youth and the other two men fording the traffic in
the street below. When the tram was once more on
its way he observed the people in front of him,
people with whom he had been travelling on the
same tram for years and who all knew him by sight,
look round at him furtively as if they felt it necessary
to place him anew. Were they all silently but
consciously hostile towards him ? When he had to
get off the tram he tried to go quite unselfcon-
sciously as usual, and with a complete indifference,
but as he reached the back of the car an old Native in
tattered clothes leant forward and raised a shabby
hat to him. He felt then that a seal, a Cain's mark,
had been put on his action, that his identification
with the other side, not the side of the blustering
European, was definitely established in the minds
of the people on the car. And he almost hated the
old man for drawing his attention to it.

For several days van Bredepoel expected hourly a
summons to appear before the magistrate's court,
but as the weeks passed and no summons came he
thought no more about the incident, and assumed
that the people on the afternoon tramcar had
forgotten it too. Then one morning just as he was
getting ready to leave his office for lunch, he saw
through the glass doors behind which he worked
a tall, awkward figure, stooping as though ashamed
of its height, pass and repass the entrance nervously.
He thought it was someone looking for information,
and taking his hat and stick hurried out to ask him
what he wanted. As he pushed the door open the
stranger turned round quickly, and van Bredepoel
recognised him at once. So completely had the

incident of the tram gone from his mind that he felt
like someone who, having forgotten a particularly
unpleasant task, is suddenly faced with the immediate
necessity of performing it. If it had been possible
he might have gone back quickly into his room,
but the stranger, striding forward, greeted him
with a large, awkward handshake and an anxious
ingratiating smile.

" I must apologise," he said, in the same high-
pitched voice van Bredepoel had noticed that
afternoon on the tram, " for not having come to you
before, but I've been away on work and only
returned to Port Benjamin last night. I hope you
didn't think I had forgotten the support, the moral
support, you gave me. As soon as I got the chance I
stole your name and address from the policeman's
note-book, for I had every intention of coming to
see you as soon as possible. So here I am."

The " so here I am " was said with a repetition of
his nervous laugh, and a girlish twist of his shoulder.
Looking at him van Bredepoel wondered how he had
ever had the courage to do what he had done. He
looked so timid, so diffident and essentially nervous
now that he had no obvious conviction or principle
to guide him. Something of his awkwardness communicated itself to van Bredepoel, who was not
prepared to like him.

" Oh! That's all right. You shouldn't have
bothered."

" Oh, no, but I had to. I'm glad I've done so.
Say, won't you come and have lunch with me ? "

" I'm afraid I have an appointment," van Bredepoel began, but seeing an expression of undisguised

disappointment on the stranger's face he found himself adding impulsively: " But I think we could lunch together all the same."

" Good! But I'm sorry, I forgot to give you my name. ' Name, occupation and address,' as our friend the policeman would say. You will find it all here."

He had become much more natural and the laugh which accompanied his remark sounded less girlish. He gave van Bredepoel a card which seemed pain- fully white in the sunlight on the stairs. It read:

J. BURGESS,
Secretary, Union of African Workers.

" What happened to your Indian friend ? " van Bredepoel asked as they walked away together.

" He wasn't a friend of mine exactly," said Burgess, " I had never seen him before. But that sort of thing always makes my blood boil. Do you know I couldn't get the police to prosecute ? And neither of us had money enough to start a prosecution on our own. In any case, the police, who seemed to know a great deal about me, as good as told me to mind my own business."

" I thought it was very brave of you to interfere," van Bredepoel told him.

" Rubbish! It's my job to do things like that. Besides, I got a very good recruit for my organisation. Now *you* did a plucky thing. Tell me why you supported me ? "

His old perplexity returned to van Bredepoel.

" God knows," he said, " I did it on the impulse,

and I certainly wouldn't have done it at all if you
hadn't asked me to."

"But I didn't ask you. I didn't know you existed,
a second before you stood up."

"I'm afraid I don't know why I did it. All I
know is that I hated doing it, but I did it in spite
of myself."

But as he spoke, for one instant the image of Kenon
had seemed to flicker at the back of his mind.

CHAPTER III

FROM that day forward a close association grew up between van Bredepoel and Burgess. Van Bredepoel soon realised that Burgess had many qualities he himself lacked. Superficially it was Burgess with his awkward gestures, his tortured manner, who gave an impression of irresolution and changeableness, but van Bredepoel soon learnt that his life had a rare consistency, that his enthusiasms were as steady as they were warm. All that nervousness was in reality disciplined; Burgess knew what he wanted and worked unswervingly to get it; was in short what van Bredepoel called " a long-distance character." In his own opinion it was he himself who, beneath his surface patterns of order and punctuality, was the confused, groping character. Beside Burgess', his own life seemed to him a blur.

Often, when his work allowed it, van Bredepoel would go to fetch Burgess at the office of the Union of African Workers. To get there he had to turn down a side street, away from the pretentious and carefully kept business thoroughfares of Port Benjamin, and go through a quarter whose squalor was as unpicturesque as it was unexpected. The streets there had broken and damp surfaces and the stale, rotting rubbish lying about, the numbers of badly clothed, ill-nourished children who played cheerfully in them, testified to a neighbourhood both poor and overcrowded. The first time, he had some

difficulty in finding Burgess' office, for the houses
here were irregularly and indistinctly numbered.
After a long search he discovered next to a second-
hand clothes shop, in a narrow, dark side entrance,
a white notice-board on which a black fist, clenched
except for the forefinger, pointed at the words,
hand-printed in thick block capitals:

UNION OF AFRICAN WORKERS, THIRD FLOOR.

He climbed up the narrow stone stairs, between
faded walls on which the glow of the afternoon light,
entering from somewhere above, left an air of
desolate tranquillity, and found Burgess sitting in a
large dusty room, behind a long table covered with
papers. In the corner of the room was a native,
dressed in black clothes, typing on an archaic
typewriter. The walls were covered with posters,
most of which depicted muscular natives tottering
under impossible worlds of burdens, while a well-fed
European with Semitic features, a complacent over-
fed expression on his face and a gold chain on his
stomach, calmly puffed cigar smoke at them.
Under most of these posters were inscriptions like
this: " He has too much. You have not enough.
If you want justice, join the Union of African
Workers."

" Daniel," Burgess said to the native when van
Bredepoel entered. " I'd go now if I were you."

Daniel went, taking with him a frayed bowler hat
and a soiled black overcoat, which together with
his black suit and high starched collar gave him the
air more of an evangelical candidate than a revolu-

tionary worker. But before he went, he startled van Bredepoel somewhat by saying familiarly: " What time do you want me to-morrow, Burgess ? "

" You had better come early to-morrow," Burgess replied. " I want you to take notes of my meeting with the dock-workers' people."

" O.K." said Daniel, and closed the door behind him.

" What a mysterious creature," van Bredepoel thought. It was the first time he had come into contact with a native of this kind.

Then van Bredepoel told Burgess about Kenon. Burgess listened carefully, sympathetically, obviously deeply interested. " I know now why you helped me on the tram that day," he said when van Bredepoel had finished.

" Do you ? "

" Yes, I do. But say, show me that fellow and I will make a good communist of him."

" I tell you he's gone. I have not seen him since."

" It's a shame," Burgess went on, " that boys like that should come untutored into a sink like this. Once they are here, what can you expect ? They come here and find that the things which led them safely through life in their own country are no longer valid. Outside the experience of their own race, they cannot yet get inside that of our own because our prejudices won't let them, so they drift into the mess you see. This place is like a soda-water bottle corked prematurely; bubbles of gas are continually rising from below. They cannot go back and yet they cannot get out, so they all collect underneath the stopper, and by and by when the

pressure gets too much they will either blow the
stopper off or burst the bottle. Still, I shouldn't
grumble, because the more people like Kenon come
here the better for me."

Often they sat talking in Burgess' room after
Daniel was gone, until it grew too dark for them to
see each other. Outside, the sound of the traffic died
away, and the whole district rang with the cries of
children, who, in that quiet hour, turned shabby
streets into their playground. In darkness Burgess
was in his element. Always with the approach of
night he talked better. Van Bredepoel would long
to switch on a light, but one evening when he did so
the effect on Burgess' conversation was such that he
never repeated the experiment. He remembered
afterwards that the only times he had heard Burgess
talk about himself, apart from his work, were in
darkness. Even then Burgess scrupled to let himself
go about himself, much to van Bredepoel's regret.
He would never have confessed it to Burgess, but to
himself he admitted frankly that his friend's reason-
ing was far less interesting than either his feelings or
the extraordinary depth and integrity of his devotion
to his work.

Burgess came from a family of English socialists,
who had been among the first to accept the doctrine
of Marx. His grandfather had been carried far
enough by a revolutionary enthusiasm to abandon a
schoolmaster's comforts at a respectable school for
the bleak life of a socialist preacher in the slums of
Liverpool. But his character had never really run to
extremes, and he had soon used a recognised ability
for compromise to help in turning revolutionary

agitation into a comparatively harmless and respectable higher-wage movement. His son, Burgess'
father, had followed closely in his footsteps and had
ended up as secretary to a trade union in which he
showed considerable skill as a negotiator. Burgess
had been trained for a similar career, and would no
doubt have succeeded his father if a pronounced
tubercular predisposition had not so alarmed his
family that they decided to send him to Africa.
Using all the influence in their power, his family had
managed to secure for him a nominal post as adviser
to the General Trades Union Council of Port
Benjamin. The salary attached to the billet was
exceedingly small, but his fare out was paid, and
so far everything went according to plan. His
family only intended him to keep his post until he
was sufficiently well to return to England. But once
Burgess was established in Port Benjamin, a profound
change came over him. Before long he had quarrelled
with his employers. The moderation and gift for
compromise which had characterised his father and
grandfather entirely forsook him. Socialism as
advocated and practised by trade unions, he told
his employers, was sheer humbug. It was only a
form of capitalism within capitalism, only a petty
capitalism without either the courage or the brains
of the system it attacked. The trade union leaders
were traitors to the creed they professed. Why,
trade unionism wasn't socialism at all!—his voice
would grow shrill with scorn when he talked like
this to van Bredepoel. Socialism meant revolution,
extreme economic revolution, the only real revolution possible. A higher-wage movement might be a

valuable means towards achieving economic revolution, but as an end in itself it was a betrayal of revolution, a parasitic growth on capitalism.

His father, writing from England, had vainly tried to effect a compromise, but it only made his son more determined. He resigned from his post without tact or grace, just walked out of his employers' office and never went back. Van Bredepoel often wondered why he had so suddenly run to extremes when all his training and environment laid stress on compromise, and he suspected that deep down Burgess identified rebellion against society with rebellion against his family. But nothing Burgess said directly confirmed this suspicion.

Van Bredepoel pointed out that Burgess had thrown over one trade union only to serve another. Burgess had an explanation ready: the African Workers' Union was frankly and avowedly revolutionary. There was no inevitability-of-gradualness nonsense about it. Once they were properly organised they would overthrow capitalism at the first favourable opportunity. Unfortunately, much preparation was necessary, for their supporters were drawn from a particularly backward people. But even this backwardness had its advantages; the black man was a natural communist, he practised communism much more widely and freely than anyone else. Communism was in his blood and in his traditions. That was one reason why Burgess had so eagerly seized the opportunity to work for him. Another advantage was that the black people were the only real workers in the country. " Talk about the Port Benjamin Labour Party! " he would exclaim. " Why, it's only a party of white overseers."

Whenever van Bredepoel questioned mildly the values of socialism, Burgess would shrug his shoulders. He would point out that whether van Bredepoel liked it or not socialism was going to be realised, that economic forces they couldn't control even if they wanted to were working ceaselessly for it. At heart, capitalist society was as dead as feudalism. It was, indeed, only an economic form of feudalism. One had to consider the circumstances in which capitalism had come about. It had only been made possible by the widespread insecurity of the workman's life. What had been the use of liberty to him when his bread, his security, were threatened everywhere ? So men had flocked to where, regardless of the cost, they could find the greatest security. They exchanged the Baron for the Millionaire. In justice Burgess admitted that the early capitalists too had taken a risk in employing workmen to lay down the first railways, build the first steel ships, for these things might have failed. To-day, however, risk for the capitalist had been enormously reduced; life for the workman was or should have been more secure on account of man's increased conquest of Nature, his annihilation of distance and time. The value of the service the capitalist rendered, therefore, had diminished, yet the tribute paid by the workman and society remained the same. It was just feudalism all over again, and the same forces that killed the latter were killing capitalism.

Van Bredepoel would reply that all that was very well said, and probably just, but it didn't carry them far. Man, after all, wasn't governed entirely by economic forces, had indeed often shown a shameful disregard for them when the spirit had so moved him. He doubted even if much change in the world were possible, unless accompanied by a change of heart. Hadn't Burgess himself implied a confession of the failure of the revolt against feudalism when he stated that capitalism was only another form of feudalism ? Wouldn't the revolt against capitalistic society merely be followed by yet another kind of feudalism ? What were the uses, in fact, of material readjustments, unless they were accompanied by spiritual transformations ?

He wasn't such a fool as to think all would be milk and honey under communism, Burgess responded. There would still be misery and unhappiness, but no poverty, no waste; there would be no one who had too much while others had too little. And that was progress! No one could reasonably expect more than that. When *that* was done they might get van Bredepoel to consider the next step!

Sometimes Daniel would linger in the office as long as he could, when they were talking; then van Bredepoel would leave the field to Burgess, while he watched the black man. For Daniel interested but puzzled him very much. For the first time he was coming into contact with a native who had succeeded in winning through difficulties under which thousands of his people succumbed, succeeded so well that he was preparing to lead others after him. Now Burgess had the utmost confidence in Daniel, but van Bredepoel could never get inside his mind. He observed Daniel carefully and sympathetically,

yet never felt that he came near understanding him.
Daniel gave him no help. Van Bredepoel talked to
him many times, and their conversations always
ended by Daniel agreeing with him in a way that
made him feel it did not really matter whether they
agreed or not. With strangers Daniel laughed very
easily; with Burgess and van Bredepoel he was
always a grave, evangelical figure, talking in a deep,
soft voice and accompanying his arguments with
beautiful gestures made with beautiful hands. When
he asked a question he invariably held out his right
hand, palm upwards, its long fingers slightly curved,
as if expecting an answer in such a form that he could
hold it. Each time he did that van Bredepoel
thought: " Heavens, how white the palms of his
hands are! They make me quite uncomfortable."
And he would look away only to realise, when his
eyes met Daniel's again, that he was being carefully
appraised with a sombre yet warm look.

Once Daniel cut his wrist and as there flowed
over his smooth black skin a dark glistening stream,
van Bredepoel believed that he had never seen blood
more crimson. He was surprised to find that he was
slightly shocked. Had he imagined that this massive
creature was made of flesh and blood ?

One thing van Bredepoel did discover about
Daniel quite soon. He found that Daniel's outlook
was strictly limited, but amazingly clear and accurate.
The black man's vision was focused on only one
aspect of life and never left it for a moment. He had
before him always, as under a microscope, the point
where white and black people came into contact.
Often Burgess and van Bredepoel, reading through

the newspapers, missed news that would have interested them. Daniel missed nothing. Sooner or later he would draw their attention to some paragraph they had not seen. Once they were on the point of leaving the office when Daniel said:

" Anything of interest to us in the newspaper this evening, Burgess ? "

" Nothing in particular," replied Burgess. He knew from long experience that something had escaped his eye.

" You did not see, then, what was going on in Campbell's Town ? " There was almost a note of accusation in Daniel's voice.

" No," replied Burgess, " read it out, Daniel."

Daniel began reading as if he had a Bible in front of him. Gradually the newspaper account took shape in their minds. They learnt that in Campbell's Town there had been a court trial in which a black woman and a white man had been concerned. The black woman and the white man were charged with having had sexual intercourse with one another, a thing which is forbidden under the anti-miscegenation laws of Port Benjamin. The black woman had pleaded guilty. The white man not guilty. They were tried by a judge and a jury, all white men. The black woman was found guilty and sentenced to four years' hard labour; the white man was found not guilty and acquitted.

" Isn't that strange, Burgess ? " Daniel said gravely, when he had finished.

" Bloody strange," replied Burgess. " Thank you for showing it to me. We'll look into that and see what we can do."

" Not much, I expect," said Daniel.

" We might get that woman to appeal. Make a note of it and we'll see what we can do to-morrow."

" He never misses anything like that," Burgess said to van Bredepoel when they were outside.

" Where did you pick him up ? " van Bredepoel asked.

" He was a minor native chief. When the war broke out he took a small labour battalion of his people over to France. After he came back he started a small native school here, sold his rights and his property to get the money to do so. When I started this work I found him and persuaded him to come in with me, and I've never regretted it."

" I don't understand him."

" You'll never understand him if you consider him as a man. He's not a man, he's an animated principle or if you like a man with only one idea. And so cautious."

Burgess, Daniel and van Bredepoel were alone in the office of the Union of African Workers one day, when there came a loud knock on the door. Daniel got up and went outside. In a few moments he came back with a card three times larger than an ordinary visiting card. On it was written in large gold Gothic letters:

> GEO. P. HALTMANN, ESQ.,
> Member, Port Benjamin City Council.
> Chairman, Ways and Means Committee.

Hard on the heels of Daniel, who had vainly tried to observe the ordinary formalities of the office by not showing him in until he had Burgess' permission, came the owner of the card, casting a surprised and disapproving glance at the black man. Burgess looked up and saw a small middle-aged man, solidly built, with grey-black hair, little green eyes and tight lips.

" Your name is Burgess," said the man in a loud confident voice, helping himself to a chair on which he seated himself astride, after turning it round so that its back faced Burgess. He leaned forward on folded arms. " You'll find my credentials on the table there."

" I have read your card," replied Burgess, " but I don't know what you could want with me."

" I asked him that, Burgess," said Daniel, " but he refused to tell me."

" I'll tell you that in a minute when I'm alone. I am not accustomed to explain my actions to . . ." —it was evidently on the tip of his tongue to say " niggers," but he hesitated and then added, " to fellows like that."

" I have no secrets from my secretary," said Burgess.

" But I have," Haltmann replied, laughing as if he had made a great joke.

" Will you go into the filing room for a few minutes, Daniel ? " Burgess said gently. " You don't object, I suppose, to my friend remaining here ? "

" No, not at all," said Haltmann and then began : " Look here, Burgess, I'm a plain self-made man. I call a spade a spade, so you won't mind if I tell you the truth right away. There's no nonsense about me, I warn you. I don't mind telling you right at the start that I've no time for all this Bolshie muck you go in for. To my mind the only way you can run a nation is to run it on sound business lines, by recognised business minds. But I have often thought there might be a good deal of truth in what your organisation has been saying about the deplorable housing conditions in the native and coloured people's quarters. And I think that perhaps I could help you, and you me. We've at last got rid of those time-servers on the City Council and got some young blood into it. We mean to run the city on business lines, and it seems to me a good business proposition to see that one's employees are decently housed. Look at what Ford's done. You mustn't think that I tolerate for a moment any Bolshie sentimentality, but I stand, at the same time, however, second to none in my desire to do justice to the city's employed. About that there can be no question of a doubt. Now tell me, as man to man, forget that you've an axe to grind, forget that you've read those fellows Lenin and Trotsky, and tell me, are things really as bad in the native quarters as you say ? "

" Why don't you go and see for yourself ? Why not ask your own sanitary department ? " Burgess said.

" That's just the point, man." The visitor moved impatiently in his chair. " Before I commit myself I want to study the question from all points of view. The official point of view is easy enough to get. What's difficult is to get the point of view of people like yourself and then blow the froth from the beer on both sides—I told you I was a blunt-speaking man. Now, will you undertake to show me these places you say are so bad ? "

So a visit to the native quarter was arranged. But while Burgess was showing the visitor to the door, van Bredepoel heard Daniel in the next room turning over one newspaper file after another. Burgess was hardly back when Daniel came in with a file and placed it before him, indicating silently a certain passage. It contained the following paragraph.

"Among the most energetic of the new-comers to the City Council is Mr. Geo. P. Haltmann, the founder of the well-known Port Benjamin firm of building contractors, G. P. Haltmann and Sons. Mr. Haltmann was elected unopposed for the Bluebell Ward."

They both observed that Daniel had underlined heavily with a blue pencil the words "building contractors."

"He heard it all," Burgess whispered, and smiled at van Bredepoel.

Van Bredepoel accompanied Burgess and Halt-mann to the native quarters of Port Benjamin, but he did not afterwards remember many details of the visit. One remembers best when one's feelings are not too strongly aroused by what one sees, when each reaction in feeling is balanced by as keen a reaction in curiosity. But when feeling has been strong enough to possess itself of the whole being so that, from one moment to another, the objective faculties of the mind are overwhelmed by the necessity of defending the desire to know and to observe against attacks of pity, disgust and shame, then memory loses its clarity, clutching at trifles, things hardly noticed at the time, and is afterwards evoked more successfully by a fugitive odour, a fleeting note of music, lamplight on a faded wall, than by any conscious effort of the intelligence. So that evening spent in the native quarters left no clear, no organised or detailed picture on van Bredepoel's mind. He remembered walking through streets so narrow that at sunset they anticipated night by half an hour, casting deep shadows which the scattered street lamps could not penetrate. He remembered wondering at the courage of children who could laugh and play so cheerfully in such streets. Everywhere there had been the same oppressive odour of rubbish and stopped drains, the same overcrowded rooms ; Malays, Hindus, natives, half-castes, shabby white men, sleeping with their heads in filth on broken and damp pavements. He remembered a room in which a woman was sleeping naked with two children in her arms, her body covered with festering sores. He remembered, too, Haltmann's matter-of-fact voice at his elbow as he made notes: " No. 4. Reebok Street, single-storied house, four rooms; front room, one window, 12 ft. by 10 ft. No beds, father, mother, seven children, no lavatory, paraffin-tin in yard, drains not functioned for years; total number of people thirty-three." He heard Halt-mann repeat the same thing over and over again.

At the end of the evening, Burgess had led them straight from a house, just like the one Haltmann's notes described, to a large concrete building on the opposite side of the same street.

" Here," Burgess said to Haltmann, " the City

Council of Port Benjamin keeps its mules. Will you get permission for us to enter ? "

They had gone inside and seen clean concrete floors, neat stalls, and well-fed, well-groomed mules eating contentedly out of full cribs.

" These stalls," Burgess said, " are cleaned twice a day. Where would you prefer living ? In the places I've shown you or here ? "

" I would much prefer being with the mules," said van Bredepoel.

" That's an excellent point," Haltmann remarked. " I'll make a note of it. And mark my words, I'll rub it into those old fogies! If you don't have better houses for these people within a year my name is not Haltmann."

Neither of them had seen Haltmann again; but some months later Burgess, reading the afternoon papers, suddenly turned to van Bredepoel with an exclamation of disgust. " Really! What a terrible town! Just look here. The City Council has turned down Haltmann's £90,000 scheme for putting up new houses in the native quarters. They say they've not got the money to spend on that now. But look, at the same meeting they voted £300,000 for building a new entertainment park and esplanade for visitors! "

" Ah! " remarked Daniel in his grave voice, somewhere from the back. " And do you know who has the contract for building the new entertainment park and esplanade ? "

" No, I don't," said Burgess, puzzled.

" Messrs. George P. Haltmann and Sons." Daniel pronounced the name very slowly and deliberately.

" Where did you hear that ? "

" I got it here." And Daniel showed him the announcement in a small paragraph at the back of the same paper Burgess had been reading.

" That is not all," said Daniel. " Here is a short account of Haltmann's speech on his housing scheme. He admits that the housing scheme can wait, and reminds the Council that anybody with guts who is born in a slum can get out of it. He said he himself was born in one, and look at him now ! "

" It's a crying shame ! " Burgess exclaimed.

Daniel said nothing, but van Bredepoel watched him closely, and noticed that he was looking strangely out of the window, as if he saw approach from the other side of the world something which gave him pleasure.

CHAPTER IV

THERE is in Port Benjamin an organisation which
calls itself the "Bantu-European Approach Association." Its members call it among themselves
"The Bee." The preamble to the constitution of
the B.E.A.A. contains among other things: "The
purpose of the B.E.A.A. shall be to endeavour by all
the means its executive committee think fit to
improve the deplorable condition into which the
relations between white and black and coloured
people have sunk in Port Benjamin. The Committee
responsible for the difficult task of drafting the constitution has agreed by a unanimous vote to lay it
down that the B.E.A.A. shall have only one enemy:
that anomalous and ignoble relic of barbarous days
commonly called colour prejudice. The Committee
can do no better here than affirm that it shall be the
sacred duty of each member of the B.E.A.A. to do
his or her best for the total suppression or extermina-
tion of the aforementioned prejudice. It considers it
its duty to recall here to each of the members of the
Association the following words of a great and
glorious declaration: 'We hold these truths to be
self-evident: that all men are born equal, that they
are endowed by their Creator with certain inalien-
able rights, that amongst these are life, liberty and
the pursuit of happiness.' It follows hence in view
of what has gone before that it is hardly necessary to
state that any man or woman, whatever his or her

class, race or colour, shall be eligible for membership
to the B.E.A.A. and that the only qualification shall
be the common humanity of all. The draft committee suggest that the membership fee shall be
10s. per annum for Europeans and 5s. for native
and coloured people."

One of the means the executive committee of the
B.E.A.A. thought fit for improving the relationship
between white and coloured and black people was to
hold on the first Friday of every month a " social
evening " in a suburban church hall. On the
Friday morning, one member would be sure to ask
another on the telephone: " To Bee or not to Bee
to-night, my dear ? "

Van Bredepoel had heard of them, and had once
even been asked if he would like to Bee, which had
entirely put him off the Association; so that when
Burgess telephoned inviting him to a B.E.A.A.
" evening " his first instinct was to refuse.

" I don't think I can come," he told Burgess.

" But you must," Burgess replied. " It isn't the
meeting I want you to see. I've something important
to discuss with you, and to-night will be my only
chance for a long time to come. I'm leaving to-
morrow on a three months' tour."

So van Bredepoel was persuaded to go, and at
eight that evening he met Burgess and Daniel outside
a small suburban church hall. Daniel was carefully
dressed, had changed his working clothes for a clean
but slightly frayed morning coat and striped
trousers, and carried a top hat in his hand. He
looked even graver and more evangelical than in the
day-time. But neither Burgess nor van Bredepoel

had changed their clothes. Daniel bowed stiffly as
he shook van Bredepoel's hand, but in his eyes there
was a new look of welcome, an expression which
almost seemed to say: "Soon you and I may
understand each other." The moment van Bredepoel saw Daniel he knew instinctively that what
Burgess wanted to discuss with him somehow concerned the black man too. They all three went into
the hall, Burgess and Daniel talking softly to each
other. Grouped round tables, on little benches of a
Protestant discomfort, were about sixty Europeans
and twenty or more native and coloured people.
Van Bredepoel noticed that a great many of the
people there were women, and he whispered: "Why
are the women all so unattractive?"

"They've got all their beauty there"—Burgess
tapped his forehead.

They had not been inside the hall long when a
very tall, thin woman, with protruding teeth, came
up to van Bredepoel, thrust herself between him and
his companion and said—with her elbows, it seemed
to him:

"My name is Katherina Primrose. What's
yours?"

"Van Bredepoel."

"No, the other," she said, giving him a virile
handshake.

"Johan," he said.

"Well, Johan, are you happy? Where do you
come from? Have you been in this country long?
What do you do? I'm sure you must do something interesting! Of course you're revolutionary.
Everybody is who comes here. Do you like your

work ? I'm sure you don't. No one who is intelligent
can ever be happy, don't you think ? "

" I'm a shipping clerk," van Bredepoel told her
when the machine-gun fire of questions had died
down.

" You're joking," she exclaimed, an expression of
acute disappointment on her face.

" No, I'm not. Ask Burgess."

But suddenly hope returned to her. Her face
cleared for action.

" You must give up your work ! " She spoke
quickly, earnestly. " I can see you aren't happy.
You don't like it. You must do something else. I'm
sure you could do something great. You might
write a novel."

She would not let him go. He replied to her
questions almost mechanically, and found himself
listening instead to the conversation around him.

" Come and sit next to me, Blankin," a woman
student was saying to a perky young man who stood
in front of her.

" I would like to," Blankin replied, " but you
know when I sit next to you, I sort of get excited,
sexually, you know."

" That's nothing," said the girl, determined to
show that she was more emancipated than he.
" All the young men who sit next to me get much
more than that." But she could not prevent herself
blushing, particularly when she saw van Bredepoel
looking at her.

" But it's more serious for me than for them," said
the young man, also blushing but laughing osten-
tatiously all the same.

" You probably take love too seriously."

" Do I ? " asked the young man, who had not been thinking of love.

" I think you do," stated the girl. " After all, what is love ? It's only a conditioned reflex."

" That's rather good! " The young man seemed impressed.

" Yes, a conditioned reflex, and if it's conditioned, it can be unconditioned again. So why be serious about it ? "

" You're quite right, van der Boel," Miss Primrose interrupted suddenly, forsaking van Bredepoel. " Happiness is only a drug."

Released, van Bredepoel walked up to Burgess and Daniel. They were standing beside a woman whose appearance was if anything more masculine than theirs. She was doing most of the talking and seemed to ignore Burgess, reserving all her attention for Daniel, who said little, but always agreed with her laughingly.

" You black people are so witty," she was saying, ignoring van Bredepoel too the minute they had been introduced. " You have such a natural spontaneous form of wit. I heard such a good story the other day. You know the politician, Bladder-man ? You know that he represents a division in Bambuland. Well, he wanted to get the black people in his constituency to give him a very good nickname, because a good nickname gives a man a high prestige among you black people, don't you know ? So he told his black servants to call him the Big White Bull and to tell all the black people they knew that that was his name. Well, ever afterwards he was known throughout the length and breadth of Bambuland as the Little White Calf. Now isn't that good ? It's a great quality that; a very great quality you black people have, and it's something we whites have lost."

Daniel laughed as if he had never heard the story before. As it happened the story had originated with Daniel himself, and by way of Burgess had spread, and made the full circle back to him.

Some minutes later when they were once more alone another woman came up to them, and ignoring Burgess and van Bredepoel, said to Daniel: " Oh, Mr. Bambatie, I'm so glad you managed to come. You black people are such good company and you're so witty. I heard such a lovely story the other day. You know the politician Bladderman, who has a constituency in Bambuland ? "

Daniel listened to her gravely and at the end laughed again as if he had never heard the story in his life.

" Listen to this," said Burgess. Two journalists were talking to a group of women. One of them, a pale young man with earnest blue eyes and a sad expression, which might have been caused either by a heavy heart or a sluggish liver, was saying: " People often reproach me for talking too much about the native question, but I always ask them: ' How can I help it ? ' We are all unconsciously focused on the native question. I've only been back in Port Benjamin three weeks. I was away in Europe for three years and had forgotten the native question existed. The afternoon on which I landed I went into the Houses of Parliament. There was a very

dull debate on. If I remember rightly they were
discussing railway estimates, and you know how
exciting they are. There was hardly a quorum, and
half the House was asleep. From the gallery I could
see below me the Prime Minister reading Edgar
Wallace. Suddenly the Minister of Railways said:
' In conspicuous contradiction to the black labour
policy pursued. . . .' He got no farther; the House
was immediately in an uproar. The Prime Minister
dropped his book, for the word ' black ' excited him
even more than Edgar Wallace. Everywhere the
members who had been smoking in the lobbies came
rushing back into the House. On the Opposition
side four or five men were on their feet shouting:
' On a point of order, Mr. Speaker.' One of them
was given the floor and he said: ' On a point of
order, Mr. Speaker, surely the Honourable Minister
for Railways was speaking with his tongue in his
cheek when. . . .' He got no farther, for again there
was an uproar. The Minister of Railways was on his
feet now, shouting : ' Mr. Speaker, I must ask for
your protection on a point of order! Has the
honourable Member for Waterkloof the right to
insult me and make statements such as that I'm
talking with my tongue in my cheek ? After all, I'm
a responsible minister.' ' I must ask the Member
for Waterkloof to withdraw his statement,' answered
the Speaker. ' I withdraw my statement,' said the
member for Waterkloof, ' and beg to substitute for
it: the honourable Minister was not serious.' A
new lot of cries of ' on a point of order ' arose, so I
got up and left. But all that fuss was over the word

' black.' They couldn't have been more shocked if
someone had informed them that their wives were
whores! Now, how can you expect us not to talk
about the native question when we suffer from that
sort of neurosis ? "

"Fundamentally observed," said one of the
women.

"The point you make is elemental," stated
another.

" Did you hear that ? There's truth in what he
says. What do you think of a system like that ? "
Burgess asked van Bredepoel.

" Ridiculous," replied van Bredepoel. " Still, it
isn't my affair."

" It's people like you with a high-almighty
indifference who make a system like that possible."
Burgess was disappointed and getting both angry
and unfair. " Give me a good healthy opposition
every time, but from indifference like yours, God
preserve me."

All the time, women were getting on and off the
platform to sing. The songs were invariably
American Negro spirituals or modern Russian and
German revolutionary songs. One would have
thought no other music existed.

" Let's go," van Bredepoel said. " Why on earth
do you waste your time coming here ? "

" You're wrong," Burgess told him very seriously.
" It isn't a waste of time. Haven't you noticed that
almost everyone here is either a teacher, a school-
mistress, a student, a journalist, a painter or a
musician, in fact the kind of person the ordinary
man regards as a representative of the intellectual

and cultural life of the country ? Now these people
help to spread an intellectual and cultural prejudice
in favour of the revolution. They make the ordinary
man, who doesn't want to feel stupid but mistrusts
his own judgment, believe that he cannot be intelligent and cultured unless he is revolutionary as well.
All good revolutions begin that way."

They began to make their way through groups of
chattering people to the door.

Outside on the steps, three white women and a
black girl were saying good-bye. The white women
all kissed the black girl heartily, but merely shook
hands with one another.

" Did you see that ? " van Bredepoel asked
Burgess.

" Yes. What about it ? "

" Prejudice begets prejudice," said van Bredepoel.
" Outside it may not be a good thing to be black,
but in here it is a disadvantage to be white. The
white people here have a prejudice against their
own colour."

" It won't do any harm. The scale is far too
heavily weighted on the other side. Besides. . . ."

Burgess wanted to go on talking, but something
distracted his attention. There was a sudden clatter
of horses' hoofs in the street below them. They had
been so absorbed in their own affairs that neither
had noticed that the street was unusually crowded;
people were moving past the hall in dense, eager
masses, all set in the same direction, and a squadron
of mounted police was hurrying through the crowd.
At the head of the squadron rode an officer on a
large white horse, his bearing quite in keeping with

the synthetic dignity prescribed in paragraph (E), sub-section D, of the Amended Police Ordinance of 1911, his stomach resting like a bundle of dirty washing on his saddle. The horse was a splendid, nervous creature. Whenever the officer's spurs touched it, it bounced sideways into the crowd, lightly like a blown leaf, a quicksilver vibration running over its skin.

Burgess evidently recognised the officer, for he exclaimed: " There's something wrong somewhere, or that fellow wouldn't be about."

He had hardly finished the sentence when from somewhere close by came a long, violent scream of hate, uttered by many people. By tacit consent, they started down the steps, forgetting all about Daniel, and began to follow the crowd. The street was so congested that they had to submit themselves entirely to the movement of the people around them. In a few minutes they emerged, with the rest of the crowd, in Shepherd's Place, where van Bredepoel had once listened to the speech of a Native agitator. On a wooden platform in the centre of the square stood van Bredepoel's old acquaintance, the Doctor, his hand held in vain above his head for silence. Round the platform were drawn up in close formation many hundreds of black and coloured men, the light of street lamps falling on their hungry and attentive faces. A thin cordon of foot policemen was flung round the square, and against it leaned and pushed an excited crowd of white people. The Doctor had apparently been speaking a long time, for the hostile mood of the crowd was not a sudden outburst. It was too sustained, deep and uniform to be anything but a growth of many moments, and very near its climax.

At first it looked as if the Doctor would not get a hearing again, but after a time the shouting died down considerably, and in the lull one heard horses clattering ceaselessly round and round the square. Suddenly the Doctor's uplifted hand dropped to his side, his body stiffened, and he shouted loudly: "If the white women. . . ."

He got no farther. The mood of the crowd heaved immediately like a big ship caught in a submarine convulsion.

"Leave the women out of it, nigger!" To van Bredepoel that scream, a mindless, sub-human scream, sounded as if it came from one throat. Around them were people in evening dress, sports clothes and blue overalls ; next to the cloth caps of workmen, blonde and shingled heads on slender shoulders covered with silk shawls. But all the odds between one individual and another had gone; here there were neither rich nor poor, but only cells of a single organism.

"If that old humbug isn't careful," Burgess shouted at van Bredepoel, pointing at the Doctor, "he'll get into trouble!"

And, indeed, stones and bricks and bottles were already beginning to fall round the platform on which the Doctor stood. A large brick even landed at his feet, but he stooped down, outwardly unperturbed, picked up the brick and held it above his head. When he could once more make himself heard, he shouted, shaking the brick at the crowd: "You ask the white man for bread, and all he gives you is missiles. So, as I was saying, if the white women. . . ."

They were the Doctor's last words. The sound of several revolver shots floated up from the depth of the crowd. A deep silence fell for an instant over Shepherd's Place and everyone looked round in amazement and horror, as if revolver shots were the last things they had expected, while the Doctor pitched forward on to the platform, his stiff, peda-gogic figure twisting in the most unpedagogic manner. Two or three times he tried to get to his feet, and then rolled slowly over the edge of the platform. At once the silence was broken. Grasping anything they could lay their hands on, the Doctor's supporters charged the Europeans, and the white people, not to be outdone, burst through the cordon of policemen to meet them. But before the two crowds could clash, a large white horse came vaulting over the railings at the far end of the square, bounced sideways as its feet touched the ground, was pulled round and headed straight up between them. Behind it came other horsemen. The half light over the centre of the square began to sparkle with the glint of brass and nickel, and immediately the mood of the opposing crowds changed. In their anxiety to get away from the police, they fused peacefully and ran as hard as they could in the direction of van Bredepoel and Burgess. The two friends also turned to run, but they had not gone far when people began to push violently round them.

A cataract of sound and mob hysteria flowed over them. Van Bredepoel felt as if he had been caught

by a breaking wave and was rolling and shaking
helplessly in a stormy surf. All co-ordination
between his mind and his actions disappeared. His
feet went backward when he had deliberately
ordered them forward, he stumbled sideways when
he had planned to cut quickly through an opening
in the mass before him. He reached out to steady
himself by someone's shoulder, and a snarling face,
with a slobbering mouth and eyes in which all
evidence of consciousness had disappeared, jerked
round and snapped like a wolf at his hand. Trying
to get past a group of young men in evening dress,
who were charging through the crowd, arms locked
together, he received from one of them a violent
blow which was not accidental. People fell at his
feet and he trod on them without any hesitation or
qualms, for the herd which attacks with such
solidarity, disintegrates when pursued. For many
moments he was a helpless, frenzied contributor to
this chaos, until there came the sound of horses'
hoofs directly to his ears. The violence of the pushing
increased a hundredfold, a scream of despair from
mindless depths shook the crowd, and the faces of
the people around him went green. Suddenly he
received a violent blow on the head and was flung
with great force sideways. It seemed to him that
he fell a long time, had the sensation of falling after
his body had hit the ground. When he sat up, he saw
the back of the police squadron going through the
crowd like a plough, throwing people up sideways
as if they were no more than dry earth. Then it
went quiet very abruptly, and a public clock near
at hand began striking out the hour, filling the street

with a sound of banal normality, for time is nothing
if not indifferent. Slowly van Bredepoel got to his
feet. He tried to dust himself casually, to behave as
normally as he could, but he was trembling violently.
He felt deeply outraged, as if the little integrity and
dignity he had tried to own as an individual had
been shattered irremediably, and when he thought
of the black man rolling limply over the edge of the
platform, tears came to his eyes. He looked round
and saw Burgess getting up from the ground.

" Are you hurt ? " Burgess shouted.

" No. Are you ? " he called back.

" No," answered Burgess. And he stood there for
a while, his back turned to van Bredepoel, flicking
dust off his clothes with deft, nervous gestures as if
nothing had happened except that he had stumbled
on a banana skin. But van Bredepoel could not see
his eyes.

Suddenly van Bredepoel doubled up and sank on
his knees in a gutter, shaking violently. Burgess
rushed up to him, and found that he was being sick.
When van Bredepoel looked up again Burgess was
bending anxiously over him.

" It's all right," van Bredepoel said, " I feel much
better for that."

" I'm not so sure," exclaimed Burgess, helping
him to his feet. " I think we'd better try to get a
drink somewhere. We both need one."

Together they turned down a side street, and
walked along without saying a word until two
parallelograms of light on the pavement, the sound
of glasses clinking and a confused murmur of conversation made them turn towards a large building

of grey, ornate and faded pretentiousness. Burgess
walked quickly ahead, entered the building with
long, quick, light steps, opened the glass door with
his left hand and held it thus, while he showed van
Bredepoel in with his right, like a doctor ushering a
patient into his consulting-room. Once inside he
again hurried on ahead and found a corner between
the bar counter and the far wall.

" I think brandy, don't you ? " he said curtly, and
without waiting for a reply ordered the drinks.

Their drinks came, and they drank in silence.
They were at a loss how to begin. Round them
people were talking lavatory obscenities and race-
course news, and also discussing what van Bredepoel
wanted to forget, the riot at Shepherd's Place. He
heard the Doctor's name often, and his mind reached
out in vain for something that could make him
forget. On his glass, against the amber liquid, lay
a bar in miniature, a portion of reality with the sting
taken out of it. There the lamps from the roof were
minute dancing flakes of ice; the smoke drifting
against the ceiling, a blue arctic mist. Carefully he
analysed each reflection, as if in that way he could
forget; soon, however, he was saying to himself, but
loud enough for Burgess to hear: " Can he really
be dead ? "

" I'm afraid he is," answered Burgess, and ordered
more brandy. When it came he raised his glass and
held it towards the light. For some minutes he stood
like that, turning the glass slowly round, so that each
portion of the liquid was transfused with light. To
van Bredepoel that gesture seemed very old,
traditional, ceremonial almost: an outlaw pledging

his outlawry. But he did not pursue the idea far.
The transition from one thought to another in his
mind was becoming diffused. His head felt on fire
and he raised his glass, pressed it against his forehead and closed his eyes. He listened thus to the
conversation in the bar. Was it his imagination ?
The movement of sound was retarded, unrolled
with a great reluctance, like a slowly played record.
He opened his eyes. The lamp was swaying like
something in a slow-motion picture and Burgess'
glass was being lowered to the counter like a crate
at the end of a crane. Time became reluctant, for
it is not only a movement in and through space
but also a movement in feeling, and when feeling
is fixed in one unforgettable moment, time only
half exists.

" I wouldn't worry about that fellow," Burgess
said slowly. " His troubles are all over." It was
unnecessary to mention names.

" Or they might be only beginning," van Bredepoel
replied.

" What do you mean ? " Burgess' tone was almost
aggressive. He was watching van Bredepoel closely.
Both doubt and anticipation were in his eyes.

" You think only about this life, don't you ? " Van
Bredepoel answered with a question. His inward
confusion showed in a slur in his speech.

" And you, I suppose, if you had twenty lives,
would waste each one thinking of the next ? "
Burgess waited, hoping that van Bredepoel would
deny this. But his friend was very quiet for some
moments and then said unexpectedly:

" What a disgusting, sickening spectacle that riot

was just now! What a revolting exhibition of sub-
human hysterics, mindless neurotics! No wonder
you want to reform the world! "

Burgess banged his glass down on the counter, and
taking van Bredepoel by the arm said, " Look here.
Let's get outside, I want to talk to you."

The streets were deserted, the night quiet. Burgess
walked along quickly and van Bredepoel had
difficulty in keeping up with him. Absorbed in some
inner excitement Burgess did not notice that his
companion's steps were faltering.

" There's something I want to ask you, but before
I do so, I wish to talk to you frankly," he began after
a few moments. " Look here! Your way of living
distresses me a great deal. I've never known anyone
with such good instincts as yours, or do as little
about them as you do. No sooner do you have a good
impulse than you allow some doubt to cancel it out.
Your interests are all away from your work, yet what
do you do about it ? You tell me this riot we saw
to-night was disgusting, but where does your disgust
lead to ? You have often told me that you hate the
injustices under which people like Kenon suffer, and
what do you do about your hate ? You see, it's all
negation with you."

" You mustn't expect me to be like you," van
Bredepoel interrupted. " With you, everything is a
question of reforming the world, with me mostly one
of making my living and of minding my own business.
You're quite sure that something is wrong with the
world and that you can make it better, so you can go
straight ahead. But I, you see, I don't quite know
what I have to do with it all. I can't see myself in

relation to it all. I feel such an anachronism, anyway. . . ."

" You would have felt an anachronism in whatever age you had lived," Burgess broke in warmly, and then, as if frightened of going too far, held his peace.

The sound of their footsteps filled the street, and the echoes jumped from wall to wall. Van Bredepoel had a feeling that each had someone else at his side. Suddenly Burgess stopped him, and put a hand on his shoulder.

" Johan," he said, and it was the first time he had ever used his friend's Christian name: " I have sometimes been terrified that you might kill yourself."

" What a silly idea! " van Bredepoel exclaimed loudly, too loudly, and the wall echoed back: " Idea! "

" Listen," Burgess said. " You have more doubts than are good for you. If they were doubts arrived at objectively I wouldn't worry, but they all seem to me only the measure of your failure to reconcile your thoughts, your interests, with what you are doing. Listen! When one has nothing but your sort of uncertainty, it's a sure sign that there's something wrong not with life as a whole, as one persuades oneself, but with one's own life. You seem to me nowadays terribly trapped between disgust and the need of making your living."

Burgess wanted to go on, but van Bredepoel interrupted him: " Man cannot live by bread alone, but without it he cannot live at all."

" Yes," Burgess said, " but it's possible to reconcile the flesh and the spirit. I confess that if I had to live in the duality you are in, I wouldn't be able to work.

It's your duty to yourself to work for something you respect. If there's nothing in this life you love, there must be something it lacks that you love, and you must work to give it one day the thing you love. If you haven't got the courage of your love, God help you, for no one else can."

Van Bredepoel did not reply. It seemed to him a mist hung between Burgess and himself. He would have liked to reply, but in his heart there were no answers.

" I know," Burgess said to him again, " that you hate oppression as much as I do, that you are perhaps more moved by social injustices than I am. Why not come and work with me and Daniel ? You will have your bread, and work I think you could respect as well."

" There's truth in what you've said," he answered very slowly. " I don't know that you have converted me yet, but I am sufficiently interested to think over your offer very seriously. Give me time."

" Excellent ! " exclaimed Burgess, encouraged. " I'm going away for three months to-morrow. Give me your answer when I come back."

" I'll do that," van Bredepoel replied, and said good-bye.

He went on, walking slowly towards Mrs. Harris'. The night had gone blacker, and now that it was late the glow of electric light over Port Benjamin had sagged on to the harbour front. Over squalid housetops, avoiding a chimney here, a tower there, appeared stars, very large and very clear. A breeze from the mountain brought with it the essence of long summer days, the memory of mosquito-winged nights, and raised from dirty paper rags a faint crackle of protest—unwound over rubbish tins the stench of discarded food. The houses stood over the streets with shuttered and barred fronts, and where a window showed it caught a cheerless glitter from the street lamps. Turning down a side street and feeling the breeze, van Bredepoel felt like a man who alone of all the passengers on a great liner had come on deck to watch it plunge on its voyage through the night.

Outside Mrs. Harris', a gust of wind carried his hat away and blew it over to where a gang of black men were digging up a drain. He ran after it, but before he could reach it one of the black men dropped his pick-axe and jumped out of the drain to catch the hat. He came over laughing to van Bredepoel and gave it to him. Van Bredepoel looked attentively at him as he took it. The man was in rags, his eyes red and swollen and his face yellow with dust. Pity assailed van Bredepoel. He put his hands impulsively in his pockets and emptied all the money he had into the palms of the black man, who was holding them cupped together as Kenon had done years before. Then he turned away, and for the second time that evening there were tears in his eyes.

That night van Bredepoel did not know whether he was awake or asleep. His thoughts seemed to be passing through the yellow light which hangs between night and day, but never passing into utter darkness. He himself was in an enormous cathedral in the ceiling of which hung the stars and the moon. Its pillars soared like mountains and between the pillars was a great crowd of people. Some of the

people were playing golf, some polo, some selling
oranges and apples, some playing at cards, others
carrying on aimless conversations, text-books in their
hands. Suddenly he saw crawling down the aisle,
unseen by the others, a young black man, bowed
down with burdens. Leading him by a dog-chain
was the capitalist of Burgess' posters, puffing out
clouds of cigar smoke. When the black man came
near, van Bredepoel was horrified to recognise the
features of Kenon. His impulse was to run and pick
him up, but he turned away, muttering with tears
in his eyes: " It isn't my affair." Hardly had he
spoken these words than he became aware of someone at his side and a voice like Burgess' saying:
" Your pity is a sham. You allow yourself to feel
sorry only because otherwise your essential indifference would be intolerable to you. No pity is worth
the name of pity unless it has the courage of the
actions that pity demands."

" It isn't my business," he murmured back, and
then, getting angry, shouted: " And neither is it
yours!" The ceiling above echoed: " Neither is it
yours . . . is it yours." Then all the people suddenly
stopped their various activities. A golfer in the act of
hitting the ball stood motionless with his club over
his shoulder, and everyone shouted: " It isn't our
business. Neither is it yours!" With these words,
the golf player swung his club and a white ball
soared with a magnificent curve over the heads of
the crowd, landing in the pulpit. " I have beaten
bogey by three. Not bad?" the man said. Van
Bredepoel looked no more: he turned to argue with
the person at his side, but he was not there, he was

floating over the crowd, calling back: " I can't wait,
it's time for the music to begin." In the pulpit there
appeared a priest who held up his hands and said:
" Only through the love of Christ and the inter-
cession of the Holy Virgin, brethren, can ye attain
salvation, only through love, my brethren. . . ."
But his voice was drowned by a mighty peal of music
from an organ played by the person like Burgess,
who was pulling wildly, ecstatically, at long ivory
stops. Every time he pulled out a stop, a long
fountain of blood shot out with it. " Won't someone
turn off that gramophone ? I don't like that noise,"
remarked a bald-headed bridge player. " I don't
like that noise, it's bad for trade, it drives customers
away! " cried an orange-seller. " Silence in the
court! " called a huge, pompous policeman. " The
Prime Minister can't hear his own voice! " But the
music grew louder, the echoes rolled over van
Bredepoel's head like a thunderstorm. He saw the
capitalist deflate, the cigar drop from astonished
lips, and heard the sharp angry scream of chain
dropping on stone as a huge black figure rose up,
growing bigger and bigger until it filled the cathedral. Somewhere in its body a light appeared,
rendering the skin transparent but neither black
nor white. " I don't like that music. I contend that
no organ music has been written since Bach," an
elegantly dressed woman said just behind him. As
she finished speaking all the people in the cathedral
rose to their feet and sang triumphantly: " Long
have you waited, long have you slept, O Africa!
But now you shall awake! " Van Bredepoel felt a
tremendous exaltation. He seemed to be sweeping

upwards like the flames of a large conflagration, and each movement of his body was subtly counter-pointed by a complex stream of music. Below him people were beginning to rush wildly about, and he saw old Karel Steyn, of Steyn, Berger and Stumpf-kopf, running hatless to the door, shouting: " Police! The Fire Brigade!" And then he was lying in his bed at " Vergelegen," and his uncle was reading to him out of the Bible: " When I was a child I spoke as a child, I understood as a child, I thought as a child, but when I became a man, I put away childish things." A candle flickered slowly at his side, and the voice of his uncle went on and on until it merged into the bleating of sheep, a helpless herd scampering terror-stricken over a twilight plain. Lightning hemmed him in, and somewhere near at hand was the thunder of a great battle.

In the morning van Bredepoel had a heavy fever on him. A doctor bent over him, feeling a large swelling on the back of his head, and Burgess, on his way to the country, did not know if he would live.

CHAPTER V

Who can say what depths you touch in delirium ?
What spiritual transformation parallels that awful
contortion of the flesh ? Even in health, the mere
action of lifting your feet from the ground, getting
into bed and turning off the light, releases the mind,
the spirit, from routine considerations. Strange
flowerings of what has been, of what can be, hang
over you like clouds horizoned by the Orient. Your
ears catch the sound of something which you are not
accustomed to call reality. The world trembles like
a million-stringed guitar. Some unknown thought
from an unfathomed deep bursts the surface of the
mind like a phosphorescent octopus the water of a
moonless sea. But when this process is syncopated to
the rhythm of a fever, the body, pedestrian symbol
of terrestrial liaisons, finding its everyday com-
munications interrupted renders thought doubly
libertine. It is doubtful if the mental state which
then arises deserves the name of thought, for thought
presupposes organisation, and here there is no
organisation, only an abysmal dissociation. Each
idea, each memory, rebels against the unity your
twisted self had of old imposed in its daily balance of
necessities. In rebellion they regain their original
velocity, recover all the power of their first impulsion,
and, regardless of one another, regardless of the
organisation in which they have so long rested,
Morse-code all together their eagerness, their

anxiety, to be received. The face which bends over
you merges into all the faces you have ever seen.
A spoon tinkles on the floor, and a Niagara of silver
falls across your vision. You turn your head, and
shut your eyes to shield them from so much bright-
ness. The action is futile. You shut your eyes to
the world in which your body moves, but when your
eyes are looking inward the lids which fall to shield
them betray you, for they merely dome a space as
vast as the sky, in which there is room for more than
one Niagara, for all the Congos and Zambesis
too. The outward world alone, which balanced for
so long with a life of subtle contacts an inward world,
is excluded. The balance sways, shudders and then
plunges. You, or a thousand things which clamour
to be you, fall. A clock strikes the hour but as there
is for you no longer any time, for time is necessity
and you are in revolt against necessity, each sound
orchestrates for you merely a depth beyond another
depth. The world falls, perhaps it soars; that is a
question for terrestrial mathematics, not for you.
There is a movement somewhere. A uniformed
nurse at your side thinks she has measured it by a
zigzag of ink on a temperature chart, but you, since
you are part of the movement, have become the
movement itself, you do not measure. Why measure
yourself? You plunge with indifference. You
change from split second to second and each new
state is as good or as bad as the previous one, for
you no longer have standards of comparison. Each
condition is its own standard. And meanwhile, to
the world, you are a ghastly caricature of yourself.
Your mouth, your eyes, ears, nose, outposts between

you and this outer world, do not renounce their
functions so easily. This machinery does not stop
so soon, for it has a long biological tradition behind
it. But, now you are ill, it is a tradition which no
longer has any internal mandate. It acts as the tail
of a lizard acts, long after it has been shed by the
animal. Your mouth forms words, but your inner
self is too preoccupied to make with this mechanical
movement the liaison that is meaning. Your eyes
look out at a world which to the people at your side
has meaning and order, but again the inner support,
the inner sympathy, is withheld, and they fail to
focus. You are a robot, a ventriloquist's robot,
whose master can no longer ventriloquise, but worse,
because the people around you cannot forget the
coherence that went before. To them this confusion
is terrible. You, in a world without values, know
neither confusion nor order. Even the dividing line
between your senses goes. Your ears signal that a
fish-cart, whose wheels fill the morning air with a
faint hysteria, is passing near by. Your ears receive
the sound of the fisherman's trumpet, but to you
the sound traces the outline of scarlet Atlas peaks,
mounting in a sulphurous light. Suddenly a thought
plunges upwards like a man from a sunken submarine: " I'll be late for school! " Your nerves
gather as if to register consternation, only to
produce at your mouth a twisted grin as the recollection of a long-forgotten obscenity collides with its
predecessor; you see, mounting towards a collision
in twilight air, two snow-white tennis balls. Your
mouth signals that it is dry; the soft, cool air, which
brings colour to the cheek of the palest child, passes

like powdered glass down your throat. But the
world with which you are occupied won't let you
hear. It throws a smoke-screen of reminiscences
round each signal of distress. You struggle instead
with the shadow of an Eton collar which once
worried your throat. If others did not give you water
you would die, without ever having known that you
needed it. Yet a day comes when your eyes, which
have so long looked without seeing, are arrested
by an object on the wall opposite. Slowly they focus.
The outline of a picture-frame is formed before you.
Soon your eyes shift to the picture itself. A pleasant
gold-blurred light shines upon it, and a sense of
wonderment possesses you. You look for some time,
enraptured. Yet suddenly you are unreasonably
agitated. The picture does not hang straight. It is
at least twenty degrees out of position. You have
known chaos long enough to be now a fanatical
disciple of mathematical order. All your consciousness fastens on this simple observation, like an army
on the first gap it has made in the enemy's trenches.
Inside there is still turbulence, but here in one small
instance you have at last admitted to yourself the
necessity of order. You demand at once that the
picture should be hung straight.

So long is it since you expressed coherently a
desire that the people near you are bewildered and
wonder whether it is not merely another form of
delirium. Their hesitation irritates you all the more.
Your tone becomes imperious. You will have that
picture hung straight, and afterwards, whenever
you open your eyes, you look to assure yourself that
it is still hanging straight. That night the nurse

notices that the graph on your temperature chart is taking a downward trend. The chart had, after all, some relation to the state in which you had so long existed. One by one you learn to sort out the noises that enter your room from outside. With these and the faint light that hangs in your room, you build up a picture of the world outside, a world of twilight reality. The voices of children in the street suggest to you games on which the night must soon fall. The afternoon sun alone is allowed to enter your room, and its rays, balancing particles of round dust that slide up and down like those translucent marbles on a wired frame from which you learned to count, remind you that the Earth is in motion and unknown to you has changed. You would, if you could, arrest the march of time. You have belonged too much to shadows lately to want them now. You hear with regret the noises of the world outside accept the coming of night, sort themselves out and settle down to a gentler measure. The candle which is brought into the room because your eyes are not yet strong becomes a terrible symbol of isolation, and you watch with dread the shadows eating up the long white stem. You begin to listen anxiously to each footstep in the passage, hoping mutely that one person at least will stop at your door, turn that lock which is so easily turned, and come inside. At last you blow out the candle, admitting only now that you are forced to admit it, that you have to face the night alone, that, in fact, you are alone.

And then your first day out of doors. So much beauty is more than you can bear. The day is something almost tangible, the object of an appetite as real as hunger. You could weep. You think of your old indifferences, and you realise that indeed you have changed. For you, that begins another story. Carefully you try to retrace your steps, but you cannot hope to retrace them all; for though time and memory in their short, unequal juxta- position run on parallel courses, the reality of one is not the reality of the other. In this simple truth there is tragedy for you. While you live, you and time seem to be practically one, and if it were not for memory which gallantly measures each gap, each difference between one moment and another, you would perhaps not have known that the trajectory of your own life thins away, while that of time soars unimpeded. Only memory, by a series of selections, by opposing an apparently irrelevant recollection to one long discarded, never allows you to forget that once you felt that, and now—this. Imperceptibly the two of you have moved. So much has happened on the way, so much that you have forgotten. Yet you are like those travellers who do not remember how they suffered, the day they set out on a long and uncertain voyage, but who still feel inexplicably sad when the afternoon gathering over a lighthouse repeats somehow the conditions of the hour when they saw the shores of their homeland sink into the sea. Even at the point where your individual memory disappears, the conservations of other memories widen the standard of your measure. The gap between you and time deepens, the sense of the brevity of your partnership quickens. Listening to the oars of a fisherman's boat coming home with the evening's catch and seeing the sunlight on its sails, you quote involuntarily:

> " The barge she sat in, like a burnish'd throne,
> Burn'd on the water; the poop was beaten gold,
> Purple the sails, and so perfumed. . . ."

The link between the fisherman's boat and that vessel on the Nile is only you, not even you but the words of a poet uttered through you. You see both the fisherman's boat and that other vessel recede with you in time. That ship was once seen flaming in Egyptian sunlight, and other men than you were so moved by the sight that they carried an impression of untold splendour with them to their graves. So strong indeed was their impression that their memory lived on in other memories, finding in the collective memory of mankind an immortality which neither they nor the barge, nor she who sat in it, possessed. Memory is a ripple that continues to radiate over the surface of a pond long after the stone which caused it has come to rest on the bottom. Does it resemble the reality as little as the ripples do the stone ? Ah, there you have it. Memory is not an historian. It is a poet, a poet with many prejudices. It serves its prejudices better than the verity. All that you, who have once more come to recognise yourself, can say is that the years behind you are wasted years. Looking back at them you are reminded of those travellers lost in the desert, who came back at nightfall in spite of all their determination, all precautions to the contrary, upon the ashes of the fire from which they set out in the morning. You tell yourself that it happened like that in your own case because you had no course to steer, no convictions to guide you ; the precautions you took were vain, because inwardly all was haphazard. You go over your spoor to find out where you went wrong, and, like those same lost travellers looking at their footsteps in the sand, you learn only one thing: whereas your tracks in the morning had made for the sun, they now lead into the night.

BOOK III

" Ich hasse jeden gewaltsamen Umsturz, weil
dabei ebensoviel Gutes vernichtet als gewonnen
wird.   Ich hasse die, welche ihn ausführen
wie die welche dazu Ursache geben."

GOETHE

CHAPTER I

VAN BREDEPOEL was leaning out of the window of his compartment on the Bambuland mail. The train pulled up slowly in a dimly lit station. A thick mist smoked over the platform and he read with difficulty on an iron signboard the name: " Paulstad." He had no conception of what the town and its surroundings would be like, beyond what Simmering had told him. Two hours before, towards sunset, the train had approached a long range of mountains, covered with thick forest, but long before it was dark a mist had come up quickly and shut out his view. He now leaned far out of his window, to attract the attention of the first porter who might come along. But the little he could see of the station showed it to be almost deserted. In the doorway of the booking-office, a man was standing, his back against the side-post, watching the train with an appearance of complete indifference. Farther along, people were throwing packages about in the glow cast on to the platform by the engine, and a man in riding-breeches and leggings, a sjambok dangling from his wrist, was helping a woman out of the train.

" Do you know if there are any porters about ? " van Bredepoel called out to the man in the doorway.

" I beg your pardon, cousin ? " said the man, taking his pipe out of his mouth and walking over to him. He was to find that most people in Paulstad said: " I beg your pardon," before they replied to questions.

" Are there any porters to be found here ? " he repeated.

" Yes, cousin," the man replied. " There are some hotel porters somewhere about. Which hotel are you thinking of going to ? There is the Paulstad Hotel, the. . . ."

" That's the one," van Bredepoel interrupted. The Paulstad was the hotel Simmering had recommended.

" Then I'll see if I can find him for you, cousin."

The man disappeared into the mist. He had not been gone long when from somewhere behind the station came a confused outburst of shouting, and through a doorway charged four or five small coloured men, peaked caps on their heads, crying out all together: " Royal Hotel! " " Paulstad Hotel! " " Imperial Hotel! " " Alexandra Hotel! "

" Really, this must be a bigger town than Simmering led me to expect! " van Bredepoel thought.

In a minute four porters were laughing, clamouring and jostling at his window.

" This is the fellow you want, cousin," said the man who had gone to find the porter, walking slowly up the platform and pointing at one of them. Before van Bredepoel could thank him, he had turned, and was strolling back to his stand in the doorway. The other porters, giving up the struggle, stood aside in a little group to make room in front of the window and became extremely critical of their successful rival's activities.

"My! But how that Bushman is slow!" one of them remarked, looking slyly at van Bredepoel's porter.

"Bushman!" another one called out, "you will have to eat more mealie-meal before you can do a man's work!"

They all laughed easily and long, and to van Bredepoel they seemed to be overflowing with happiness. And yet, except for their caps, they were all in rags and had thin, pinched faces.

"Slow? Slow?" van Bredepoel's porter called out, crouching as if preparing to jump, and snatching his cap off his head. "Call this Highland boy slow? Watch me, you beautiful things!" He jumped through a doorway, flung the compartment door open, and before van Bredepoel could stop him began to throw baggage out of a window, shouting: "Slow? Slow? Catch that, you yellow he-goats! Catch that! I was not bred under a turkey for nothing. Catch!"

"God! The Bushman is mad!" shouted the others and stampeded for the window. But all van Bredepoel's luggage was safely caught and landed on the platform.

"Are there any taxis here?" van Bredepoel asked his porter, who was grinning at him like a mischievous schoolboy. Instantly the man lost his look of happiness and became terribly gloomy.

"No, seur. There are no taxis here. I am so sorry, seur. There are no taxis." He looked as if he were to be blamed for the lack of taxis.

"Well, how are we to get to the hotel?"

"We will walk, seur," he said, regaining his cheer-

fulness, and jumping towards the others shouted:
" Give me the master's things! "

" But you can't carry all that ? " van Bredepoel
called out.

" Oh yes, seur! I can! Just you watch this Bushman boy! "

His companions helped to lift a trunk on to his
head, and taking three suit-cases, two in his hands and
one underneath his arm, the porter led the way out
of the station.

In the streets the mist was even thicker than van
Bredepoel had expected. There were no street lamps,
and the only light came from houses shut in by ample
gardens. The air was coldly humid, and van Bredepoel felt the presence around him of innumerable
trees. He thought that the mist testified to a well-
watered soil and said to the porter:

" It must rain a good deal here."

" No, seur. Yes, seur," the porter replied, the
trunk tilting dangerously as he tried to turn towards
van Bredepoel. " It has been terribly dry lately. As
a rule we have much rain, and we always have water
here even when it is dry, but there on the other side
of the mountains," he pointed into the mist, "there,
in Bambuland, people are dying of hunger like cattle."

" But this is very wet mist," van Bredepoel ob-
jected.

" No, seur, the mist comes up from the sea every
night. It is not from rain. No, seur."

" But you are not as near to the sea as all
that ? "

" Only four hours on horseback, seur."

Two things pleased van Bredepoel very much

about the man's manner of speaking. He liked his pronunciation, for as he said "no" and "seur" he unconsciously used the accent of the first Dutch inhabitants of the country, and though the form of the words themselves was new and belonged specifically to the country, he made them sound like the words people still use in the Netherlands to-day. The other was his method of calculating distance. He did not say that Paulstad was twenty miles from the sea, but "four hours on horseback," a way of reckoning which belonged to the days before there were motors and speedometers. Van Bredepoel was sufficiently out of sympathy with the life in Port Benjamin to warm to a village which followed the larger town's lead, if it followed it at all, with so much reluctance.

Deeper in the village, the streets became narrower, and there were no front gardens. They passed some well-proportioned houses with massive white walls and beautiful gables, which spread around them the atmosphere of grace and leisure of another age. Van Bredepoel was so interested that he made the porter stop while he went and had a closer look at some of the houses. The glass in the windows, judging by the way they let the light through, was old and not flawless. Here and there the rays of brilliant gas-lamps refracted by a flaw in the glass folded small rainbows over the mist. Outside the doors burned oil-lamps, enclosed in old iron frames, which bevelled in carefully with light and shadow the graceful lines of the gables. In one of the houses a gramophone was playing a tune which once, many years ago, had been fashionable, but had since had a hundred equally

popular and fatuous successors. Indeed, so long ago
was it since the tune had been popular that it had the
power—a power that resided not in the value of the
music, but in its association in the listener's mind
with a bygone period of life—to revive in van Bredepoel the sorrow he had felt when he first came to
Port Benjamin. And while he stood looking and
listening, he heard in a neighbouring street the
sound, once so familiar, of a cart and horses starting
out on a journey, and he felt for an instant like
someone coming home for good after a long trek.
He turned round, and there in the middle of the
street was the porter sitting on his trunk, the suit-
cases piled up around him.

" These houses must be rather old," van Bredepoel
said to him.

" Ah yes, seur! " he replied, " they were built by
the people of once-upon-a-time."

" Do you know when they were built ? "

" Yes, seur. By our great-fathers once upon a
time, before the great Kaffir War."

Suddenly the buildings that had interested van
Bredepoel ended, and they passed small shabby
structures with thin tin roofs, supported on sham
Corinthian pillars. Yet he succeeded in ignoring
them effectively, which, he told himself, was more
than he would have done in Port Benjamin. They
passed the doors of a small cinema, and so still was
it in the street that he could hear the steady flickering
of the film inside mixing with the sound of an old
piano delivering itself of pre-War dance music.

" You are going to the best hotel, seur. Yes, seur,"
the porter told him suddenly.

" Oh, am I ? "

" Yes, seur, it is the only building with two stories and electric light in the town. Look! There it is, seur."

They had walked into a wide gravelled square, on one side of which was a long, low yellow-walled building with a very wide, high veranda round it. On the veranda a woman was knitting, and drawn up in front of the hotel steps was a car covered with dust. As they passed the car van Bredepoel thought he saw on the registration plate a Port Benjamin number, but he was not sure. He noticed that its engine had been kept running. On the steps leading on to the veranda he nearly collided with a motorist, who came running out of the front door of the hotel. In turning round to apologise, the man stopped for a moment on a step lower down and looked up at van Bredepoel, who had by then mounted into the full light on the veranda. It seemed to van Bredepoel that a glimmer of recognition passed over the man's face, but he himself was convinced that he had never seen the fellow before. Instead of going on, the man turned and bounded back, muttering that he had forgotten something. At the entrance he was met by the proprietor, and van Bredepoel heard him say: " Look here, Rothman! You mustn't forget to send that letter to the Residency immediately. It's very important and he's expected home at any time now. I would wait myself, but I must get through to Port Duncan to-night."

As van Bredepoel came towards them, the man watched him slyly and very intently, but at the last

moment turned away again to his car. Just as van
Bredepoel was going to speak to the proprietor, the
motorist stopped the porter on the veranda steps
and began to examine the labels on the suit-cases he
was carrying. Disliking the man's furtive way of
trying to discover his identity, van Bredepoel turned
back angrily, but the man saw him coming and said
quickly to the porter:

" Here, Jim! Take this and get me a packet of
fifty Cape-to-Cairo cigarettes."

" You bring up my luggage first! " van Bredepoel
called out to the porter.

" Oh, damn! I can't wait! " exclaimed the man,
snatching the money back. He jumped into his car
and drove off. Van Bredepoel was a little disquieted
by the incident, but in arranging about his room he
soon forgot about it.

The Paulstad Hotel had a stale and dusty smell
inside, as if it had not been swept for a long time, and
was evidently not accustomed to fresh air. The
floors were covered with a torn, blackened linoleum.
Near the entrance, in a long passage, was a high-
legged desk on which lay a book, rather like an old-
fashioned Bible, fastened down at one corner by a
nickel chain. Without speaking to him, the proprietor
led van Bredepoel to the desk, and flinging the book
open said: " Will you please sign here ? I expect
you want a room for the night."

" No, I might want a room for a month, or eight
weeks. I don't know yet," he replied.

" Our charges are ten shillings and sixpence a day
as a rule, but if you stay a month I'll make it six
shillings," said the proprietor.

" Well, I'll take a room for a week, and think it over."

" At your service, sir." The proprietor bowed stiffly, and turning to the porter said: " Jim, show this gent up to room twenty-three."

James led van Bredepoel along a narrow passage, from the walls of which looked down on them with glassy eyes the antlered heads of many kinds of buck. At the end of the passage they climbed a staircase on which the dust crunched like sugar under their feet. Room twenty-three was at the end of yet another corridor. As they walked into it the small chest of drawers rattled violently. In one corner was a single iron bedstead, in another an iron wash-stand, on which stood an enamel jug and basin. There was only one window. Over the bed hung a lurid picture of the Judgment Day; in the top left-hand corner of the picture an enormous eye brooded like a setting sun over a world in flames, remote and aloof from those last cataclysms of sea and earth and fire and sky, which caught a wretched humanity absorbed in rape and murder and brother-hate and warfare. Van Bredepoel felt uncomfortable looking at it, and taking it down gave it to the porter.

" Here, James, hide that somewhere. I shall never sleep with that eye looking down on me," he said.

The porter looked astonished, but did as he was told. He went out of the room, but in a few minutes returned, walking in without knocking. Once inside he could not keep his eyes off van Bredepoel. His curiosity and wonder had been aroused by the labels on the bags, and van Bredepoel concluded that neither Paulstad nor Port Benjamin knew much about each other.

"You can go now, James," van Bredepoel told the porter.

"Yes, seur," he replied, but made no attempt to go.

"Here!" said van Bredepoel, giving him a tip. "I forgot; I'm sorry."

James took his tip, but still did not go.

"They say Port Benjamin is a fine place, seur," he began.

"Yes."

"The seur is going back there?"

"Yes. At least, I'm not sure."

James became gloomy. He stood against the door, watching van Bredepoel wash his hands. There was an expression of despair in his eyes.

"The seur keeps many servants," he said at last, when van Bredepoel had finished.

"None."

"I am ready to go. . . ." But James changed his mind and finished his sentence differently to what he had intended. "I am ready to show the master the bath and bar and smoking-room."

The smoking-room was large and empty, and the lights in it had a dull, dishonoured glow. There on the tables van Bredepoel found eighteen-month-old weeklies, and even a pre-War *Graphic*. On the walls were portraits of the Queen of Holland in her Coronation robes and of Princess Juliana. The queen, in that portrait, was still young and beautiful,

and like the music he had heard, the houses he had
seen, her portrait made van Bredepoel place the
hotel, together with Paulstad, farther and farther
back in time. In between these portraits were other
pictures, depicting at a glance English hunting
scenes, but when he looked closer he discovered that
the horses had large whisky- and brandy-bottles for
bodies, and that they bore inscriptions like: " Jack's
whisky first in at the kill." They, too, must have
been painted a long time ago.

" Excuse me, please, Mr. van Bredepoel." The
proprietor was at his side. " No impertinence
meant, but I saw your name in the visitors' book and
I was wondering if you were not related to Commandant van Bredepoel, who was killed at Dalmanutha."

" He was my father," replied van Bredepoel.

" Your father! " the proprietor exclaimed. " Sir!
You are my guest! You shall stay here as long
as you like as my guest! I served with your father
for two years, and I was with him when he was
killed."

Van Bredepoel feared the proprietor was going to
embrace him, but instead he turned and ran to the
door, shouting: " Maria! Maria! "

The woman who had been sitting on the veranda
when van Bredepoel arrived came slowly into the
room, knitting as she walked.

" Mr. van Bredepoel," the proprietor said, pushing
her before him, " meet my wife." Then drawing
himself up to attention at van Bredepoel's side, he
said: " Maria, a son of Wolferd van Bredepoel."

" Very happy, very happy I'm sure," replied the woman, giving him a fat hand to shake. " If there's anything I can do for you, Mr. van Bredepoel, I shall be very happy to do it."

She looked him up and down with placid good humour, turning on him eyes that were by nature and habit incurious and steady; then walked back to the veranda with her knitting. With her went an atmosphere of healthy animal contentedness. Van Bredepoel was left alone with the gesticulating proprietor, and it was a long time before he could get to his room.

He soon found that the proprietor was, for all practical purposes, two persons. In the mornings he was heavy-eyed and sulky, bade people the most stiff and reluctant of good mornings, casting around him the shadow of dull, ineradicable, unanalysable blood misery. And when van Bredepoel saw him in this mood, he thought: " He, too has been through the War." In the evenings, however, when he had enough to drink, he was embarrassingly cordial and talkative, revealing a mind into which had been dropped, as into a waste-paper basket, many a half-baked idea; haphazard results of an ineffectual self-education. Then he would begin a conversation by saying: " I'm only an hotel proprietor, but I'm a bit of a philosopher," or, " I'm something of a psychologist," or, " I'm a student and observer of men."

But his wife was always Maria the happy, the very happy, a keeper by nature and inclination, the keys of the hotel at her side; working placidly at her knitting, brooding with quiet, unsurprised eyes over the streets of Paulstad and the men and things that came and went through them. Yet only a fool would have thought that the heart which beat so steadily was not warm.

CHAPTER II

THE next morning van Bredepoel was up long before
his usual hour. The mist had disappeared, and the
sun was bright so early, warmed the air so quickly,
that he could not remain indoors. When he came
downstairs the black menservants of the hotel were
only just beginning to take coffee round to the
rooms, and James, the porter, passed him, his arms
full of boots and shoes, giving van Bredepoel an
unseen look of appeal as he went.

He lingered on the veranda for some time. From
a small house near the hotel came the sound of
people singing at their morning prayers. The air
was still and hazy with a blue morning smoke,
folding and unfolding over the town. Paulstad
seemed to carry at heart a profound peace, a contentment with both its past and future.

Once out in the streets, van Bredepoel could
hardly see the houses for the trees; and though the
porter had said rain was long overdue the scent of
their leaves was heavy and fresh. Where there was
a house without a garden it turned out to be an
office, a public building or a merchant's store. And
in most of the gardens were men in shirt-sleeves,
gathering their first crop of fruit from their own trees,
or spraying plants with water, which released into
the air a smell of earth and tender grass. The
absence of hurry in their movements, the calm
expression of their features, the slow, placid way in

which they greeted van Bredepoel, though he did
not know them, seemed to link up their lives with
that tradition which expressed itself in the beauty of
the older houses. " For once," said van Bredepoel,
" Simmering was right. This is the place for me."
As the day advanced, however, the freshness disappeared. Paulstad, like Port Benjamin, was, after
all, only an island in Africa; like Port Benjamin it
owed its beauty to the mountains which stood over
it, their backs to the stony Africa beyond. The few
motor cars that passed through Paulstad raised a
thick dust which hung in the air long after they had
disappeared. Over the mountains, there in Bambuland, where the porter had said people were dying
like cattle, the sky turned yellow, the tops of the
mountains black; the heat vapours flickered over
the country like the blank spaces in an old film.
Towards noon the evaporation of moisture from the
soil became so intense that the base of the mountain
range disappeared from view and its summits were
flung rootless into the sky, plunging like black
derelicts in a quicksilver sea. In the evening the sun
went down a blood red, and though there was not a
cloud in the sky van Bredepoel could look at the sun
without blinking; between him and it was a world
of silently drifting dust, a world of decomposed stone
floating over a world of stone. No sooner had the
sun set than once more the sky turned blue and of an
incalculable profundity, but before dusk a breeze
sprang up, carrying from the sea an impenetrable
cloud of mist, hanging it between Paulstad and
Bambuland like a curtain which is timed to fall
when the horrors of a play become more than the

audience can bear. And in van Bredepoel, who had
for so many years lived through long months of
waiting between one year's rain and the next year's,
revived all the old feeling of depression, the sort of
blood-thirst for rain, which he had felt at " Vergelegen." He began to discuss, like everyone else at
the hotel, the possibilities of rain, not as a subject of
polite conversation, but as an issue in which life was
at stake.

That evening at supper he heard a little boy say to
his mother at a table next to his own:

" Mother, do you think it's the end of the world
coming ? "

The woman laughed. " The end of the world ?
Why ? "

" The sun was like blood to-night, mother."

" But that's nothing, my child," she said, still
smiling.

" Oh, but mother ! Sarah says when the sun's like
that, something terrible always happens ! "

" Sarah's only an ignorant black woman." She
was evidently a little annoyed with her servant.

" But Sarah knows, mother. She says that in the
Great War she herself saw the sun set red like blood
every evening. She says. . . ."

" You're too young to understand. She was only
telling you a story. Now eat your food."

" Sarah says . . ." began the child again, and
this time his mother spoke to him very severely.

" That's enough, Klasie. Come ! Eat your food.
Sarah was telling you stories." But the little boy
seemed convinced that Sarah knew. He looked up

often at his mother for encouragement to speak; she gave him none.

After supper van Bredepoel met the proprietor in the corridor. The man's spirits had risen wonderfully since the morning. He was whistling and the moment he saw van Bredepoel, he took him by the shoulders and said: " Mr. van Bredepoel, I served with your father for two years. I was with him when he was killed. He was my commandant and my friend. Q.E.D. you are my friend and my guest. I would like to make you a member of the Club." He said the word " club " as if it were the Reform or the Athenæum. " We don't let just everyone into the Club, but you are my friend."

He would take no refusal. Pouring out a long series of reminiscences, he conducted van Bredepoel down a side corridor to a glass door, on which was painted in large black letters: " The Royal Paulstad Club."

" Gentlemen! " said the proprietor, when they had entered. " I want you all to meet the son of my old friend, Commandant van Bredepoel. Mr. van Bredepoel, some of the faithful."

A number of red-faced men came up to shake hands with van Bredepoel. Some of them had been lounging in deep green-leather chairs, others talking over their glasses at the bar counter, and two had been playing billiards at a small-sized table. On the walls were amateurish caricatures of the Club celebrities, among which van Bredepoel recognised the faces of some of the men present.

" What'll you have to drink ? " half a dozen voices called out simultaneously to him, and soon he was standing in the centre of a large group at the bar counter.

Waiting for their glasses to be filled, van Bredepoel looked about him and felt that by coming he had almost rendered the Paulstad Club a substantial service. A dozen men turned well-nourished and apparently cheerful and contented faces towards him. Like many men who are forced to spend much of their time in the same places and in the same circles, they had developed a sort of family likeness to one another. Such at least was van Bredepoel's impression, and he did not find it an altogether comfortable one. Next to a common misfortune there is, perhaps, nothing that binds men closer than a common boredom, and after a more careful scrutiny of his companion's, van Bredepoel was convinced that their cheerful and contented looks, the unanimity with which he was being made an excuse for drinking more than usual, were only the measure of the monotony of their lives. The most contented and satisfied people are those who like strangers least.

When all the glasses were filled, there were suddenly shouts of " Good old Reddy! " " That's the stuff to give 'em, Reddy! " and a small, fat man with a very red face, red hair and lively, greenish eyes, came pushing through the group towards van Bredepoel. He evidently had a somewhat privileged position in the Club, for the rest instantly made way for him, and looked at him with smiling, expectant faces.

" That's Reddy Brand," the proprietor whispered to van Bredepoel. " Such a good chappie. I've

never heard anyone say a bad word about him.
And he an attorney, too! He'll make you laugh.
Did you see that ? Ha! Ha!"

Like the others, he broke out into loud laughter.
Brand had gathered his short coat about him, like a
portly matron her evening gown, and was moving
skittishly over to the bar counter.

" Mitha van Bredepoel," he said, holding out his
hand high before him. " I'm thure pleathed to make
your acquaintanthe." And then looking coyly round,
he asked: " Won't thomeone pleathe fetth me a
drink ? "

His companions found him irresistibly comic. He
had only to open his mouth or make the slightest
gesture to draw their laughter. When his drink
came, he dropped his pose, put one hand to the lapel
of his coat and raising his glass with the other,
shouted out:

" Gentlemen! Unaccustomed as I am to public
speaking, it's my privilege and my pleasure. . . ."

Here everyone applauded vigorously and laughed
loudly, repeating, " It's his privilege and his
pleasure! "

It was some moments before Brand could go on.
Then he said: " I repeat, gentlemen, that it is my
privilege and pleasure to heartily welcome to-
night on behalf of the boiler-makers' union, this
distinguished stranger in our midst. I am an honest
working man of few words. . . ."

" Tell another, Reddy, have you ever heard of an
honest lawyer ? " someone called back, and because
everyone was determined to be cheerful, everyone
laughed.

" . . . of few words," Brand went on, " and though I drops me haitches, I always says it's not a man's haitches, it's 'is 'eart that makes a welcome, so I will without further ado offer this toast to our visitor as a slight token of our respect and esteem. Our visitor ! "

They all emptied their glasses like men who are accustomed to drink, not for the taste of drink, but for the condition it produces in them. Immediately the glasses were emptied someone else called for more drinks.

" You're not playing to-night ? " someone asked Brand.

" We, the Administration, has not yet arrived. We wait," replied Brand, making a pompous mock bow.

" Speak of the devil! " another man exclaimed.

The door opened, and two men entered quietly. One of them was very tall and very carefully dressed. He looked quickly over the group at the bar counter, a faint expression of distaste on his face, and then turned with a grave, preoccupied manner to his companion. Van Bredepoel searched his face in vain for that group resemblance he had observed in the others. The new-comer looked as if neither his interests nor his inclination bound him to the company. He carried with him an atmosphere of neatness and precision, a suggestion of order and thoughtfulness which the others lacked. When he came closer, van Bredepoel thought he saw in the man's cool, steady, grey eyes the shadow of a profound and intelligent disillusionment: evidence of a character in which doubt played a far bigger role than conviction. His companion was shorter, and dressed in the uniform of a colonel of the police. He walked at the side of his tall friend with a precise resolute bearing, and looked round him with an honest and harmless aggressiveness. They both gave the men in the club the most perfunctory of greetings.

" Silence in the court! " shouted Brand, springing to attention when he saw them. Once more everybody laughed.

" You must have a drink, Colonel," the tall man said in low, even tones. " We need something to wash down all that dust."

" Just one quick one, then," replied the Colonel. " I must get back to the station, and so must you."

" You're late, Mags," someone said to the tall man. " We've been waiting for you more than an hour."

" Yes, I'm sorry," he replied. " I had a job to do, and I don't think I can play to-night."

" Why not ? "

" I don't think I feel like it," he said curtly; his expression had not lost its gravity.

" You're not working up another case against me, your Honour ? " asked Brand.

It seemed to van Bredepoel that Brand had for so long been imprisoned in his role of public jester that he could not open his mouth without trying to make people laugh.

" Not unless you've been using the ninth hole on the golf course as a public urinal again," replied the magistrate.

Brand laughed heartily with the others, and tried to reply with a semblance of deadly seriousness.

" I've not forgiven you that. This is a God-forsaken spot and when a fellow gets a little tight you must allow him a bit of freedom. Besides, what is one to do when Nature calls so strongly ? "

" If you had only done it once, Brand," the magistrate said, " it would probably have been all right. But if I remember rightly, you did it at every hole and had a bet on it as well."

" Come on, Mags! Admit you were piqued because you lost to me at chess the night before."

" It'll be two weeks' hard labour without the option of a fine next time for that." The magistrate smiled at Brand with a sort of tired schoolmaster's indulgence.

" But what kept you, Mags ? It's most unusual at this time of the month," another man asked.

" The Colonel and I have been into the native territory this afternoon," the magistrate said.

" An inquest ? "

" Yes."

The questioning was obviously unpleasant to the magistrate.

" Not another murder ? "

" No! A sacrifice."

Three or four men whistled, and several shouted: " What! "

" A sacrifice, a blood sacrifice, a human sacrifice."

He seemed to want to let the matter rest there, but still the others persisted.

" But what on earth for ? "

" Rain."

" There! I've always said it," Brand exclaimed, forgetting for the moment to be funny. " Don't tell me ever that you can civilise those bastards in Bambuland. Once a barbarian always a barbarian."

The magistrate put his glass down on the counter very deliberately and turned round to face Brand. He began speaking like a man who is anxious to convince himself as well as his hearers.

" Look here, Brand, if you saw your cattle dying round you every day, and not your cattle only but dozens of your own people, through lack of rain, and you were convinced that by the sacrifice of one human life you might get rain and so prevent the death of many others, would you hesitate to sacrifice ? "

" Come on Mags, you're not going, to take the part of these murderers. You know that no amount of sacrifice'll make it rain if it doesn't want to rain."

" That's not the point. If you believed in the necessity and efficacy of sacrifice, would you hesitate ? Answer, yes or no ? "

This insistence on legal precision seemed to annoy Brand a little.

" Surely, Mags," he said, " you're not going to be kinder to these murderers than you were to me ? Surely they'll hang."

The magistrate did not press his question but said, rather mournfully van Bredepoel thought: " If they are proved guilty, they'll hang all right."

" Sure! They'll hang all right," echoed the Colonel, speaking for the first time, and swallowing his whisky.

" I don't think you fellows know how bad things are in Bambuland," the magistrate began again. " There's no grass left. The country's red, absolutely

red. There's only sand and stone and thorn-bush
left. There's so little water that I felt like a criminal
taking a gallon of it for the radiator of my car. I
tell you, once we left Masakama's Drift the stink of
dead cattle was so strong that I wanted to hold my
nose all the way."

" I haven't stopped spitting yet," interjected the
Colonel, and immediately illustrated his statement
by spitting into the fender.

" At every half-mile or so," continued the magistrate, " we met some poor devil tramping this way
for work."

" Don't like it! " exclaimed the Colonel. " Too
many blacks out of work in this place already. It is
highly—er—I don't like it."

" Don't I know it," replied Brand, " I'm sick of
turning black tramps away from my door."

" Queer gent, that," the proprietor told van
Bredepoel, nodding his head in the direction of the
magistrate. " Never been very popular. He's too
much of a negrophobolist. He fined Brand four
pounds for what he did on the golf course, and at
the same time let off a native who had stolen a
sheep for ten bob. I notice these things, Mr. van
Bredepoel, I notice them. I'm only an hotel
proprietor, but I'm something of a psychologist.
I've read psychology; I know that that fellow is
intellectually complexed. Very dangerous! You
know! When our faculties are not properly heredi-
tated, they become oppressed and we dream about
cobras and walking on tight-ropes and. . . ."

Van Bredepoel excused himself and walked over
to Brand.

" Will you introduce me to the magistrate ? " he asked.

" Try me! " said Brand, and led him over to the magistrate.

" Mags," he said, " let me introduce to you that strangest of phenomena—a Port Benjaminite who travels, who actually has the desire to see other places than Port Benjamin."

" I was very interested in what you were saying just now about a sacrifice. Won't you tell me more about it ? " van Bredepoel asked him.

" It's very simple really," replied the magistrate. " As magistrate of this district, I have to hold inquests on every death the district doctor thinks abnormal. Here the facts are evident, though they have, of course, to be further established legally. A young native girl has been sacrificed by her tribe in the belief that her death would make it rain. The people in the kraal made no secret about it. Her father told me frankly that he had assisted at the ceremony. He and his wives seemed desolate with sorrow, but they told me that they could do nothing else. The witch-doctor told them that it was their only means of getting rain and insisted on her death. She was, from their point of view, honestly and fairly condemned. It might easily have been another, only the witch-doctor picked her out in the traditional manner, and there was an end to it."

" But," exclaimed van Bredepoel, " I thought witch-doctors no longer existed! Or, if they existed, had no power, except for doing harmless medicinal stuff."

" They haven't got much power in normal times,

but I don't know if you have noticed that, even with civilised nations, a great calamity often revives the most conservative instincts of a race. A disaster like this in Bambuland, coming long after these instincts have disappeared superficially, throws races back overnight on the principles and traditions by which, rightly or wrongly, they believe themselves to have been brought safely to where they are."

Brand began whistling " Tell me the old, old story," but stopped suddenly, took the magistrate by the arm and said, seriously for once: " You know, Mags, you have far too good a heart. You shouldn't worry so much about these black skins. Honestly, they aren't worth it."

" You shouldn't complain," replied the magistrate, " seeing that most of your clients are black people."

" Shows you how objective I am," Brand said cheerfully, and walked away.

" You don't seem to like the idea of punishing these people," van Bredepoel remarked.

" I'm not trying to defend the utility of the custom," the magistrate said. " It's useless, and because it's useless, cruel. But what worries me is, can one, humanly speaking, call that murder? You see, I myself haven't much faith in an abstract conception of justice. It seems to me that between the psychological habits of people and their conception of justice there is, or should be, a very close bond. We wouldn't, with a mediæval mentality, be able to tolerate twentieth-century justice; if we were able to, we would abuse it: and it would, of course, be worse the other way round. Yet that's precisely what we're trying to inflict on these people. In their case it's doubly cruel, because we won't allow the black people to enter into the system of living for which our justice was obviously devised. By refusing to do so, we imply that they are psychologically and racially in a ᵛdifferent class. Yet we proceed very illogically to inflict our system of justice on them as if they were like ourselves. If we hadn't prevented these people from living like ourselves, I wouldn't hesitate for a moment to punish them. But you see, I feel that indirectly we have a terrible responsibility in cases like these. We forbid them the sort of life their law demands, and give them our law without the sort of life that our law demands. That's what's worrying me. But if they're proved guilty, they'll be hanged, all right."

The magistrate seemed inclined to go on, but they were interrupted by a loud noise. Brand had climbed on to the billiard-table, and was holding a glass of whisky high above his head.

"Gentlemen! Gentlemen!" he called out. "On behalf of the boiler-makers' union, it's my privilege and pleasure to propose to you a new toast. Gentlemen! I give you 'Rain,' that liquid, I must confess, which is so strange to me—in all the years I have lived in Paulstad I haven't tasted it once—but which is apparently so necessary to our black brothers!"

He looked slyly in the direction of the magistrate as he said "black brothers," and catching van Bredepoel's eye winked broadly. The magistrate, smiling ever so faintly to himself, a light ironical look in his eyes, retained a perfect self-possession in the

midst of the roar of laughter which Brand's jest
provoked. But the Colonel had stepped to his side
and taken him by the arm. He looked at Brand like
a sergeant-major at a truculent recruit, and then
said to the magistrate:

" Come on, Mags, let's get out of this kindergarten.
We've got work to do."

They went out as they had come in, aloof and
indifferent, yet turning at the door to nod to van
Bredepoel. Meanwhile Brand, his glass high above
his head, his fat, red features shining with a jester's
satisfaction, shouted:

" I repeat, that liquid which is so necessary to our
black brothers. Gentlemen! The boiler-makers'
union, with which is affiliated the ex-engine-
drivers' association and the discharged cooks'
union, gives you ' Rain! ' "

" Rain! " The club shook with the answering
shout, and in that tumult no one saw or heard the
door shut quietly on the magistrate and his companion.

The moment they had gone Brand leaped down
from the table and began to sing, " We are marching
to Pretoria." The others formed a procession behind
him, dancing round and round the table a mock
Bambuxosa war-dance. Van Bredepoel was left
alone at the bar counter, stacks of dirty glasses and
smoking ash-trays around him. No one heard him
say good night.

In his room at last, he leant out of his window.
He tried to look in the direction of Bambuland, but
between him and it hung a world of mist. Somewhere, the commando birds, those creatures whose

eyes, not strong enough for the full light of day and not penetrating enough for the night, condemn them for ever to a twilight existence, were beginning to raise their mournful cries.

" There's another who has lost faith," he told himself, thinking of the magistrate. " He has no faith, even where his duty is obvious, as in this case. He has come to mistrust so much the system of which his administration of justice is part, that he can no longer see a case by itself, but only as something in which, no matter how just he himself is, his justice will be coloured by the general injustice of the system."

He felt a sudden breeze against his cheek. The breeze was unexpectedly hot and dry. It was beginning to blow from Bambuland.

CHAPTER III

VAN BREDEPOEL saw a group of children come rushing past the hotel, laughing as they came. He was amused to see that they were playing a sort of endurance game with the heat. They were all barefooted and would gather in the shade of a tree, while one of them ran out into the sun to see how long his feet could stand the heat of the ground. Before long the soles of his feet would become so hot that he had to take comically big strides to avoid touching the ground more than possible. The other children would cheer him on mockingly and the quiet afternoon street was filled with laughter.

In the wake of the children, two natives came marching down the street. They, too, were barefooted, but they walked along as though utterly indifferent to the heat, and sought no shade. One of them was middle-aged and slightly bowed down, his steps firm but slow. The other seemed about van Bredepoel's age and was a head taller than his companion, striding at his side with an extraordinary grace. The clothes of both were in rags, and they did not speak to each other. Van Bredepoel found himself watching them very intently, forgetting even to smoke his cigarette. When they came abreast of the hotel, they turned sideways and walked slowly over to where van Bredepoel was sitting. They evidently knew Paulstad well, for when they came underneath the veranda they began searching for cigarette ends. Only the tops of their backs were visible as they stooped. Van Bredepoel was just about to walk casually to the edge of the veranda, when there came the sound of an aeroplane flying towards the town. This was so unusual that even he hurried forward to look. Both natives immediately stood up, their backs to him, and scanned the sky.

" What is that ? " he heard the old man ask his companion.

" An aeroplane," replied the other.

" It is heavy. Why does not it fall ? "

" It has a machine like a motor car which keeps it up."

" But why does not a motor car fly like that ? "

" Its machine does not go fast enough. You see, old father, the machine of that aeroplane goes so fast that before it can fall from one place it has already reached another."

" Ah ! " replied the old man, evidently satisfied. But they stood there with their backs turned to van Bredepoel for a long time, watching the aeroplane out of sight.

When it was gone the old man said: " I think it is foolish. It is cold up there, and here it is warm."

The younger native laughed. Van Bredepoel suddenly felt strangely agitated. To van Bredepoel standing there, there was as yet merely something unaccountably familiar about the old man's companion, but another van Bredepoel, who guarded carefully many a fugitive recollection and who was interested in the present only so far as it was related to the past, began to tremble with excitement. He was almost afraid to look. Yet he watched the old

man call the younger and hold out to him a handful
of cigarette ends. The younger man held out both
hands cupped together for the old man's gift. Van
Bredepoel doubted no more, for with that gesture
the native linked himself up with and merged into
that other native who many years before in Port
Benjamin had held his hands just like that to receive
a small tip as if it were a glittering pile of gold.
Slowly the younger native stretched himself and
turned round to look at the hotel. He gave van
Bredepoel a look in which there was not even the
most casual interest. Yes, it was Kenon, but so much
had he aged, so much more deeply imprinted was
the look of inarticulate despair which van Bredepoel
had noticed of old when it first shadowed the boy's
features, that he almost wished it had not been
Kenon. His eyes were sunk deep into his forehead,
and a heavy shadow lay over them; as he tried to
find a pocket for his cigarette ends, his hands
trembled violently. Van Bredepoel had not imagined,
had not pictured Kenon, who had once moved
through the shadowy corridors at Mrs. Harris' with
such a glitter, so dulled, so frail, so twisted.

"Kenon!" he called, walking down the veranda
steps.

In that moment recognition came to Kenon too.
He looked first as if it terrified him, but then, as
van Bredepoel called him again by his name, he
raised his hand far above his head as he used to do
when they met in the streets of Port Benjamin, and
said in a voice that came from far down in his
throat:

"Auck! My Inkosan'."

Van Bredepoel felt the pathos of this greeting; both he and Kenon were speaking and behaving as if no more than a summer's night had separated them. Yet he knew that every word they would henceforth say must widen in their minds the gulf that existed between them in time.

"Kenon, I did not expect to find you here," he said at last.

"Yes, Inkosan'," Kenon replied. "It is I who am here."

"Where are you going to?"

"I am just walking, Inkosan'." Kenon's hand brought North, South, East and West together.

"But where have you been all this time?"

"Working, Inkosan'," he replied like one who feared further questions, yet knew them to be inevitable.

"Working? Here? Where?"

"Here, Inkosan'. And in the mines."

"You have not been back to Port Benjamin?"

"Oh, no, Inkosan', I have not been back to Port Benjamin."

"Why did you not come to tell me that you were going away?"

"The missus told me that Inkosan' was very angry with me and did not want to see me again." And then he added, as though he feared van Bredepoel would take that as a reproach: "But the Inkosan' did right to be angry with me."

"The missus lied. I never said anything of the kind to her. And she did not tell me that you asked to see me."

"The missus spoke an untruth?" Surprise and a

faint joy looked out of his eyes, but soon the old look of despair came back. He shook his head as if he had found the gesture by long experience to be easier and more convenient for expressing a sense of misfortune than words. He tried to laugh, and said: " Auck ! "

" But where are you going ? " van Bredepoel asked him.

" I am just going," Kenon replied, not from a desire to be vague, but because he was not sure himself.

" Is there anything I can do to help you ? " Van Bredepoel was beginning to despair over the life-lessness and vagueness of these replies.

" I thank the Inkosan', but there is nothing that the Inkosan' can do for me."

" Look here, Kenon," van Bredepoel told him energetically. " Have you got work ? "

" I have not got work, Inkosan'."

" Why not ? "

" I have looked for work everywhere, but the times are bad and there are many people like me looking for work, Inkosan'."

Van Bredepoel did not ask him how he came to be out of work, but merely demanded: " You want work then ? "

" Yes, I want work if I can find work, Inkosan'."

" Good then! Perhaps I can help you. When can you come to see me ? "

" I have promised to take this old father to his hut this evening, but to-morrow. . . ." His hand again swept round the horizon.

" Good! Come and see me here at the hotel to-

morrow evening at six o'clock. I shall wait for you.
Don't be late."

He added this last sentence because he knew from
of old how little sense of time Kenon's people
possessed.

" I thank the Inkosan' and I shall not be late."

They went slowly down the street, dust playing
round their feet, the light of a tortured afternoon
flowing like a Pacific surf around them. Watching
them go, van Bredepoel thought:

" A pity, a great, great pity."

He had said the same thing five years before, and
now, as then, he had no definite plan for helping
Kenon. But he was determined this time to do something for the boy, even if he had to take him back to
Port Benjamin, always supposing he himself went
back.

Returning from his walk that evening, van Bredepoel met the proprietor on the veranda.

" Ah, there you are! " he said, rushing up to van
Bredepoel. " I've been planning such a good trip
for you to-day. I want you to come in a few days'
time with me and my wife to Masakama's Drift.
You won't regret coming. It is such a beautiful spot,
even now with the drought on. It's on the border of
Kaffirland, and you'll see there such black people as
you have never seen. You'll see. . . ."

The proprietor stopped suddenly, and asked him:
" Do you know about Masakama ? "

" Yes, I do," van Bredepoel replied. The proprietor was surprised.

" Well," he said, " you'll be interested then to see
there the great mountain which Masakama and his

impis scaled at the dead of night. God knows how
they ever got to the top. It looks terrible enough by
day. I wouldn't go up with a Swiss guide if they
paid me. But Masakama and his impis went up it
by night and as quick as you can wink your eye,
killed all the Bamangkwetsi, who had their kraal on
the top. But you know all that, I suppose. Say,
would you like to come ? "

" I would like to very much," van Bredepoel
replied, and thanked him warmly.

" That's all right, that's all right. Your father was
my friend. Q.E.D. you are my friend. And oh, by
the way, Mr. van Bredepoel, Mr. Moller sent in a
messenger this afternoon to say that his car will call
for you at half-past seven to-morrow morning. That
was all. They told me you'd understand. You were
expecting the message, weren't you ? "

Van Bredepoel thought instantly, with dismay,
that it would have been better if he had remembered
Simmering's friends, the Mollers, when he arranged
his meeting with Kenon for the next day. He realised
that they lived a long way off, and that it might con-
ceivably be difficult to get back punctually. But he
comforted himself with the thought that the Mollers
were sending their car in very early in the morning.
No doubt they would send him back in good time.
He said aloud: " Oh, thank you, Mr. Rothman. I
was expecting the message."

While they stood talking, a car drove up to the
hotel. As the driver stepped out of it, van Bredepoel
recognised instantly the motorist who had taken
such a strange interest in him the night of his arrival.
At supper this man sat alone, at a table opposite van

Bredepoel's. He often paused over his food to look very intently at van Bredepoel, and once or twice smiled to himself with the sort of disdain a person feels for people he is accustomed to outwit. Yet van Bredepoel was surprised when the man, on his way out, stopped behind his chair and said sarcastically: " So you've given up your lonely walks on the Esplanade at Port Benjamin, Master van Bredepoel!"

Van Bredepoel turned round quickly to reply, but the man was already half-way out of the room. The uneasiness he had felt the night of his arrival instantly returned, and after supper he stopped the proprietor in the corridor to question him about the motorist.

" The fellow with the waxed military moustache ? " Rothman asked.

" Yes."

" Oh! That's Major Atkins of the Criminal Investigation Department."

" A detective ? " There was both consternation and disgust in van Bredepoel's tone.

" Yes. Head of the Native Affairs Section, I believe. He's been here a great deal lately. A charming gent. Would you like to meet him ? "

" No, thank you very much."

" But he'll be at the club to-night; surely you are coming ? "

" No; I have some letters to write, and as you know, I have to be off early to see the Mollers to-morrow."

" Oh, come on, Mr. van Bredepoel, we'll have just one short quick one."

" No, thank you, Mr. Rothman."

He said good night; but it was a long time before

he could write.   He was still uneasy and rather
upset.

"A detective," he thought.   "What on earth can
he want with me ?   And why should he be so
interested in my movements ? "

He could think of no reason, no reason at all. Why
detectives should have followed him round on his
innocent walks at night on the Esplanade at Port
Benjamin he could not imagine.   "There must be
a mistake," he told himself, but the thought did not
give him much comfort.

CHAPTER IV

At half-past seven the Mollers' car called for him.
Although it was early when they turned into a
country road outside the town, the sun already held
overhead the threat of an exceptionally hot day.
Every half-mile or so ahead of the car lay a small
mirage, a quicksilver pool, which receded as fast
as they approached. The mountains were almost
invisible behind a heat mist of a shining Chinese
white. Even the vegetation in which Paulstad
wrapped itself behind them went a dirty grey
colour. Whenever he looked backwards he saw
between them and the town a long plume of dust
which unfolded itself slowly over the road. Far
away over the other roads which circled the mountain slopes, hung similar plumes of dust. Over their
heads the sky was a pale blue, but on the horizon,
over the mountain tops, it had already begun to
change into that sulphur-yellow van Bredepoel now
knew so well. The flocks of sheep they passed were
painfully thin and lifeless, and even at this early
hour the weakest sheep formed little groups and
stood there, dumb, panting, their eyes fixed on the
ground, their heads in one another's shade. There
was something terrible in the despair of these
animals, their utter subjection to this caprice of
Nature. They met even the butcher's knife without
a struggle, he reflected; their behaviour then

271

showed only how well they had learned this lesson
of their essential defencelessness.

Yet when he mentioned the sheep to the coloured
chauffeur the man replied:

" It is not too bad here, seur, no, seur. You should
see the sheep in Bambuland."

Long before they arrived at " Donkerhoek," the
Mollers' farm, his eyes were so pained by the dry,
trembling air that he no longer cared to look about
him, and for a time sat with closed eyes next to the
driver.

" There is ' Donkerhoek,' seur," the driver
remarked suddenly.

He sat up and looked out. They were circling
along the slope of one of the foothills of the Donkerberg Range. About ten miles farther ahead the
range ended abruptly in the sea. They were already
so high up the mountain slopes that an enormous
stretch of water, smooth and oily and of a dazzling
copper colour, bursting into explosions of white
along the rocky shore, came within their view. High
over them hung the dark forest-covered flanks of the
range, vibrating with light in some parts, gloomy
with shadow in others. Behind them the country
was a deep brick-red, irregularly blackened with
vegetation, herds of cattle casting listless clouds of
dust over it, while overhead flocks of crows and
vultures wheeled and turned rhythmically, measur-
ing depth beyond depth in the well of the sky. And
far below them, leaning against the slope of a hill,
appeared, disappeared and reappeared in the midst
of a plantation of oaks the walls of a substantial
house, so white it hurt the eyes to look at it. In a

few minutes they were driving up a long avenue, down a tunnel of shadow on which the sky lay like light on water.

A great heaviness fell from van Bredepoel. He walked with unusual pleasure into the Mollers' cool and shuttered home. There the welcome they gave him made him forget for the time his disquiet and fatigue. The whole family, the father, mother, daughter and three sons, pleased him greatly. He liked the obvious pride the parents took in the children, and the affectionately truculent attitude the children showed towards them. He felt that it was a family in which you would never be able to deal with one member without taking into consideration all the others, that all six of them were only cells of one unit. It did not occur to him that the children might perhaps find such a unity irksome, for wasn't that one of the things his own life had lacked? He liked, too, the European atmosphere of the home, the German tapestries and engravings on the walls, and before he was there long the mother showed him with great pride a passage laid out with German tiles.

" We brought those with us from Germany," she told him, pointing at the passage floor. The tiles his aunt had brought with her from Holland, he remembered, were very like these.

" Yes," said one of the sons, " do you know, she is so proud of them that she will never let a servant touch the passage floor. She polishes it herself every morning. At her age, too! It's a disgrace! "

In the morning he was shown round the farm, in which he saw much to admire, above all the careful,

elaborate and neat organisation. At lunch time they
had their meal on an old-fashioned Dutch stoep,
sheltered above only by some old creeper-vines
through which large patches of sunlight fell and
burst round all the silver and food in a mist of
luminous gold. He thought then that he had never
seen wine so red nor tasted food so good. So near
the sea was the house that, during the meal, they
saw far out on the horizon a liner fling its smoke like
a mirage of palm-trees into the sky. For a moment,
when van Bredepoel saw it, his disquietude returned
to him. He was reminded that Messrs. Steyn,
Berger and Stumpfkopf would be expecting him
back in some three weeks' time, and that he had not
yet decided what to do. Suddenly he found himself
listening very eagerly to something one of the
Moller boys was saying.

" I hear, father," he said, " that Strang is selling
out."

" And who told you that ? " the old man asked
like one who is accustomed to take all he hears with
the utmost reserve.

" I met Johnson at the Driefontein fence this
morning, and he told me," the boy answered.

" And what was Johnson doing at the Driefontein fence at that time of the day ? "

" He was out mending his side of the fence, with
three of his natives."

" About time too," the old man said, and added:
" Johnson ought to know, seeing that he's Strang's
neighbour."

" Yes, he said that Strang had already placed the
farm into auctioneer's hands. He did not say so,

but I suspect from the way he talked that Strang can't help himself."

" I'm not surprised," exclaimed the old man. " The way that fellow farms! He thinks of nothing but polo ponies. Why the devil did he come all this way to play polo ? He could have done that better in Europe. And such a good place he has got, too. If I had the money, I would buy it straight away. If only you children did not cost me so much! "

" Oh, come on, father," the boy said, " don't grumble so much. You'd have to pay someone else if you didn't pay us."

" Not so much," replied the old man, not without bitterness.

" Will it cost very much, that farm ? " van Bredepoel asked, feeling a great longing.

" Ach, I don't think so," the old man said. " Strang must sell, apparently, and there aren't many buyers about with this drought on. He hasn't done much to the property either, except to build some very fine stables for his horses. I wouldn't mind living in them myself. But he has brought very little new land under cultivation; besides, it's a very small farm, though very good."

" You don't know where I could find out about it ? " he asked.

The whole family turned to look at him with a new interest, particularly the mother, who was thinking of her daughter.

" Excuse me, Mr. van Bredepoel," the old man said bluntly, reading van Bredepoel's motive at once, " but what do you know about farming ? "

" I was brought up on a farm," he replied.

" Well, you couldn't do better for a start than take that place. I don't say that because I want you as a neighbour, the fewer neighbours I have the better I like it, but because Strang's place, with a little trouble, could be made into anything." The old man turned to his son: " Hans, do you know who's handling it ? "

" I'm not sure, father, but I think Johnson said Brand's got it."

" I don't know whether I can buy it, or really want it, but I'm very interested," van Bredepoel told them.

The old man looked at him intently for a minute, and then said, with a firmness and a conviction that made van Bredepoel feel ashamed of his own indecision: " You'll buy all right, Mr. van Bredepoel."

For a few minutes they were all silent. The old man seemed to look at van Bredepoel as if he were already one of the family. He began speaking to him like a father talking to one of his own sons.

" Only don't make as that fellow Strang has done. He came here not to farm but to play at being a country gentleman. He was not at rest until he had riding-horses for his whole family, and in the end the horses ate him out of his farm. He always had headaches, that fellow, and swallowed a ton of aspirins in the time he was here. I've never had a headache in my life, but I work. You must do the same."

It was nearly five before van Bredepoel could get away. He protested in vain that he had an appointment in Paulstad at six, but they all assured him that

the car could get him back in a little under an hour.
When he came out of the house to go away, he saw
the old man, his white hair shining in the sun,
shaking his stick at the chauffeur and shouting:

" How many times, creature, have I told you that
you're not to travel without that spare tyre ? "

" I know, master," the man replied, " but the
people in the garage couldn't vulcanise it in time,
and it needed vulcanising badly, so I left it until this
afternoon."

" If the baas is late, you'll be sorry for yourself
to-night, creature! "

" He won't be late, master," the man said.

" So much the better for you! " exclaimed the old
man. He went slowly round the car, examining the
paint-work with great care. He seemed to know
every scratch on it, and when he found one he did
not recognise burst out into a new tirade.

When van Bredepoel said good-bye to him, adding
that he hoped it would rain soon, he did not reply
immediately. He looked round the sky carefully,
and then said: " Two days before or two days after
the moon, my father taught me. In two days it will
rain. Your farm will be just right for you when you
trek in, Mr. van Bredepoel."

On the way back, the chauffeur said to van
Bredepoel:

" My master's words are always strong, seur, but
he's a dear master. I love him, and just you wait,
seur, he's never wrong. In two days it will rain.
Yes, seur, his words are strong, but his deeds are
good."

But a few minutes later the chauffeur's face was

seriously agitated, as there came a loud explosion from the back of the car, which began to bump violently over the road. His disbelief in his master's strong words was not perhaps so firm after all.

The clock struck half-past seven as they entered Paulstad. At the hotel there was no sign of Kenon. Van Bredepoel questioned the servants; they could not or would not tell him anything. In the dining-room he saw the proprietor with his family at table. He walked over to him, and in spite of his anxiety to know if Kenon had turned up in his absence and had asked for him, noticed immediately a marked coldness in the proprietor's attitude, a strict and formal politeness which at that time of the evening was as foreign to Rothman as surliness in the mornings was natural.

" Do you know if a native called here for me this afternoon ? " van Bredepoel asked.

" Yes, a native did ask for you, I think," the proprietor said, after some hesitation.

" He didn't wait ? "

" No, he didn't wait, Mr. van Bredepoel."

" Do you know if he left a message for me ? "

" No, he did not leave a message, Mr. van Bredepoel."

" You don't happen to know why he didn't wait ? "

The proprietor's tone suddenly became aggressive.

" I told him I wouldn't have any street loafers hanging round the hotel," he said.

" He came here at my wish," replied van Bredepoel.

" The fellow is a notorious gaol-bird and beggar,

and I frankly didn't believe him when he told me you had arranged to see him. I thought it was just another begging trick. Still, if I had known he was —er—a friend of yours, I would not, of course, have sent him away."

The proprietor reddened over his effort to insert the word "friend" in his reply. Van Bredepoel controlled himself with difficulty. He thought there was more in the proprietor's explanation than he pretended. There was only one more question he could usefully ask.

"You don't know where he has gone to, or where I could get into touch with him?"

"I don't know where you could get into touch with him, Mr. van Bredepoel," the proprietor replied.

"Thank you," van Bredepoel said curtly and walked away to his table.

"At your service, Mr. van Bredepoel," the proprietor called out after him.

Van Bredepoel arrived at his table just as the detective prepared to leave his. He had hardly opened his napkin when he heard the detective's voice behind him.

"So you're expecting your friend Burgess," Major Atkins said. "If you're wise the two of you will keep out of this town." And as on the previous night, he was gone before van Bredepoel could reply.

"Really, I shall leave, if this sort of thing goes on much longer," van Bredepoel thought. But in one way the detective's words calmed him. Here at last was the explanation of the man's behaviour; the detective was concerned with him, he felt, only

in so far as he was associated with Burgess. But was
Burgess really coming to Paulstad ? He himself did
not know, for he had not seen Burgess since his
illness and his letters had not yet received any
reply—a fact which did not alarm him. He knew
Burgess would be too busy on his propaganda tour
to have much time for writing. He wondered
whether the detective's presence at the hotel did
not also explain the change in the proprietor's
attitude to him. Probably he had told Rothman
that van Bredepoel was the friend of a notorious
agitator, and this accounted for his rudeness to both
van Bredepoel and Kenon. He thought he was
beginning to see more light. There was only one
thing that still puzzled him completely: the
proprietor's statement that Kenon was a notorious
gaol-bird and beggar. It suddenly occurred to him
that if there was any truth in the statement, no doubt
the magistrate must know something about Kenon.
He decided to go to the Club after supper, in the
hope of finding him there.

After supper he met Rothman outside, but this
time the proprietor passed him with a very detached
air and did not invite him to have a drink.

" The trip to Masakama's Drift is off," van
Bredepoel thought, and went to his room to write
Burgess a long letter telling him what had taken
place.

He had not been there long when someone knocked
quietly on the door.

" Come in," he called out, but as no one opened
the door he got up and opened it himself. Before
him stood the proprietor's wife, the hotel keys

dangling at her side, her knitting in one hand and in the other a small green bottle.

" I'm sorry to disturb you," she said, looking at him with steady, friendly eyes. " But I want to know if you're feeling well, Mr. van Bredepoel."

" I'm quite well, thank you, Mrs. Rothman. Won't you come in ? " he asked, and stood aside.

She shook her head.

" You don't look well. I saw to-night at dinner you weren't well. So I've brought you this small bottle of 'Life's Essence.' It has seen my mother and myself through many illnesses, and you won't regret taking it. Please try it. Three drops in half a glass of water, three times a day."

" Thank you, Mrs. Rothman." He took the bottle.

" Happy, very happy, to be of service to you, Mr. van Bredepoel."

She walked on slowly down the corridor. Van Bredepoel watched her go. He knew that it was not so much the medicine she wanted to give him as to dissociate herself from her husband's action. When she reached the top of the stairs she stood still, one hand on the banisters, and called back without turning round :

" Three drops of essence in half a glass of water, three times a day. You won't forget, Mr. van Bredepoel ? "

" How on earth did she know I was watching her," van Bredepoel thought, and went back to his writing.

The clock in the passage of the hotel struck half-past nine when he opened the door of the Royal Paulstad Club. As he walked in, he heard someone say: " There'll be trouble if he comes here. The place is full of discontented unemployed niggers." He closed the door behind him quietly, and saw a group of men talking round the bar, their backs to him. In their midst was Major Atkins and the proprietor, who was waving his hands wildly about. On one side, away from the group, the magistrate was seated in a deep arm-chair, smoking a pipe, a light, ironical smile on his lips. He nodded slightly to van Bredepoel as he came in, but the others did not see him immediately. Van Bredepoel liked the magistrate's position, there apart from the others. It seemed that he was not only sitting away from them, but was also separate from them in spirit.

While he stood there at the door, hesitating what to do, a wealthy farmer called van Copenhagen began speaking with great energy. Van Bredepoel had met him before and had been told by Brand that he was an incorrigible liar and boaster, only respected for his wealth and his capacity for standing strong drink.

" He'll be put against a wall before he can shay ' mama,' " van Copenhagen was saying. " We don't shtand any nonshenshe in Paulshtad."

Atkins was on the point of replying, when he saw van Bredepoel and stopped in confusion. The others, noticing his confusion, looked round and were embarrassed in their turn, particularly the proprietor.

It was obvious to van Bredepoel that they had been discussing both him and Burgess. For a few moments no one said a word, feeling perhaps that any action of friendliness on his part now would be too obvious a contradiction of the sentiments he had been expressing a minute before. Only Brand, to van Bredepoel's surprise, detached himself from the group and came towards him with an outstretched hand.

" I'm so glad you have come, van Bredepoel," he said, greeting him. " Atkins. . . ."

He did not get farther because someone shouted " Oh! shut up! Reddy! "

" . . . Atkins," said Brand, ignoring the interruption, " has been trying to persuade us that you are a desperate Bolshie, determined to disturb the peace in Paulstad. If I hadn't known you, I would have pictured you from his description as dirty, bearded, and with a couple of Mills' bombs in each pocket."

" Oh, come on, Brand, don't exaggerate," Atkins called out.

" You aren't going back on what you said ? " Brand looked at him as if to say: " I might have thought so."

" No, but you needn't turn my words like that. Why not repeat exactly what I said," Atkins replied.

" You can do that for yourself." Brand turned his back on Atkins. " What will you have to drink, van Bredepoel ? "

" Ask van Bredepoel himself if he isn't this fellow Burgess' closest friend ? Ask him if they aren't both well known to the police ? " Atkins went on.

" Police ? " Brand feigned surprise. " I thought you were a detective. In any case I'm not interested; you can ask him yourself."

" He's right, Mr. Brand," van Bredepoel said, speaking only to Brand. " I am a friend of Burgess."

He knew he could honestly have added that he did not necessarily share Burgess' political convictions.

" Well, what does it matter, anyway ? " exclaimed Brand, " you aren't a political agitator, are you ?"

" No, I'm not," replied van Bredepoel.

"Mr. van Bredepoel was very disappointed not to find his native friend here this evening," said the proprietor, for the first time taking part in the conversation.

His words were followed by a loud crash. Van Copenhagen had banged his glass down on the bar counter and came swaying slowly over to van Bredepoel.

" Look here, young fellow," he said when he came up to him, " thish ish no plashe for nigger kishersh. We won't shtand for any mucking around with our nativesh. If you try anything of the kind, we'll run you out of town, perhapsh worsh, yesh, worsh. And look here, don't you go and shtick any more poshtersh round about thish town."

" He's drunk, van Bredepoel," Brand said. " They're all drunk, except me and Mags there. Don't take any notice. What'll you have to drink ? "

" Nothing, thank you very much, Mr. Brand, I'm just going," van Bredepoel replied. He was turning towards the door, when Atkins' voice stopped him.

" I'm not here to-night officially," he said, " but speaking unofficially. . . ."

" I can't imagine you being unofficially anywhere, Atkins," interrupted the magistrate, who had risen slowly from his chair and was speaking very evenly and very deliberately. Then reaching for his stick and hat, he looked at van Bredepoel and said in the same slow, even voice: " If you'll just wait a minute, Mr. van Bredepoel, I'll come with you."

As the door closed behind them they heard: " Birdsh of a feavver. . . ."

But van Bredepoel forgot to ask the magistrate about Kenon. His thoughts had for the moment taken a new direction. As he lay in his bed that night he asked himself: " Sticking posters round about this town! What on earth did that fellow mean ? "

CHAPTER V

VAN BREDEPOEL was up early the next morning. He had hardly slept during the night. He woke up thinking of Kenon. He knew how much importance black people attach to the keeping of a promise, and he feared that Kenon might have thought his absence deliberate. He suspected, too, that after what Mrs. Harris had told Kenon he would have a tendency, in spite of himself, to doubt van Bredepoel's word. Furthermore, van Bredepoel did not know what the proprietor had said to Kenon. Was it inconceivable that Rothman, repeating perhaps Mrs. Harris' very words, had told Kenon that van Bredepoel did not want to see him? His only hope was to seek out the magistrate. If Kenon had been sentenced by him, as the proprietor implied, he might be able to help van Bredepoel to trace him.

When he came out into the streets, he found that while he had been away the previous day someone had stuck a great number of posters on to hoardings, lamp-posts and trees. One glance at these left him in no doubt that they were the work of Burgess' organisation. On each one was a reproduction of the design he had first seen years ago in Burgess' office. In the corner was painted by hand the notice of a meeting to be held in the native quarters of Paulstad the following day. When he saw the date of the meeting, November 6th, he realised with a

shock that it was the anniversary of the final victory
of the early Dutch Trekkers over the Bambuxosa
nation. It seemed to him that whoever was holding
that meeting could not have chosen, from a propa-
gandist's point of view, a better time. He knew that
this anniversary, observed for nearly a hundred
years, made the whole country acutely conscious
of the wide gulf fixed between white and black;
made it conscious, moreover, in the most dangerous
way, by reviving in the white people all the pride
which they felt in the victory of their forerunners,
and in the natives all the shame of their defeat.
And as the conflict, which nearly a hundred years
ago had made a quiet country brook run red with
blood, was by no means ended but had only been
transformed into a long, dreary and unequal
political and economic fight, this celebration revived
a hatred inflamed both by tradition and everyday
reality. It was an anniversary celebrated not
merely by the people of the old republics, who had
gained that victory, but by all the white people in
the country. It was to the black man both the
celebration of the victory of the white man over a
branch of the black race, and a bitter reminder of
the subjection of all. Van Bredepoel knew that on
that anniversary, in the midst of all the bitterness
and distrust the white and the black people felt for
one another, would surge up, with all the pressure
of the past behind it, the sense of a blood conflict.
On that day, more than on any other, people would
be inclined to say: "I am white," or "I am black."
And all the misgivings the sight of those black
letters "November 6th" aroused in him were

sharpened when he remembered the detective's
warning, coupled with the words of a swaggering
drunkard uttered the night before. Had he known
where to find Burgess, if it was Burgess, he would
have set off there and then to persuade him not to
hold that meeting.

It was in the vague hope that he might be able to
discover news of Burgess that he went to buy, for
the first time since his arrival in Paulstad, some
newspapers. He bought not only that morning's
but all the papers published during the last fortnight. In one of the oldest of these he read an
account of a violent discussion in the Houses of
Parliament at Port Benjamin. A new Bill had been
introduced by the Minister of Justice, asking for
" extraordinary and arbitrary powers " for his
department to deal with " political agitators," but
it had met with a very strong opposition on the
grounds that nothing in the state of the country
justified it. In the end the Minister of Justice had
agreed to a postponement of the debate until the
New Year, " after which time, he hoped to place
before the House sufficient evidence to convince it
of the grave urgency and necessity of the measure,"
apart from the fact that the subject naturally
interested him, the report made no deep impression
on van Bredepoel at the time. It was an obscure
back page of another newspaper that gave him some
indication of what he wanted. He read there that,
two days ago, the municipality of Port Duncan, which
was only thirty miles from Paulstad, had refused to
allow a " notorious communist and agitator to hold
a meeting in any of the buildings and public places

under its control." He felt intuitively that the
"notorious communist" must be Burgess, that—
alas!—Burgess was coming to Paulstad, might be
there even at that moment.

In the afternoon, on his way to see the magistrate,
he passed Brand's office and decided to go in and ask
him for information about Strang's farm. Brand,
unusually pale and blear-eyed, was sitting uncom-
fortably behind his desk, wiping incessantly at his
face with a large red silk handkerchief. The attorney
immediately began a long apology for van Bredepoel's hostile reception at the Club the night
before.

"They're not bad fellows," he concluded, "but
they were so soused that that tick Atkins, whom
nobody likes here, worked them up quite easily. I
hope you'll forget about it and come again."

"I'm very grateful to you, Mr. Brand," van
Bredepoel replied. "But I didn't come to see you
about that. I wondered if you could give me any
information about the sale of Strang's farm?"

Brand instantly became very alive. "I can tell
you everything you want to know. I've been
authorised to put it up for sale. Say, come along
to the Club, and we'll discuss it over a glass of
whisky."

"Thank you, but I would rather discuss it here,"
van Bredepoel told him.

"A pity, but if you wish it, here we go," Brand
said. "Strang wants to sell. I don't mind admitting
he has got to sell. If you want a good place cheap,
here's your chance. It's one of the best places for
its size in the district. It has. . . ."

He was about to go into a long description of the farm, when van Bredepoel interrupted.

" I saw the Mollers yesterday, and they gave me all that sort of information. What I want to discuss with you chiefly is the question of the price. What is the least Strang will take ? "

" He is prepared to take a good offer for two-thirds in cash, the rest in five instalments paid yearly."

" What do you call a good offer ? "

Brand laughed and hesitated.

" That depends," he said, " but will £3,500 be too much for you to pay ? "

" It is too much for me. I think I could, at a pinch, pay you £1,500 in cash, and an equal sum in five years."

" I shall have to discuss that with Strang, but I will, if you like, give you the option of a first refusal on the property."

Van Bredepoel agreed to that, and went away. He had no doubt that the little money he had saved, together with a sum his aunt had left him on her death, would enable him to buy the property. But he was cautious. He wanted time to think it over. Great as his reluctance was to go back to Port Benjamin, the revolution in his life that buying the farm would involve was obviously so big that he hesitated. Yet he suspected that his hesitation was only a rational formality, that in the end he would buy the farm. He arrived at the Magistrate's Court just after the afternoon session was over. At the entrance were two policemen marshalling a group of handcuffed black men, but in the building no one was about. He walked down a corridor until he came to a door marked " Magistrate," knocked and went in. The magistrate was at his desk writing, the scraping of his pen filled the room. The light against the window was a brilliant yellow, framed in the window panes; the red surface of Paulstad's Main Street was just visible, shining with heat and wrapped in the silence of that placid afternoon.

" Sit down, won't you, Mr. van Bredepoel. I shan't keep you a minute."

The voice was friendly, low and cultured, the room neat and orderly, the harshness of the early summer light mellowed by the sombre colours of immense racks of law books and official records. Somewhere just outside children were playing, and forgetful that night would soon fall on their games added happiness to the peace of the day.

" Well, Mr. van Bredepoel, is there anything I can do for you ? " The magistrate had finished writing, and was looking intently at van Bredepoel.

Briefly he explained what he wanted. The magistrate heard him in a silence which needed no words. Then he said:

" If that boy's a criminal, we're sure to have his record here. I don't recollect his name offhand, but we shall soon see. Atkins, by the way, gave us quite another interpretation of your interest in the boy last night."

He stood up and walked over to a book-rack.

" What is his name again ? Kenon Badiakgotla ? " he asked, and as van Bredepoel nodded drew out a large yellow file and brought it to his desk, where he turned over its index slowly, stopping every now and then to wipe his hands with a quick fastidious gesture.

" You know, Mr. van Bredepoel," he said, while he went through the index, " to anyone who knows anything about the black people there is part of their history just in these names here. I remember when I first came to Paulstad as a magistrate's clerk— it wasn't long after the Boer War—how thrilled I was by the names of the native criminals here; I say criminals, but for the most part they were people given criminal punishment for civil offences such as breaking the Pass Law and failing to pay their hut tax. You see, I hadn't been out from England long, so you can imagine how struck I was by names like—" he paused and ran his fingers down the index—" like Bwakabana, Linchwe, Kwabozayo, Ndlhambi, Xolilizwe. Then I went away. Some years later I came back as magistrate, and one of the first things I noticed was that in the index the names I had liked so much were very rare, the crimes much more serious. I was faced daily instead with an ever-growing number of Aprils, Februaries, Januaries, White-Boys, Grey-Boys, Samuels, Daniels, Josephs."

The magistrate stopped suddenly: " There is a Joseph Badiakgotla here. Is it. . . ."

" It is," van Bredepoel confirmed.

The magistrate pressed the two sides of the file down, and smoothing the pages over with his hands said: " Well, I regret very much that here are one, two, three, seven convictions against his name. I remember the case quite well now. All seven convictions for smoking insangu. Yes, I remember it

very well. So that's the boy. Do you know, he
interested me very much. His employers all gave
him excellent records. They all praised his honesty,
but they all stressed this one failing: he could not
keep away from insangu. I don't know if you know
that drug—the hashish to which we owe the word
assassin. It is a terrible thing once it gets hold of
one, and more terrible still, as I have so often seen
here, because it gets hold of natures that are in many
ways better than the average. This boy, for instance,
always appeared to me more intelligent than the
natives who usually come before me, but he seemed
very highly strung. I had the impression that inside
himself he had got terribly tied up, and didn't know
how to straighten his nature out again. I suspected
that he felt very keenly something had gone wrong
with him. He never tried seriously to hide his guilt.
I think he was so divided between a sense of something having gone wrong and an inability to understand even the sources of his trouble that he lost the
will to fight himself, and attempted instead to forget.
I say this, because the first time he came before me I
had a long talk with him, and let him off lightly. He
kept away for about a year, but after that he came
back again and again, and each time I had to increase
his sentence. The last time, indeed, I increased it
considerably. I had no option, for the drug had
begun to make him violent. He assaulted his
employer, who caught him smoking insangu, and I
had to give him a year and a half. The next time,
I'm afraid there will be a next time, it will be two
years. He is the sort of type insangu never leaves at
rest again. And he isn't the only one. This file is

full of the names of others like him, and I have only
to shut my eyes to see a procession, twelve years long,
of others, and the procession grows and grows each
year. I have often asked myself what is the use of
sentencing people like that, when the conditions
which drive them to it still exist, but in the court I
am a magistrate, not a man. Thin comfort it is to
me. To-day these things are bad, to-morrow they'll
be worse. . . ."

" Still, I should like to find him again, if it's
possible," van Bredepoel said, and added, more to
himself than to the magistrate: " I feel in some way
responsible. If there was anyone who could have
helped him years ago and prevented this, it was I.
But I didn't know, and I couldn't foresee. Couldn't
you help me to trace him ? "

" I can't, I'm sorry, but the police might. Look,
I'll give you a letter right now to the Colonel of the
Police. If anyone can help you he can, and he will
be only too willing to try. He's a very, very good
sort."

The police headquarters at Paulstad are situated
right on the southern limit of the town, at the end
of a street which divides the native and coloured
quarters from the houses of the white people. It is
a long double-storied building. Its walls are covered
with a white plaster made out of a mixture of
cement and well-crushed gravel. It is the one
building in Paulstad which has a red-tiled roof, and
on an afternoon like this the sunlight on the red
tiles and rough white walls is so strong, vibrates so
consistently, that it is almost more than eyes can
bear to look at it long. Behind this building is a

large square parade-ground, covered with a gravel
which is at once green and blue, and which glitters
like a field sown with crystal. It is shut in on one
side by the main building itself, and, on the two
sides which run at right angles to the offices, by a
barbed-wire fence and two rows of a giant species of
aloe. The leaves of the aloes at a distance have the
same colour as the gravel, but at closer quarters one
finds that they are blue, striped with yellow and run
into a long purple thorn. From the centre of the
leaves there soars with the curve of a sky-rocket a
long yellow stem which bursts in the austere air into
a branch of gold blossoms. Both these lanes of aloe
lead from the main building to a single low-storied
barracks, where the unmarried policemen have their
quarters. Almost always one sees in this parade-
ground groups of tattered and shackled natives
trying to find some shade against the aloes while
passing constantly from one building to the other
are young policemen whose spurs and leggings rival
the glitter of the gravel. One sees almost always, too,
a group of saddle-horses held by a black constable,
whose surroundings have made him desperately
grave. As one enters the police station one finds
oneself grave also. One feels that it has been forbidden to laugh there; the atmosphere is not unlike
that of a Protestant church.

Van Bredepoel showed the magistrate's letter to a
uniformed clerk. The handwriting on the envelope
appeared well known to the clerk, for the moment
he saw it he gave van Bredepoel some directions and
told him to announce himself to the Colonel. Van
Bredepoel climbed up a concrete staircase and at the

end of a long corridor came to a door, made partly
of wood and of a thick white painted glass. On the
door were the words: " District Officer Commanding." He was on the point of knocking when the
sound of voices inside stopped him. Two gesticulating silhouettes were thrown on to the glass in front
of him. He decided to wait until the Colonel was
alone. He was about to begin pacing up and down
the corridor, when something familiar in one of the
voices made him lean forward to listen. In a few
moments he realised that it was Atkins' confident
voice addressing the Colonel, almost angrily.

" There's no danger," he heard Atkins say, very
emphatically. " The three of them were caught
smoking the stuff red-handed. They've all been
convicted for the same offence umpteen times. They
know that next time they come before the magistrate it will be three years or nothing. Isn't that
so ? "

" Yes," the other silhouette replied.

" Very well, then. If they know that by doing
what they are told to do, and keeping their mouths
shut afterwards, they will get off scot-free, they'll
keep their mouths shut, and do what they are told.
Besides, we're not asking them to do anything so
very outrageous! "

" We ? "

" All right, me if you wish it. All I want them to
do is to walk about the place with three useless old
carbines. There's nothing so very outrageous about
that, is there ? "

" I told you before that I don't like it, and the
more I hear you talk about it the less I like it. I'm

only a policeman. My job is to prevent trouble, not to make it. What the hell are you after anyway ? "

The Colonel's silhouette disappeared from the door. Van Bredepoel heard him pacing up and down the room.

" I told you before," Atkins resumed, " I just want to make an excuse for breaking up the meeting. You know very well how the damned law ties our hands on these occasions."

" I know that. But it doesn't seem to me a sufficient reason. There have always been these meetings. Must they all be broken up in this way ? "

" Well, those are my instructions from head-quarters. If there's anything behind it I'm not supposed to know, that is, not officially, of course. If I was sure, I'd tell you. But you know the rule— think, but don't say what you like."

" Still, I think I would like to consult the magis-trate about it first, Atkins. If he consents, I'll feel safer."

" You'll do nothing of the kind, I regret. Here are my instructions. They're all that concern you. If you like you can get through to headquarters on the telephone and ask the Chief himself. You are not under the magistrate, and I have orders not to drag that softy into this."

" All right, then, all right! But you'll give me a statement in writing, please, and before two witnesses, and you'll include in it a note to the effect that I take the strongest possible exception to your action."

" I'll do that with pleasure. But you know you're not doing yourself any good, Colonel."

" I'm a policeman, not a detective."

Van Bredepoel marvelled at the scorn the Colonel
put into that word " detective."

" Well, it's settled then. You'll see that it's all
arranged ? They must be at van Zyl's Corner at
2.45 to-morrow afternoon at the latest. I'll call
early to-morrow morning to make my statement,
and please see that the witnesses are men you can
trust."

Atkins rose to go. Van Bredepoel quickly turned
and ran down the corridor. He had only one wish
—not to meet the detective at the door of the
Colonel's office, indeed not to meet him anywhere
at all. The affair of Kenon could wait a day or two.
He wanted to get away to think over what he had
learned alone, to calm the disquietude which the
events of the last three days could not have aroused
more thoroughly if they had been designed for that
purpose. To the clerk who called out to ask him
if he had seen the Colonel he replied briefly that he
was engaged, and hurried out into the street.

But instead of returning to the hotel he took a
road that led away from the town and in the
distance circled the slopes of the mountains. He had
not heard enough to grasp the detective's plan fully,
but enough to understand that he meant to break
up Burgess' meeting the next day. How three
criminals armed with old rifles could give the
detective the pretext he wanted was not clear to van
Bredepoel, but the more he turned things over in his
mind the stronger grew his foreboding of disaster.
He went over all the fears and the reasons for those
fears he had felt in the morning, when he first saw a

zinc hoarding covered with posters of the African
Workers' Union. It was most strange that one of the
heads of the Criminal Investigation Department
should be sent to an obscure village to break up an
agitator's meeting. Surely a minor detective could
have done that equally well. Was it because Paulstad was on the borders of Bambuland ? He remembered that even the Colonel, who knew more than
he himself did, had not found Atkins' explanation
satisfactory, that the detective himself had hinted
at a bigger motive. No explanation occurred to
him. He could only decide to do his utmost to
find Burgess and persuade him not to hold the
meeting.

He sat on a stone at the side of the road for a long
time. He saw a tall native followed by three of his
wives and two daughters pass by him. The native
walked alone in front; he had a large black and
white blanket wrapped round him like the toga of a
Roman senator, and bore himself with immense
dignity. As he walked along he smoked a long pipe,
and the copper bangles round his wrists and ankles
flashed in the late afternoon sun. His wives and
daughters carried on their heads large bundles of
goods, and as they passed van Bredepoel looked
modestly on the ground. He was amazed by the
sensitiveness of feeling that showed in their faces,
the heavy grace with which they walked. Once they
had passed him, their bodies were between him and
the sun, and the dust raised by their feet spread
around them a halo of gold. They looked then like
the figures on the wall of an Egyptian tomb; so
might have looked the handmaidens of Pharaoh

when they walked down to the Nile for their evening bathe. They walked slowly along the road which led to Masakama's Drift, and that luminous mist of dust which gathered round them seemed to him a symbol of all the mystery and attraction that unknown Africa held for him. He wished now that he could shed his way of living, like a suit of old clothes, and be walking in the evenings as calmly as they, on just such a road, whose course seemed to be set into the sun.

While he sat there the sun went down. Once more it turned red as blood, but before it went down, before its lowest rim touched the horizon of distant mountains, there spread slowly over its surface, like a stain of ink, the peak of a thunder-cloud, poised far away over the shrinking interior of Bambuland. And he found himself recalling quite involuntarily the words of a little boy: " Sarah says when the sun is like that, something terrible always happens," and the mother's reply: " Sarah is only an ignorant black woman."

As he turned back towards Paulstad the smoke hung reluctantly over the house-tops, and a tide of blue shadows, broken by patches of yellow light, ebbed heavily over the town. Quickly the sky in the west turned yellow, and he felt on his face the first slight movement of the evening breeze. Over the downs, from the direction of the sea, the first clouds of mist came, elongated and low, speeding towards the town. Behind him he heard for a long time the cries of the commando birds, bemoaning their twilight existence. But in the end all was quiet and at peace, except he with himself.

At the police station, instead of taking the road by which he had come he turned into one leading through the native and coloured quarters. He had not walked far and was passing a house larger and more imposing than the rest, when the sight of two men talking in its doorway made him stop. Both were outlined against the glow of lamplight in the room behind; there seemed to hang over them the mystery of an El Greco picture. One was in shirt-sleeves and, judging by the sound of his voice, a coloured man; the other was very tall, his shoulders bent forward, his hands accompanying his words with many a restless and awkward gesture. Was it Burgess? He decided to wait, and leant over the little wooden gate that led into the garden in front of the house. When the door was at last shut, the tall man came walking towards the gate, whistling cheerfully.

" Burgess! " van Bredepoel called, as he came near.

" Van Bredepoel! You're not dead then! "

" You didn't get my letters ? "

" Not one. Did you write ? But I've travelled. God knows where I haven't travelled since I saw you last. And, I tell you, the great day is near."

" I know you've travelled, but I've been expecting you. I was only afraid you would be gone before I found you."

" Expecting me ? What made you expect me ? "

" Come with me." Van Bredepoel took him by the arm. " It's a long story, but I'm so glad I've found you. It's my first real stroke of luck for many days. Come on, I've got a lot to tell you and you've got a lot to do."

Farther along they found an old bench at the side of the street and sat down. It seemed to van Brede-poel that never had the night been as black as now. He wished he could see Burgess' face and measure the effect of his words, but he could only make out a dim shape against the half-light of a neighbouring window. The houses spread around them a peaceful, domestic murmur. Burgess listened without interruption to what van Bredepoel had to tell him, and then asked:

" But what do you expect me to do ? "

" Don't hold this meeting to-morrow! "

" Impossible. I've made all the arrangements. I've so much to do that I won't get through my programme unless I hold it to-morrow."

" Well, give it up then."

" Impossible. I wouldn't even if I could."

" If you thought there was the slightest possibility of blood being shed, only the slightest possibility, don't you think it would be your duty not to hold that meeting ? Don't you think the avoidance of bloodshed is more important than your pro-gramme ? "

" I take that risk every time I hold a meeting. It's a risk I've got to take. Don't you think you're taking bloodshed too seriously? Don't you think you take the life of the individual too seriously ? Don't you think that the interests of the whole are far more important than the interests of the units ? Surely it's a simple question of social mathematics, and nothing more. Even if I knew for certain, which

I don't, that there would be bloodshed to-morrow, I would hold my meeting. Don't you see that you are putting an alternative that should not in common justice be put to me ? If people are killed it won't be my fault, but the fault of the pigsty system under which we live."

" Listen, Burgess, it seems to me terrible that you should consider this question so academically. Have you no feelings apart from your principles ? But even academically I don't think you can disclaim responsibility as easily as all that. In Port Benjamin there might be a chance of your words being taken for what they are worth. People there have long since learnt how to listen to men like you. But Paulstad is a hundred years behind Port Benjamin, it was one of the first things that struck me when I arrived. It has never occurred to the white people here that anyone could seriously criticise their relations with the natives. Everything you say or do will be obscured on either side by a cloud of virgin passion. You'll be merely an excuse for an explosion of passion. They won't listen to you reasonably, as you want people to listen to you, and so whatever you say won't do any good. Why incur all this risk if it's going to be futile ? "

" I know there's always a risk of that kind in the beginning, but, you see, there's got to be a beginning. I believe that what I've got to say to these people, what I'm going to ask them to do, is in their interests, that it's just and true. You mustn't blame me if there's a fuss because I speak the truth; you must blame all those liars and exploiters who live on the blood and misery of six million black people. If they want to sit on the truth and on justice, and get bucked off in the end and hurt themselves, it isn't my responsibility, it's theirs."

" Yes, but the trouble is that the people you're trying to help are the very people most likely to get hurt, and they might be a great deal worse off afterwards than before. Listen, hold your meeting later. Come back here. Do you want me to feel that people were killed only because Master Burgess didn't want to change his programme ? This town is not normal now. It's abnormally behind the times, and to-day is abnormal even in its abnormality. It hasn't rained for nearly two years. The town is full of strained, discontented, hungry people. Even the day you have chosen is not an ordinary day. It's November 6th, and you know what that means! Even those who bring food to the starving are responsible for seeing the starved people don't kill themselves by eating their food too quickly. From your point of view, your position is no different. You have only to substitute for food what you call truth and justice. Remember that many far greater men than you haven't been able to prevent their justice and truth becoming merely an excuse for murder and anarchy and bloodshed."

" You're only providing me with more arguments for holding the meeting to-morrow. If these people are hungry and discontented, whose fault is it if not the fault of a system which lets one section of the people swine in plenty and the other, and by far the biggest, starve? Do you know that the white people who are suffering from the drought have been helped liberally by the Government, the black people not at all ? If people like you would spend your time rubbing that in, instead of always shouting caution to me and my like, you would spend it more usefully and more justly. These people shall be told the truth to-morrow. I shall tell it to them."

" The truth?" replied van Bredepoel, feeling utterly hopeless. " What is the truth ? Is it an abstraction for which you sacrifice life and peace and order, or is it something which you make serve these things ? "

" Oh, curse you and your like! It's difficult, I know ; but because it's difficult to bring these things about rationally and calmly, that's no excuse for not trying. I can't change my programme even for you, and that says a good deal."

" Have you forgotten what I told you about the police ? You'll be just walking into a trap."

" That's the first sensible thing you've said. But I'm used to police traps. It isn't the first time they will have tried something of the sort. I'll take steps to see that those criminals never get near the meeting, but even if they do, I don't see what good that will do the police."

" I wish I felt as confident as you do," van Bredepoel said, giving up hope. He felt like someone who had tried in vain to signal an express train to stop, knowing well that farther up the line it would run head on into disaster and that he could do nothing now but anticipate the number of casualties.

" But then, Johan," Burgess said, speaking softly and putting his hand on van Bredepoel's shoulder, " you've never been confident about anything. It isn't your nature to be confident. All your life you've

been sitting on your little liberal fence, with your
fears on either side. I know that you hate as I do
the misery which the system in this country produces,
but you hate the thought of the temporary misery,
that must accompany any reform, just as much.
You must come down on one side, for your happiness' sake. Even the monkey in the popular legend
was more philosophic than you when he said:
' No pleasure without pain.' There is no greater
wisdom than that. And don't think you are unique.
Your problem is the problem of our entire generation. We must all decide now, once for all, to
commit ourselves either to the past or to the future.
No one shall have rest, no artist, no writer, no
worker, no politician, no one, until he has taken this
decision, for the individual is subordinate to society,
and when the structure of society is breaking down
the peace of the individual goes with it. Look anywhere you like and you will see the truth of this.
Take any representative writer or painter or musician
and you will find evidence of a sociological pre-
occupation. Commit yourself and you'll be happy,
but don't let me go on thinking of you as typical of a
generation whose most conspicuous characteristic is
its obstinate determination to avoid committing
itself to anything! "

But van Bredepoel was hardly listening, he was
murmuring to himself: " The system, once more the
system. I wonder. . . ."

" What's that ? " Burgess said sharply.

" Nothing, I was only thinking."

" Shall I see you at the meeting to-morrow ? "

" No, but come and tell me about it afterwards."

" Why not ? "

" Well, if you want to know why, I've had enough of these conflicts, which can only lead to more bloodshed, more licence for instincts which perhaps a thousand civilisations have perished to organise. I think you're terribly wrong. You're playing with forces you neither understand nor can ultimately control. You've no right to play with things that are potentially out of your control, even in the name of truth and justice. I refuse to help you even as a spectator; I won't add one more cell to that mass-mind you'll have before you to-morrow."

" Don't take it so hard," Burgess replied. " It's only a difference of opinion and they aren't rare between the two of us. But I'll say good night now, I've got a lot to do. I shall come to you to-morrow immediately after the meeting."

In his room that night, van Bredepoel looked back over the last three days. He felt that a definite period of his life had come to an end, that he was like a man who had come to the eve of a very long and un-certain journey, who has made all his dispositions, said good-bye to all his friends, and had now only to put the labels on his baggage and count his change. Late in the night he woke up, and heard a group of men being let out of the Paulstad Club. As they marched up the street they began singing in hoarse maudlin voices:

" We are marching to Pretoria,
    Pretoria, Pretoria,
We are marching to Pretoria,
    Pretoria rules the way."

He knew that it was a song sung by the English troops in the war in which his father and mother had died, that once, many years ago, they might have been listening to it too with heavy hearts. In his highly-strung state, he felt as if an army was marching outside, as if Paulstad had been invaded, and never had his room seemed so black.

CHAPTER VI

THE following morning van Bredepoel tried to rest and read at the hotel. But he could not settle down to anything. Fear and disquietude had now such a grip on him that, try as he would, he could not throw them off. The day had begun so hot that sitting or lying on the bed in his room was like being in a turkish bath. Round him, the heat brought out of everything an old and dusty smell, which made it difficult to breathe. The woodwork on the veranda, in the hall, on the stairs and in the stifling bedrooms creaked from time to time as it contracted; and people too seemed to creak as they moved woodenly about. " Everything is creaking," thought van Bredepoel. " Soon something will crack! " In the end he went out into the streets. He had expected to find the town very quiet in the morning. He knew that on November 6th, shops and public buildings were shut, and that usually all the Europeans gathered somewhere in the country, where they celebrated the anniversary of the victory of their forefathers by combining picnicking with praying. But the streets were surprisingly animated, filled with horse-carts and motors. He noticed that the occupants of most of these vehicles were men, that for so many people, particularly such family people, there were remarkably few women and children about. He was just about to turn into a side street when the sight of a man on horseback coming round a corner towards him made him stop. The man carried a rifle and bandolier filled with cartridges slung over his shoulders. Farther along he came across another horseman, similarly armed. Before he had walked three hundred yards he had seen seven horsemen like the first two. Outside the back entrance of a general dealer's shop he came across the Mollers' car with the boy Hans busy packing parcels into it.

" Father's so determined that it's going to rain," he said to van Bredepoel, greeting him, " and rain so much that the roads will be impassable for days to come, that he insisted on my coming into town for extra provisions."

" You haven't come in then to parade with these armed fellows on horseback I've seen about ? " van Bredepoel asked him.

" What fellows on horseback ? "

" Well, I haven't walked three hundred yards from the hotel and I've seen seven, armed to the teeth. You don't know what it's all about ? "

" Ah! That must be van Copenhagen's circus," replied the boy, laughing. " You know van Copenhagen has been spreading some wild rumour that there's a Native uprising timed to begin to-day. You see, we are so near Bambuland here that there are always rumours like that going about, particularly on Anniversary Day. Yesterday we received a frantic note from van Copenhagen asking us all to turn up here with fifty rounds of ammunition and rifles. But father only tore up the note and laughed. He said he was sure van Copenhagen was drunk when he wrote it. He said that he wouldn't be surprised if there was a revolution on van Copenhagen's farm, but that he would kiss van Copenhagen the next time they met if there was an uprising anywhere else. And you know, for my father, that says a lot. I think that's what it must be."

" But what has van Copenhagen to do with it ? Has he got the power to call up armed people like that ? " van Bredepoel asked.

" He's deputy-commandant of the district, or something of the sort, but you can take it from me that anything he's in is bound to be just hot air and bluff."

At lunch time the hotel was full of strange men. There was hardly room for them all. In the centre of the dining-room several tables had been put together, and van Copenhagen and about forty men had gathered there with much laughing and shouting. Van Bredepoel could not hear what they were saying, but he saw that they were drinking heavily, and looking frequently, too frequently, in his direction. He hurried over his food and left the room long before they had finished theirs. On the veranda the proprietor was talking excitedly to a man on horseback, but he gave van Bredepoel no greeting. Van Bredepoel seated himself on a bench, but before he had smoked half-way through his cigarette he threw it away. His mouth was dry, his lips parched as if he had fever. If anyone had there and then tried to convince him that he was conscious not in his head but in his solar plexus, he would probably have agreed with him, for he felt all the time that his uneasiness had gathered in a dull and very heavy pain in the pit of his stomach. He got up

from the bench and began walking up and down the
veranda. A twig which had blown on to it and
lay in his way he kicked savagely into the street
without having been conscious of any motive or
desire for his action. He began to stare at the street
and his mind instantly started analysing a hundred
insignificant details without keeping step with the
analysis from one detail to another. " That house
there has a green roof and lace curtains," he said
to himself, but a current of feeling, deep and strong,
swept the observation away like a cork before a
Yangtze tide, almost before he was aware of it.
Without taking his hat, he descended into the street.
The afternoon was like polished steel, the trees and
white-walled houses trembling reflections on a
buckler of steel. Round the church tower the sunlight exploded like a stream of electricity at the end
of a radio-telegraph mast. Suddenly a deep shadow
fell over the street. He looked up. A large cloud,
purple in the centre, ringed with white, lay there,
a coral island in the surf of the Pacific of the skies.
Over the mountains were flung other clouds as
smoke and dust over a terrible explosion of dynamite.
The air vibrated like a high-powered engine: the
day trembled like a violin string in his ears. A
swarm of birds were circling overhead wheeling
and wheeling on to ever-higher planes, and he
thought of bats trying to beat their way out of a
bottomless pit. Against the walls of the houses, in
narrow bars of shadow, lay dogs panting, their pink
tongues wide out before them. There was not
enough calm in him to balance this twisting world.
He returned to his room. He turned over the pages

of a book at regular intervals without knowing what he read. He got up, put his book down and placed himself in front of the mirror without seeing his reflection. He arranged his room, which needed no arrangement. He leant out of the window and looked out into the yard of the hotel.

The clock in the dining-room struck half-past two. Thank God, it was about to begin. Never before had the hotel seemed so quiet. A clock ticking near by, the rattle of plates in the kitchen, and the creaking of the tin roof overhead were the only sounds to break that strenuous silence. A Native came into the yard from the kitchen with some pots and pans and began to scrub them with wet sand. The fellow did his work with a placid, methodical air that irritated van Bredepoel. Then he descended the stairs and went into the dining-room. There was no one there. He looked at all the portraits on the wall, and when a servant came into the room and asked him if he was looking for anything, he replied almost angrily, " Nothing, no, nothing." He returned to the window of his room. The Native was still scrubbing his pots and pans. This time he noticed that the veld and mountain slopes beyond the town were streaked with bars of purple shadow and quicksilver light. He looked at them for some time, and so rapidly did light and shadow alternate that he felt like someone walking along a railed fence between him and the sun. He heard the first explosions of thunder, saw the wind far away add its power to that of water and electricity. It seemed to him that the earth was beginning to plunge forward like a dreadnought, with flags flying, to take part in that far-off Trafalgar of the skies. He was about to go downstairs once more, when a movement of the Native below attracted his attention. He had stopped work and was listening carefully, his head on one side. Van Bredepoel, too, suddenly heard something, someone was approaching at a run. In a few moments there passed by the yard entrance a Native running hard, with two sticks and an assegai in his hand. As he passed he shouted something at the Native in the yard. Immediately the hotel Native ran into the kitchen with his pots and pans, then came running out into the yard again; vanished into the servants' quarters and reappeared quickly with two clubbed hunting-sticks. For a moment he looked round to make sure he had not been seen and then dashed into the street. In front of the hotel there was a sudden clatter of horses galloping very fast, but a loud rumble of thunder fell over the town and van Bredepoel could not hear where the horses came from or were going to. Quickly he descended into the street. On the veranda were the proprietor's wife and a companion, knitting. At the entrance to the Royal Paulstad Club, tied up or held by little boys, stood about fifty saddled horses.

" Do you know whose horses those are, Mrs. Rothman ? " he asked the proprietor's wife.

" Van Copenhagen's commando's," she replied.

" I thought so. But I am surprised to see them there. I thought I heard them galloping past the hotel just now," he told her.

" Oh, no. Not past," she replied. " They came

charging up to the hotel and hurried into the Club
to hold a meeting."

" A meeting! Why ? "

" I understand the Colonel of the police has
prevented them breaking up a Native meeting, and
they're very angry about it."

" What do you think they'll do now ? "

" If you had to believe van Copenhagen, Mr. van
Bredepoel, there will not be a Native left alive in this
town this evening."

" But aren't you nervous ? "

He was amazed at her placidity. In his agitation
it seemed extraordinary that anyone should remain
calm.

" I know van Copenhagen," she said.

" Thank you, Mrs. Rothman. Excuse me, please.
I shall have to be going."

" Happy, very happy, Mr. van Bredepoel," she
replied and went on with her knitting.

Over the mountains the clouds had melted into
one. They rose into one silver-crested formation far
into the sky, scribbled and zigzagged with lightning.
The mutter of thunder had become almost incessant,
but the earth was hushed and quiet, only its trees
and bushes moaning faintly as they flagged the
storm on.

When van Bredepoel had told Burgess the previous
evening that he would not go to the meeting, he had
been absolutely sincere. But he was finding the
suspense, the flights of imagination which turned
events like the arrival of van Copenhagen's commando into infallible portents of disaster, so painful
that he now decided to seek out some place where

he could get more reliable and direct news. He at once thought of the home of the coloured man with whom he had seen Burgess the previous evening.

He had no difficulty in finding the house. As he approached it, he heard screams of approval and hate mixing in terrible confusion in a near-by street. Though Paulstad was more than a thousand miles from Port Benjamin, he thought instantly of the night when he and Burgess had seen the Doctor killed. There seemed no difference between the sounds uttered then by a Port Benjamin crowd and those of the invisible mob close at hand. The similarity in no way helped to calm him. With every step he took the din increased, till as he pushed open the garden gate he thought it must come from immediately behind the house. He ran up to the door and knocked loudly. The noise had become deafening. Could they possibly hear him ? Suddenly the face of a woman, yellow and sickly pale, looked round the corner of the door with wide, shining eyes. As she saw him she flung the door wide open and gasped: " Little Lord in Heaven! I thought it was the police! "

" I'm a friend of Mr. Burgess," van Bredepoel told her, " and I would like to wait for him here until the meeting is over."

He passed through the door straight into a small room with a green dung floor. Round the table covered with a faded green plush cloth were five trembling but silent children. The walls were hung with religious texts, and opposite van Bredepoel was the picture of a woman clinging to a rock on which

Christ stood, holding a shining torch towards a stormy sea.

" I have asked the Lord all afternoon," the woman said, a mystical light in her eyes, speaking at the picture more than at van Bredepoel, " to see that nothing terrible happens out there."

She stopped, turned upon van Bredepoel and shouted at him as if he had contradicted her:

" And you'll see, nothing will happen! Nothing! "

" Have you any news of how it's going?" van Bredepoel asked. The conviction she had just uttered suddenly left her and tears came into her eyes.

" The police are there with their guns," she told him, " the white commando are there with their guns, the black men are there with their sticks and assegais, and soon they will begin shooting. I know it."

" Why do you say you know it ? "

" I've been watching them from the back garden, but when the police and white men came with their guns I went away."

" How from the back garden ? "

" From over the wall. There's a pigsty there. I climbed on to that."

" Show me," he said. He almost had to shout the words, to make himself heard above that hideous noise.

She led him into a small back garden, at the end of which a pigsty was built against the wall.

" Get up on that," she said, pointing at the pigsty, " and you'll see it all."

Van Bredepoel climbed up a thin, sloping tin

roof, and was able to lean with his elbows on the
wall and look over. Below him was a long narrow
street shut in with low squalid huts, except immediately in front of him where it opened on to a
rough football ground. But this playground, too,
was shut in beyond by houses. The space in front
of him was occupied entirely by a crowd of wildly
shouting Natives, brandishing sticks and assegais at a
mass of Europeans huddled together further down
the street. Between the Europeans and the Natives
was drawn a thin cordon of policemen, armed with
rifles and a machine-gun. In front of this cordon
paced up and down, like a buffalo in a zoo, the
Colonel of the police, and at his side, or rather at
his heels, trailed a gesticulating Atkins, trying in
vain to make the Colonel listen to him. Farther
down the street, on the corner of the first side alley,
was another thin cordon of policemen, also with
fixed bayonets. On the opposite side of the street,
in a similar position, were more policemen. Van
Bredepoel did not understand this division of the
meagre police force into three, until he saw that
facing one of the outside cordons was a commando
of about one hundred and fifty horsemen. He
thought he recognised at the head of the commando,
threatening the police with his clenched fist, the
corpulent figure of van Copenhagen, a large ostrich
plume stuck in his hat. The meaning of the disposition of the police immediately became clear.
The Colonel had split up his forces like this in order to
protect a hostile crowd of Natives from van Copenhagen's commando. Furthermore, as van Bredepoel learned later, he had instructed the outside

cordons not to hesitate to fire on van Copenhagen's
men if they should try to interfere. This threat
alone had prevented van Copenhagen from " shooting up the niggers," as he himself expressed it.

Just below van Bredepoel, at a distance of about
fifteen yards, was Burgess, standing hatless on an
ox-wagon. He was surrounded by ten or twelve
coloured men. The sight of this little group did not
reassure van Bredepoel. Most of the coloured men
had lost their heads and were all trying to shout wild
advice to Burgess at the same time. And Burgess ?
He was standing there, his head bent, his eyes on the
ground. Van Bredepoel was so used to seeing him
self-confident in his deceptive, nervous way that
he read the worst into that attitude. The fact that
Burgess no longer made any attempt to address the
crowd was the worst possible sign, implying
as it did that he had already admitted defeat
inwardly, was no longer in command either of
himself or of his audience. And then as he looked
and listened, it seemed to van Bredepoel that all
through these confused noises certain groups of
sound returned at regular intervals, that the pattern
of something more organised was slowly taking
shape. He listened more carefully. Here and there
he began to catch a word or two, chanted in deep
bass voices. At first it sounded like those chants
Natives improvise over their work in the streets of
Port Benjamin; but certain words were coming
back over and over again, and as his agitated mind
began to translate them, horror sank like a stone
into the midst of fear. He could no longer ignore,
however much he had wanted to, the significance

of the chant, when into the open space round the wagon jumped three black men holding three old carbines like assegais over their heads. One he did not know; of the other two, he knew one at least too well. It was Kenon, and with him the old man who had helped him to look for cigarette ends in front of the Paulstad Hotel. But it was Kenon transformed. His lifelessness had gone, his eyes, which before reflected only his habitual despondence, were wide and vivid.

" My God, he has been smoking that stuff again! " van Bredepoel exclaimed. Atkins and the Colonel had come to the same conclusion, particularly Atkins, who was weak with dismay. It was right in front of these two that the two younger Natives began a slow, primitive dance, while the old man, stamping his feet rhythmically on the ground, chanted in a hoarse, blurred voice. With their tattered coats slung over their arms and held before them like shields, their rifles pointed like spears, they stalked towards the police as if they were stalking big game, only each step they took was timed to the rhythm of the old man's chant. When it seemed that they were about to clash with the police, both jumped high into the air, whirling their bodies round at the same time. The moment their feet touched ground, they bounded back to the front ranks of the crowd. And now the entire crowd had taken up the old man's chant. The front ranks were already stamping their feet with him, swaying and shaking their arms and bodies to the rhythm of the dance. Other natives were beginning to break away and to execute movements similar to

Kenon and his companions. It seemed to van
Bredepoel that all the faces in the crowd had lost
their individual expression. Every black man
looked alike. The mob no longer saw outside themselves; they were a people possessed by a rhythm,
possessed by a vivid racial memory.

" Eh! You men of the Bambuxosa! Have you kept
watch in the night ? " the old man chanted, shaking
his assegai in the air, while Kenon and the other
native stalked the police again.

" Ay, we have kept watch, kept watch in the night,"
the crowd replied, and thunder joined in their reply.

" What have you watched for, men of the Bambuxosa ? "

" We have watched, have watched for the Eland! "

" Do you want to kill the Eland ? "

" Aye, we want to kill, kill, kill the Eland!"

" Where shall you kill the Eland, men of the
Bambuxosa ? "

" Here ! Here ! Here ! "

" Then let us kill the Eland ! "

The old man in his turn stalked carefully towards
the police. For a moment a deep silence fell over
the dark mass of Natives. Their bodies, released
from the rhythm of their chant, stiffened. They
made no attempt to follow. A flash of lightning
and its thunder crashed over the town, but the crowd
did not hear. It was listening in to another world,
to a succession of worlds, through which the Bambuxosa had slowly come, the great Masakama at
their head. The three leaders felt they were not
being followed and turned round.

" Are you bred from polecats, have you become

old women, men of the Bambuxosa ? " the old man
shouted at the crowd, and pointed upwards with
his rifle. " See the Great Chief Masakama comes on
the clouds with all his warriors! Will you shame
yourselves before Masakama ? "

Van Bredepoel saw the Colonel turn round and
give an order to the police, saw the men undo the
magazine locks of their rifles and push cartridges
into the barrels. And in that moment a decision
came to him. He jumped over the wall. The crowd
at his feet instinctively scattered, and he ran quickly
up to the Colonel.

" I know the leader of those three," he told the
astonished Colonel. " I think I can calm him."

" He knows him all right," said Atkins, for the
first time looking welcome at van Bredepoel.

" See what you can do," the Colonel replied
curtly, but all the same he undid the flap of his
revolver pouch. Van Bredepoel walked forward
slowly. Afterwards he realised that he must have
felt and looked like someone going to put salt on a
lion's tail. As he came forward, the three natives
turned round and looked at him, flinging their coats
like shields before them, and putting themselves
in spear-throwers' attitudes. Van Bredepoel saw
Kenon look straight before him, like someone who
had long since lost touch with earth.

" Kenon! " he called.

Kenon did not reply.

" Kenon! " he called again. " Don't you know
me ? "

Kenon's eyes did not waver.

" Yes, I know you," he said in a voice that sounded

inhumanly detached. " I know you, but," he tapped his rifle, " my assegai knows you not."

Van Bredepoel tried no more. He knew that he could do nothing. He walked back to the Colonel and shook his head. He felt weak and that he would cry.

" You get out of this," the Colonel said to him gruffly, and pushed him swiftly through the police ranks. Van Bredepoel made no resistance.

" I'm going to arrest those fellows myself," he heard the Colonel say to the police. " I'll give them three warnings first. If the crowd make any movement to interfere, shoot, and shoot to kill. Major Atkins will take charge while I'm away, and one of you had better go and tell the outside troops to fall back slowly on this position here."

He turned to face the crowd, and called out three times to Kenon and his companions to give themselves up. Their only reply was to begin to stalk forward slowly towards him. The crowd still stood silent. It had gone beyond the point where words could sway it either way. Action alone would get it to act. Slowly the Colonel walked out towards the three Natives. It seemed to van Bredepoel that there was something infinitely heroic about his action, that this obscure Colonel of police in an obscure country village had suddenly become great, not because of anything attaching to his own life, but because he placed himself like a bridge between the conception and execution of a duty that was greater than himself. Bearing himself like someone inspecting a troop on a fashionable parade-ground, he continued to move forward until he reached the old Native, who had danced into position ahead of his companions. The black man raised his rifle to strike the Colonel, but before it could fall the Colonel caught his arm and said coolly: " Jan Makatese, you're a fool. I always thought you were a fool, but now I think you are a bigger one. Give me that rifle and go over to Major Atkins there."

The old man gave up his rifle and walked over to the police cordon very slowly, ashamed and crestfallen. Hope returned to van Bredepoel. He knew how sensitive black people were to individual qualities, he knew that, unlike many Europeans, they saw and judged men purely and directly as men, that there were few social associations to interfere with the clarity of their judgment. He knew, too, that they had in them a great and instinctive longing to be led, and he began to hope that the Colonel might still manage to calm them. But unfortunately everything depended on Kenon and his companion, and on the quantity of insangu Atkins had arranged for them to smoke. They were watching the Colonel very attentively and with no sign of fear. As he walked quietly towards them, his eyes never leaving their faces, van Bredepoel saw once more that terrible look of detachment on Kenon's face, a look which seemed to have long since seen and reconciled him to the inevitable conclusion of this incident. The Colonel too may have noticed it. For one second his step slowed down, and in that brief moment Kenon's body stiffened, he raised his rifle with both hands and jumped at the Colonel. Atkins shouted a warning and the police took aim, but could not shoot because the Colonel was between them and Kenon.

Van Bredepoel saw the Colonel tugging at his revolver but before he could raise it the butt of one of Major Atkins' carbines descended on his head. He doubled up and fell slowly forward. Before his body reached the ground Kenon had hit him again. Van Bredepoel heard Kenon shout out wildly, but he could only distinguish the word " Masakama," for in that moment the crowd broke and charged the police. Kenon, his face transfigured, his eyes wide and shining, his black skin a-glitter, threw himself forward at the moment the police opened fire. The machine-gun began to play lightly on the crowd, producing casualties as easily as a concertina notes. The crowd overflowed towards the police, like a river over a precipice. It seemed to van Bredepoel a many-footed monster with a single voice. He began to feel himself very detached, and if the crowd had broken through the police ranks he would doubtless not have moved. He was seeing only what he had anticipated. He was like a man who has arrived on the scene of a terrible railway accident, who hardly hears the cries of the wounded and the shouts of other spectators, and knows only that he must go in among the wreckage and search for his brother. But the crowd did not break through. It came to within five yards of the police, in conflict even with one of the cordons, but then turned and ran, as suddenly as it had charged, the policemen pursuing with fixed bayonets. Van Bredepoel mar-velled at the swiftness with which the black people now disappeared from this narrow street. Soon he

was left there, standing alone. Far away he saw van
Copenhagen's commando turn down a side street
to head off the fugitives. Overhead the sky darkened,
the rumble of thunder was continuous, lightning
lassoed the world. The first drops of rain began to
fall round him like bullets in the dust. Not fifteen
yards away lay the Colonel and Kenon. The
Colonel's body was facing the fleeing crowd, Kenon's
the original position of the police. Kenon had one
black foot on the Colonel's back, the other drawn up
at his side, his head supported and hidden in his
arm, lying like someone who had settled himself in
his favourite position for sleep—a sleep in which he
might easily have been dreaming of that summer's
day many years before when, well rubbed with
lion fat and full of hope, he came out from his
father's hut, and amid cries of admiration from his
sisters turned into that blood-red footpath which
leads through the valley, to the other side of the
valley, to that wonderful, very wonderful Port
Benjamin.

Van Bredepoel saw the wind throw up a spiral of
dust over their bodies. And then he heard: " Van
Bredepoel! Van Bredepoel! "

He tried to look up, but the voice sounded to him
as that voice must have sounded which called
" Samuel! Samuel! " from the darkness of a temple
in Palestine. He looked and listened, but he found
it difficult to see.

" Van Bredepoel! Van Bredepoel! " he heard
again.

" For Christ's sake come and help me."

It was Burgess, crouched forward against the

wheel of the wagon. He hurried towards him. Burgess' face was very white, his left shoulder red with blood.

"Help me, please, to get into that house. It's nothing serious, but I'm afraid to use my left arm."

Van Bredepoel got Burgess over the wall with difficulty, and might not have succeeded if the coloured man and his wife had not come to help him. They were hardly in the garden when van Copenhagen's commando raced down the street; following the trampling of hoofs sounded the shrill bell of the first ambulance car.

"They have sworn they'd kill Master Burgess," the coloured man told van Bredepoel. "Van Copenhagen has sworn he'll kill all of us. Oh, what can we do, master?"

"We'll attend to Master Burgess' wound first, and then see what we can do," van Bredepoel replied roughly.

When they were inside the house, the rain came down in full. The tin roof vibrated loudly with the force of it: they had to shout to make themselves heard. The house swayed to every flash of lightning. Sometimes the thunder cracked like a gigantic ox-whip overhead, sometimes it sounded like a deep subterranean explosion. The woman gathered her children round her in one corner of the room, shut her eyes and began to sing hymns to them. In the few lulls that did come in the storm they heard horses splashing ceaselessly round and round in the streets outside, and very far away, almost like the bleating of a flock of sheep, the cries of a fugitive crowd.

Van Bredepoel and the coloured man laid Burgess
on the sofa, gave him a glass of brandy and milk,
and began to undress him. They found that he had
only a slight wound high up in the left shoulder.

" It's nothing," he said, " it's not that so much
that hurts."

" You'd better go for a doctor immediately, while
I dress the wound," van Bredepoel told the coloured
man.

" Master, it isn't safe for me. They'll kill me."

" But we must have a doctor as soon as possible.
I've got to stay here to dress the wound."

" I'll get my eldest son to go," the man suggested.

" If it's not safe for you, will it be safe for
him ? "

" They wouldn't harm a little boy."

" Be quick, then ! "

The woman began to cry when she saw her eldest
son, a boy of about eleven, getting ready to go, but
she did not stop him. He had no coat of his own, so
van Bredepoel lent him his. When he had gone
they dressed Burgess' wound as best they could and
made him comfortable. Soon the colour returned
to his face and after a time he called van Bredepoel
to him. He began to talk slowly, almost apologetically.

" There would have been no trouble," he said,
" if it hadn't been for those three fellows with the
carbines. Everything was going well until they
turned up. I've never been so careful about what
I said. The crowd was quite calm. I had ten men
on the look-out for those three. When they arrived
my men held them back, until the three of them—

they were either drunk or mad—clubbed two of my
people with their rifles and broke through the
rest. You know how quickly things of that kind
excite crowds, particularly Native crowds. These
black fellows have some uncanny way of transmitting
news. In half an hour the crowd was doubled and
out of control. I can't understand what the police
were after. They must have mismanaged things
terribly. Three of them dead, I hear, and one of
them the commanding officer! Hell, what a lot of
trouble there is going to be for us! What a noise
this is going to make! I wish I knew what the police
were after."

"Do you know who one of those three fellows
was?" van Bredepoel asked him.

"No."

"Kenon."

Burgess sat up suddenly.

"Then . . ." he exclaimed, but changed his
mind and said: "I'm so sorry, Johan."

He was silent for some minutes and then added:
"So that was why you walked out towards them!"

Van Bredepoel nodded.

"Yes, it was Kenon. He was well known to the
police here. He has been up many times for smoking
insangu. The magistrate told me that only yesterday. He said, too, that the last time Kenon was up
before him the evidence showed that smoking the
stuff had made him violent."

"I understand," replied Burgess. "Hashish plays
the devil with black people."

"Yes. I think that's the one thing Atkins forgot.
He didn't foresee they had ample time between

their release and the meeting to get thoroughly drugged; in fact a golden opportunity, for weren't they doing it more or less under the protection of the police ? "

Van Bredepoel paused; an idea had occurred to him, throwing light on many things which before had seemed inexplicable.

" Have you read the papers recently ? " he asked.

" Yes," Burgess replied. " You know Daniel and I never miss one."

" Well, did you read the discussion in Parliament on the Minister of Justice's new Bill ? "

" I did."

" Well, you must have noticed then that the opposition to the Bill was so strong that the Minister had to postpone the final reading till the New Year, saying he hoped to place before the House later sufficient evidence to convince it ' of the urgency and necessity of the measure.' "

" Yes, I did, but what are you driving at ? "

" Don't you think that he will now have all the evidence he wanted ? "

" My God! That's it! " exclaimed Burgess. " We were blind not to see it before. My God, what swines they are! Still, I think they got more than they wanted. I'm only sorry Atkins wasn't wiped out as well."

" Yes! They forgot the insangu. They probably intended only to break up the meeting, on the pretext that you had incited the natives so much that they began arming themselves with rifles— you know how we always fear a Native uprising in this country. Then the Minister would only have

had to say, ' Look, the agitators make the niggers
arm,' for the Bill to be passed."

Here we may add that afterwards, when Burgess
read the official version of the riot, he was entirely
convinced that van Bredepoel's explanation was the
right one. For Atkins stated, in his report, that he
had long been on the track of a huge organisation
which smuggled arms, supplied by ' certain well-
known Communist agents," into Bambuland.   In
proof of this, Atkins claimed that there were present
at Burgess' meeting not three but scores of armed
Natives, who had been worked up into such a state
of wild excitement by Communist agitators that they
were preparing to fire on the police. And this
report was not long out when Burgess was arrested
and charged with " having deliberately and wilfully
incited an assembly of Natives to riotous conduct,
dangerous to the public safety." At the trial,
Burgess tried to repeat what van Bredepoel had told
him, but the Attorney-General, who was prosecuting
in person, got the Court to silence him on the grounds
that " prejudiced hearsay of that kind is inadmissible
as evidence." The official evidence, however, was
not sufficient to secure a verdict against Burgess,
and when the trial was over he persuaded an English
newspaper in Port Benjamin to start a campaign
for reopening the investigation into the causes of
the Paulstad Riot. The newspaper hinted strongly
that the police and Atkins had played an extremely
provocative role in the riot, but in the end it had to
withdraw these statements under threat of libel
actions from half of the Port Benjamin officialdom.

" If only you had seen that boy." Van Bredepoel's

thoughts had gone the full circle: back to where he had started. " If only you could've seen him when he first came to Port Benjamin. I used to think there could be no one happier in all the world. He was so honest, so diligent, so loyal to the gratitude that any act of kindness roused in him. I don't know what went wrong. I don't know what could have brought him to this. He must have suffered terribly before he came to this. You should've seen the way he looked this afternoon. There seemed to be an inhuman sort of logic in his eyes. I felt that, given all the unknown that had happened, given Kenon as he was, he could not act otherwise."

" I'm terribly sorry, Johan. But what do you expect under this benighted system. If you allow—"

" Burgess," van Bredepoel said bitterly, " you went into this with academic justifications, you come out of it with an academic explanation. It's the system, always the system, and yet again the system, for you. You are always beating your wings against the system. I'm sick of hearing about the system. The system is only an approximation, a reflection of the rules that govern the little acts of each one of us. Only it's an approximation so big that if you place all the emphasis on it, the individual loses the sense of the responsibility for his little share in it. It seems to me fatal. The starting- and finishing-point is in the heart of each man. At one time the responsibility for action was placed on the individual, and I think the world was relatively a good deal happier. But to-day if a man is a thief or a murderer, we no longer blame the man, we blame his environment. If a man is poor and hasn't

enough to eat, we don't say that he has been lazy
or has made no consistent effort to better himself,
we blame the system. If a man rapes a woman or
walks down the street and opens his fly to a crowd,
we don't blame his lack of self-control; we say
'What can you expect of a system which forces
such terrible sex-taboos on us?' It's always the
system. Even scientists and philosophers have
rushed in to help people like you. Man, they tell
you, is only a machine; put him in a certain environment and he must react in a definite and calculable
way. He cannot help himself, only his conditioned
reflexes can. And what conditions these reflexes?
Environment. Oh, yes! The ground has been well
ploughed! You have all the rationalisation for your
attacks on the system that you can want. Only man
is losing the sense of his integrity, the sense of his
responsibility to himself. He is already, for you,
someone who can be improved merely by increasing
his income. Everyone wants to improve the system
under which he lives and not himself, and as he, or a
collection of people like him, makes the system, it all
ends in no improvement, no responsibility. Take
you yourself. What have you done this afternoon?
I haven't heard you utter a word of reproach against
your share in it, all you've done is to come back
howling about the system again!"

"I'm surprised at you," exclaimed Burgess,
visibly distressed. "You've so often agreed with me
about the palpable social injustices in this country.
Are you going to blame this poor Native devil, for
instance, for everything that happened to him?"

"I would blame him, perhaps, if it hadn't gone

beyond blaming," van Bredepoel replied. " And
you ought to know it's not easy for me to say that.
But I *am* going to blame myself. I was the only one
who felt affection for him and could have learned to
understand him. I had a bigger responsibility there
than I knew, because when one's the only person
who can help, one must help. I quite see that our
social system inflicts many injustices on people like
Kenon, but I cannot see that it's entirely responsible
for their reactions to those injustices. Moreover, your
conception of the system is to me, now, an unreal
abstraction. I have thought it over a great deal
since my illness, for I was at one time tempted to
come in with you and Daniel, but the more I think
of it the less I believe in it. Listen, the unjust man,
the selfish man, the cruel man, will act always
according to his lights. The system is only a garment
round the human heart; it doesn't give the shape
to the heart, it takes its own shape from the heart.
I agree with you that some garments fit better than
others, but yours seems to me not a garment but a
strait jacket, which man will have to burst if
he is to survive. Under your system the just will
still be just, the unjust still unjust, we will be no
farther forward and you'll have put the world
through a period of bloodshed and anarchy in vain.
Your enemy and mine in this country is not the
system but the heart of every white man.   You
can't legislate a man's heart away."

" So you would just let the white people in this
country go on having too much, and the black
people not enough ? You would just let——"

" I think it's terribly wrong. But Burgess, Christ

knew what you don't when he told the rich man to give up his riches of his own accord. He asked no one to legislate against riches. He placed all the responsibility for his riches and for their renunciation on the rich man himself."

" Ah, van Bredepoel, you're again speaking for the exceptions. Most people have little will, few strong desires ; they are what the system makes them. They are the people you have to protect from the system."

" A fat lot of good it will do giving people things they neither will nor desire strongly! But we could go on like this for ever; we're both upset, and you need rest. I shall go and see if I can't hurry up the doctor. That boy's been a very long time! "

The boy's mother, when she heard van Bredepoel's words, rushed up to him and keenly urged him to go. Van Bredepoel had to borrow a wool-sack to wrap round him, for the rain was still coming down heavily. Every flash of lightning lit up the window with a green-yellow light, and showed the battered rain smoking against the glass. Out in the streets he kept carefully in the shadows. Twice he had to draw back under the trees, as patrols of horsemen came clattering towards him; their silhouettes against the lightning showing the barrels of their rifles sticking out behind their shoulders. But at the border of the European quarter five men armed with rifles suddenly walked out of the shadows and stopped him.

" Who are you ? Where are you coming from, and where are you going to ? " a strange aggressive voice demanded.

" I was caught in the storm out walking this

afternoon, and had to take shelter in a Native hut until it calmed down a bit. I'm on my way home now," he told them.

"You look it," the man laughed. "But I haven't seen you before," he added suspiciously. "You don't belong here."

"No, I don't," van Bredepoel replied. "I'm on a visit here. I came to negotiate with Brand over the sale of Strang's farm."

"He's right," another man said. "Strang is selling out, and Brand's doing it for him."

"You're lucky not to be that Bolshie agitator or his friend; they won't get out of this place alive," his interrogator said.

"Why, what's wrong?"

"What's wrong? Why, man, we've had a war here this afternoon through that fellow's monkey tricks. Three policemen are dead, five in danger of their lives, fifty-three niggers killed, and God only knows how many wounded."

"I thought I heard the noise of shooting, but I wasn't sure, the storm made such a row."

"You can go. We won't keep you and I'm sorry we stopped you, but we must get that Bolshie and his friend. We'll beat them up at dawn, no doubt."

In the doctor's consulting-room he found the little boy, shivering in front of a large fire. The doctor's wife came herself to speak to van Bredepoel, and he explained to her what it was they wanted.

"Do you know," she said, "I couldn't get out of that little boy what he wanted the doctor for? All he said was, would the doctor come with him. I am surprised to hear there's still another wounded

man, and a white man, too! My husband has been
in and out all the afternoon since four, attending
to the wounded. But I don't think he'll be long
now."

She left van Bredepoel and the child together.
The moment there was no need for action, van
Bredepoel's thoughts resumed all their previous
activity. He could not forget the sight of the bodies
of the Colonel and Kenon. He felt an immense
pity for the Colonel. He admired his rigorous
conception of duty, which had lifted him slowly into
place, like a bridge over a gulf, in that last moment
before his death. He admired his determination to
be just to both white and black. It seemed to him
there was some compensation for the Colonel in the
way he had died. But what was there for Kenon? The
sorrow he felt, the sorrow over a past in which
Kenon had entered, a hesitating figure, half civilised,
half savage, was reinforced by a sense of guilt.

" Ah," he thought, " we were brothers in mis-
fortune and inadaptability, but I could have helped
him, and I didn't. Remote from one another we
passed through life like two shadows over a hill,
darkening it, but not altering it at all. Our lives
were set in a corridor shut at both ends. He has
broken out and I am left, but not for long. These
bodies which give us so much pain, shock us by
contortions so violent that we half believe our flesh
will never die, are frail. Life, like a brief and dis-
cordant bar of music, is only a fugitive structure in
time, a fragile counterpoint of flesh and blood and
spirit. This flesh which looks so solid is only the
white edge round a flickering flame of blood. Wait,

Johan! Sit still. Don't complain. Soon you will
have peace. You have come to the frontier of the
last ' Why,' and you need something more than the
knowledge that has brought you there, to carry you
on beyond. You are but *one* in two thousand millions,
and what are you to two thousand millions, you and
two thousand millions to life, and life to the universe,
the universe to God, and God to . . . what ? Ask
yourself that and you'll see how little *one* is, and be
still."

He leant forward and looked into the fire, listening to the deep, steady hymn of the rain from
clouds washed yellow with lightning, and the little
coloured boy's eyes opened wide when he saw tears
on the white master's face.

" Master Burgess must be dead," he thought.

But van Bredepoel was trying to remember his
conversation with Burgess. He felt he would break
down unless he could stop thinking about the riot.

" Burgess is always telling me to take a long view,"
he thought. " But what good is a long view to us
whose lives are conceived in terms of a short view ?
If we try to look farther than the life that is in us, it
merely lands us in confusion, in a vague speculation
which is only too easy since the reality that must
qualify it does not yet exist. Isn't it better to look
around our feet, there where we can see clearest,
not there where we can see farthest ? If we look
at the steps, won't the miles and the years take care
of themselves ? Anyway, I am going to begin there.
I'm going to begin by minding my own step. Each
one must take heed for himself, and the system will
in the end take heed for itself. If the system per-

petuates a colour-prejudice, we can counteract it by refusing to admit a colour-prejudice in our own lives, we can live as if no colour-prejudice existed. If we are too rich we can counteract riches by leading a simple life and helping the poor. I am tired of people who still point me only to a cross in Palestine, tired of people who are always telling me to keep my eyes on the horizon, looking for a justice which never comes. I don't know if I want justice, lest in justice being done to others justice should be done to me. It is not justice I need, but forgiveness. Never again shall I reject, or not recognise, affection offered me, but take it and go on alone with my love. That's all; no more. I shall buy Strang's farm. I shall mind my own step."

When the doctor came at last, night had deepened the darkness of the storm outside. He entered the consulting-room, water dripping from his coat. He looked tired and upset, but only stayed to gulp down a glass of whisky and milk, and then led van Bredepoel and the little boy to his car. In the car van Bredepoel explained who it was he wanted him to visit, and added that the coloured quarter was carefully guarded, that if the patrols knew where they were going they would not let them pass.

"They shan't stop me," the doctor told him, speaking with a broad Scotch accent. "Just let them try."

As they passed the street where van Bredepoel had walked into the patrol, five men rushed out and signalled them to stop. The doctor slowed down the car, leant over the side and shouted " Doctor "

—then accelerated. The men made no further attempt to stop them, and returned to their shelter.

Burgess was asleep when they arrived at the coloured man's home. The memory of the afternoon's events seemed to have left no shadow on his mind. Van Bredepoel woke him gently, and helped the doctor to remove the rough linen bandages.

"Nothing serious," the doctor told Burgess. "You'll have to be careful, though, not to use your arm for a week or two. I'll clean out the wound now and give you an injection. But you'd better see a doctor again to-morrow."

"But doctor, surely, you'll be able to do it for me again to-morrow?" Burgess asked, surprised at the last phrase.

The doctor did not reply immediately. He seemed to be thinking.

"Look here, young fellow-me-lad," he said at last. "I will, of course, dress that wound to-morrow if you're still here. But see, you've made enough mess to-day as it is. If you stay here until to-morrow, you'll make a bigger mess. The Colonel's dead and Atkins is in charge. I've spent my whole afternoon among the wounded police and natives at the police station. Atkins will do nothing to stop van Copenhagen, van Copenhagen is drunk and out of control, and he and all his men are determined to put you up against a wall. I'm using his own words. You had better get away to-night. It'll be painful for you, but not dangerous. I'll call here to-morrow at ten in any case, to see if you're here. But if I were you, I'd get out of this, both of you."

"I think he's right, Burgess," van Bredepoel

urged, after the doctor had gone. " You must get away to-night. Give me a letter to the magistrate, and I'll see that he gets it first thing to-morrow morning. You'll have nothing to reproach yourself with then."

" But how am I to get away ? You know the station is on the other side of the town, and every train will be carefully watched."

" I know, but we must make a plan," van Brede-poel told him. " You try and sleep, and I'll see what can be done."

Burgess closed his eyes, but a few minutes later he raised himself suddenly and asked: " You're coming too, aren't you ? "

" No, I don't think so."

" It's just as dangerous for you to stay here, Johan. You can't. If I go you must come too."

" I don't think it is dangerous for me. In any case, I must stay."

" No, you can't. There's no 'must' about it. Come back to Port Benjamin with me. I shall give up my tour for a bit. It won't be any good going on now."

" No, I can't," van Bredepoel repeated. " I'm not going back. I'm not ever going back."

Burgess watched him intently, and then said:

" You're mad. You have your work. You must come back. What could you do here ? "

" I've just enough money to buy a piece of land and plant potatoes."

" Plant potatoes! " Burgess tried to laugh, but van Bredepoel stopped him.

" You must sleep now. I shall tell you about it later."

In the kitchen, van Bredepoel found their host and his family sitting before the stove. They were all very quiet. They seemed incapable of speaking. The woman was sitting on the floor and holding her husband's right hand, while she stroked with the other the head of the boy who had gone for the doctor. Every now and then she sighed deeply. Rain still fell heavily on the roof, but it had steadied considerably. The lightning was far away, and the thunder was pleasant to hear. A smell of rain and refreshed earth drifted into the kitchen from outside.

" Man," the woman said suddenly to her husband, " do you think the rain has washed all the blood away ? "

" I think so, vroutjie," he said and stroked her hand.

" I thought God was going to strike this town with thunder and lightning to-day. I thought he was going to send it up in flames like Sodom and Gomorrah. But God has been good to us, hasn't he ? "

" Yes, God has been good to us, vroutjie," the man replied.

" And you will not go to any more meetings?" She seemed on the point of crying again.

" I don't think so, vroutjie."

" Then I shall go and cook some food for us." She got up and went over to the kitchen table.

" I want to speak to you, please." Van Bredepoel beckoned to the man.

" We must get Burgess out of this to-night, it isn't safe for him here," he said when they were alone. " Do you know how it can be done ? "

" I've been thinking about it," the man replied.
" The doctor's right. While you were away one of
our committee members came to see me; he told
me the police are expecting big reinforcements from
Port Duncan. There'll be trouble for all of us
to-morrow, but it will be worse for Master Burgess."

" But what can we do ? "

" There's a railway siding six miles from here,"
the man explained. " The trains all stop there for
water, because it's on the banks of the river. I
think it's the only place. We can get there without
going through the town."

" But Burgess can't walk there. You saw yourself
how difficult it was to get him into the house this
afternoon."

" I know, master. But Barendse, one of our committee members, is a cab-driver. He has some horses.
I'll go and ask him to lend us three. We won't be
able to go by cart, because there isn't a road for a
cart, but with the horses I'm sure we can get through.
Can you ride, master ? "

" Yes, I can, and so can Master Burgess."

" I'll go then and ask Barendse for the horses."

At half-past eight it was very dark and the lightning had gone far away, but still the rain fell. The
three of them left the house carefully; fortunately
it was one of the last houses in the town, and
Barendse's house, too, stood only a little outside the
native quarter. Behind his house was a large horse-
camp, whose farthest gate gave on to the open veld,
beyond the reach of van Copenhagen's last patrol.
Burgess' horse they put in the middle, and van
Bredepoel was prepared to support him at the side.

Luckily it was an old harness-horse, which could be
trusted to take care of itself and its rider too.
Barendse conducted them to the gate and leaned, a
shadowy figure, against the post, calling out a low
" God go with you, my masters ! " And then they
were out on the veld, alone with their horses, the
sound of the rain, the far-off flashes of lightning and
the distant mutter of thunder. The lights of Paulstad
became indistinct, fused by the rain into a luminous
mist. The farther they went the louder became the
sound of the rain, the splashes of the horses' hoofs,
the rushing of swollen streams. When lightning
flashed, it revealed an immense plain of water,
flanked by jagged outlines of mountains, dark yet
insubstantial like summer clouds. The world sounded
like some thirsty person who had long since drunk
enough, but was still gurgling the water round in
his throat, just for the pleasure of feeling it. For a
long time no one spoke. The coloured man was too
busy finding the footpath that was their road,
Burgess too occupied with his pain, van Bredepoel
with his thoughts. But suddenly van Bredepoel
felt Burgess' hand moving over his saddle.

"Johan!" he said. "You will come back with
me to-night, won't you ? "

" No, Burgess, I can't."

" You can't stay here. If you do, you'll only get
into trouble to-morrow. And even if you don't get
into trouble, you'll be miserable. You can't uproot
yourself suddenly like that."

" No, this is final. I can't go back."

" Don't say that. You were once so interested in
all I did. Come and help me. Give me the answer

I asked you for in Port Benjamin. We could start all
over again."

" No, Burgess. I might have believed in your
principles once; I don't believe in your methods.
You fight hate with hate and the result is only more
hate. You think you're destroying a colour-prejudice,
but you're only putting a white-prejudice in its
place. You think you're destroying a lust for riches,
but you're only putting a lust for riches for all in its
place. On your road there is only more disorder and
hate and blood. I'm going to begin here with myself.
I've been thinking to-day of all those times I paraded
the streets of Port Benjamin, looking at those shops
in which there was nothing I wanted to buy, those
theatres and cinemas in which there was nothing I
wanted to see, those bookshops without books I
wanted to possess. And now, even if I wanted to
buy the things they have there in Port Benjamin, I
wouldn't touch any of them. They're all part of
that world of hate and blood. There's not a thing
there that isn't tainted for me by the sweat, the
misery, the hunger and blood of those who produced
it. I shall never touch all that again. I shall stay
here and grow potatoes and mind my own step."

Burgess was about to speak, but the coloured man
whispered:

" Please! Please, my masters, don't talk here!
The great road to Port Benjamin makes a wide
curve here and we might be heard. Please keep
your horses walking quietly!"

Hardly had he uttered the words, when the veld
in front of them was brightly illuminated. Their
horses stopped short, snorting with terror. About

fifteen yards away shone the lights of a powerful
motor car, standing in a well-made road. They
heard a low murmur of surprise and someone say
hoarsely:

" What did I tell you, you fellows ? What did I
tell you ? "

" Quick, masters! Quick! Get your horses
round! " the coloured man shouted.

" Halt there! " someone called out, and seven
men with rifles in their hands came running round
to the front of the car.

Van Bredepoel and his companions got their
horses round with difficulty and started to gallop
away, but they could not go very fast because of
Burgess.

" Stop, or we shoot! " the men shouted after
them.

" Oh God! Be quick, my masters! Turn your
horses away from the light. We are riding dead
away from them. We can't make a better mark
than like this. For God's sake, ride away sideways! "

But they could not get their horses, blinded by the
light, to turn into the darkness. A first, a second
and a third volley were fired after them, before the
light dimmed sufficiently for them to turn their
horses aside. Then the men started in pursuit, but
once off the road their car stuck in the mud.

" Are you two all right ? " called out Burgess,
when they were well away.

" I'm all right, Master," answered the coloured
man, but van Bredepoel did not reply at once. He
found his voice with difficulty and said hoarsely:
" Faster! "

"Are you all right, Johan? Why don't you speak?" Burgess called out again, frightened by the strangeness in his friend's voice.

"Yes! Faster!"

To van Bredepoel it seemed that his own voice was coming from a distance. He felt his knees weakening. He was receding slowly from himself; somewhere in the darkness he was brooding like a cloud over himself, spreading and melting into something infinite beyond. From afar, he heard Burgess say to the coloured man:

"My God! He's not all right. They've shot him. Stop my horse for me!"

"No master! Don't! There's a light there beyond. I know there's a coloured man's farm there. Ride, master, and let's get him there. Quick!"

"Hold out just a little longer," Burgess called out to van Bredepoel.

"Yes, faster," he repeated, but his voice was so far away now that he hardly heard it. He was at the bottom of an endless steel pipe; far above, its grooves rose like a cyclone towards a disc of light. The rain began to sing like the air in a sea-shell at his ears. The disc of light began to whirl round. The world was a merry-go-round, turning and turning to the music of a steam-organ. There were people dancing round and round, caught in a music of wild abandon. The light went out, came on again. A candle threatened by many shadows held a swaying pillar of flame before him and a voice that filled the world, filled a little room that was the world in far-off "Vergelegen," read out of a book slowly:

" And though I have the gift of prophecy, and understand all mysteries and all knowledge, and though I have all faith so that I could remove mountains, and have not love,[1] I am nothing."

The light became steadier. It whirled round no more; it did not go out immediately; it only rose and fell rhythmically like the poop-lantern of a wind-jammer caught in a typhoon. The world is a " Vergelegen " ; the roads that lead from it long. Again the light went out, again it came on and the voice continued:

" For we know in part, and we prophesy in part. But when that which is perfect is come, then that which is in part shall be done away.

" When I was a child, I spoke as a child, I understood as a child, I thought as a child; but when I became a man I put away childish things.

" For now we see through a glass, darkly, but then face to face: now I know in part, but then shall I know even as also I am known."

The voice, or memory of a voice calling through the years, faded, and music and light became one. It was the music of his childhood; the music born out of one of the tragic platitudes of the existence of his people. There round the disc of light, people were singing:

" Vat jou goed en trek, Fereira,
Vat jou goed en trek.
Daar agter die bos staan 'n klompie perde,
Vat jou goed en trek.

[1] The author has preferred the word " Love " to " Charity " here, as it corresponds in his opinion more closely to the Dutch version of the text.

Swaar dra, Oh al aan die eenkant swaar dra,
Oh al aan die een kant swaar dra ;
Vat jou goed en trek, Fereira,
Vat jou goed en trek."[1]

" We are nearly there, Johan, please hold on,"
Burgess pleaded. His voice was infinitely remote.
Far above, from down that long tunnel of steel which
is the sky, van Bredepoel was murmuring " I'm too
late." But it was a wordless, voiceless murmur.
The light had once more begun to whirl, the music
rose to a screech, a great wind swept over him and
then the light went out for the last time. Van
Bredepoel, or he that had been called van
Bredepoel, fell from his horse.

" Stop! He has fallen!" Burgess shouted to the
coloured man.

" You stop, master. I'll ride for help. I can see
the lights and hear the people dancing."

Slowly Burgess got off his horse. He groped
over to van Bredepoel's side and fell on his knees,
feeling for his friend's pulse. He held van Bredepoel's
wrist for a long time, but there was no movement.
He heard the dance music stop and saw people,
waving lanterns, come running towards them, but
their coming gave him no hope. He looked straight
before him into the darkness, and said to himself:

" They shall pay for this, when the revolution
comes."

---

[1] Which we can only translate freely in prose:
Take your goods and trek, Fereira, take your goods and trek.
Behind the bush there are some horses, take your goods and trek.
They are heavy to carry, they weigh you down on one side,
Fereira, so take your goods and trek, take your goods and trek.

Round them the rain fell steadily and gently, even in Bambuland the stones would be dripping with water and in the morning the vleis would vibrate with the croaking of frogs, the call of wild geese and the bleating of sheep, and there would be washed for a time from the minds of all, except, I fear, mine, the last memory of blood-sacrifice and blood-hate, and of that old, old Africa which had lain there so long, its stony face turned to the sun. And I wish that I, too, could forget. But when I look back, the memory of Johan and Kenon stalks like a sunset shadow at my side, and I wonder if they are still uncertain and unhappy and perplexed, and I want to call out to them, if only they could hear:

"Johan! Kenon! Poor, unhappy children of life, courage! People like Burgess still sow out of their love of the oppressed the seeds of a terrible hate. Life is bent low with hate. But take heart. For here, where your footsteps disappear, so near that if you stretched out your hands you could almost feel them, come the feet of the generations that trample the dim future, and there may be love at their side."